**W9-BCI-155**

3/20

The
GRACE
KELLY
DRESS

Also by Brenda Janowitz

The Dinner Party
Recipe for a Happy Life
The Lonely Hearts Club
Scot on the Rocks
Jack with a Twist

The GRACE KELLY DRESS

A NOVEL

BRENDA JANOWITZ

GRAYDON
HOUSE

GRAYDON
HOUSE®

Recycling programs
for this product may
not exist in your area.

ISBN-13: 978-1-525-80459-5
ISBN-13: 978-1-525-80466-3 (Library Exclusive Edition)

The Grace Kelly Dress

This edition published by arrangement with Harlequin Books S.A.

Graydon House
22 Adelaide St. West, 40th Floor
Toronto, Ontario M5H 4E3, Canada
www.GraydonHouseBooks.com
www.BookClubbish.com

Printed in U.S.A.

To Doug, Ben and Davey, always

The
GRACE
KELLY
DRESS

"Our life dictates a certain kind of wardrobe."

—Grace Kelly

PART ONE:
PICK YOUR PATTERN

"When designing a wedding dress, the first step is to decide on a pattern. Do not make this decision lightly. This is the most important step, as all other decisions you make will flow from this very first choice. This dress is the most important dress a bride will ever wear. Choose carefully."

—Excerpted from *Creating the Illusion* by Madame Michel,
Paris, 1954

ONE

The bride
Brooklyn, 2020

She hated the dress. She did not really like the veil that went with it, either. Yes, she understood that it was made of rose point lace, the same type of lace that was used on Princess Grace's wedding dress, the most iconic wedding dress of all time, but no, that did not sway her opinion.

She did not want to wear any wedding dress, for that matter. She thought that wedding dresses were stupid and overly expensive and a symbol of the patriarchy and a million other things her mother just would not understand. But she could never say any of those things to her mother. Especially since it was *her* dress that they were talking about. The dress Joan proudly wore down the aisle on her wedding day. The dress that was passed down to her by her mother, Rocky's grandmother.

How could a girl tell her mother that she didn't want to wear that dress?

Rocky wiped her hands on her black jeans as she puzzled over what to do, what to say. Perhaps she should just be honest with her mother, tell her the truth. This could end right here and now.

She could hear her father's gentle laughter echo in her mind. She didn't need to speak to him to know what his reaction would be: *Is that the plan, Kitten?* No, that wouldn't work. That wouldn't work at all.

Rocky took a deep breath as she arrived at the bridal boutique. This salon was the one her mother had picked out, of course, not the one Rocky had wanted. But she could never say no to her mother.

Rocky slowly opened the door, so slowly, as if she were afraid to walk in (wasn't she, though?), and a gentle chime rang out. Her father was right: she would need a strategy to tell her mother the truth. She couldn't just blurt it out. She'd have to visit her father this week. He'd help her come up with a plan.

"This is my daughter, Rachel," Joan said, beaming with pride as Rocky entered. Rocky felt like Dorothy, walking into Oz and seeing things in color for the first time. It was as if the streets of Brooklyn, where she lived and worked, were sepia tones, and the bridal shop, a store she'd walked by hundreds of times without noticing, was in full Technicolor. Rainbows bounced off the tiaras in the display case onto the mannequins wearing wedding dresses in delicate shades of white, ivory, and blush. There were ribbons, and tulle, and taffeta, oh my!

"Rocky," her daughter corrected her, arm extended for a handshake. The old woman standing next to her mother regarded her, arms carefully folded across her chest. She examined Rocky from the tips of her toes to the top of her head and then offered a small smile in return. "I'm Greta."

"Oh, yes," Joan said. "I was just getting to that. She likes to be called Rocky. Rocky, Greta. Greta, Rocky." And then, sotto voce, she delivered her usual line: "It would make more sense if her name was Raquel, but who am I to judge?"

Truth was, they'd been calling her Rocky since the third

grade, and it had nothing to do with the fact that her given name was Rachel. They named her "Rocky" one day at recess, after she punched Jimmy Timbers squarely in the nose for calling her sister, Amanda, a dyke.

Joan put her arm around Rocky's shoulders as they walked towards the back of the salon. "Did you need to wear combat boots into a bridal boutique?" she whispered.

"They're motorcycle boots," Rocky said, and then looked down at her feet, as if to prove it were true. She glanced down at her mother's shoes: pale pink ballerinas.

"Combat, motorcycle," Joan said. "Same difference. Wouldn't it be lovely to wear a nice pair of heels for a change?"

"These are my dressy motorcycle boots."

"Shall we get the dress on?" Greta asked, and Rocky couldn't help but think: *What, no foreplay? We're just doing this?* But she simply allowed herself to be led to the slaughter. Which is to say: a fitting room where she would be forced to strip down, nearly naked, in front of her mother and Greta and try on a dress she had no intention of wearing.

"She's going to dye her hair back to brown for the wedding," Joan said to Greta, as she pulled the bodice onto her daughter's lithe frame. She pressed her hands to Rocky's waist, to show her what it would look like once it was tailored to fit her body. The dress had been made for someone with more of an hourglass figure, someone more like her sister, Amanda, and everyone knew it. But no one would say it. No one would dare say it.

Rocky wanted to say something about her hair color—she was not planning to dye it back to brown for her wedding day—but she couldn't get the words out.

"Great," Greta said, as she slowly helped Rocky step into the skirt of the dress. Greta's hands showed her age, and Rocky didn't want her bending over and straining herself on her behalf. She looked to be around the same age as Rocky's grandmother. Rocky wanted to tell Greta that she could do it on her own, but then reconsidered. Would it offend her if Rocky offered to do it on her own? Greta was old, but she moved as if she were a young woman, as if nothing could kill her. "We'll use these clips to get a sense of what it will look like once it's been tailored."

"Oh, Greta," Joan said, as the woman stepped back to admire her handiwork.

With the aid of the clips, the dress actually fit. Rocky gave her short hair, cut into a messy shag and dyed dark green this week, a tousle, and looked at herself. She didn't look terrible. That much she had to admit. But there was something bothering her, something she couldn't put her finger on.

Her eyes traveled down her body. The rose point lace was beautiful, just as her mother had described. Rocky had never been the one to try on her mother's wedding dress as a child—that was Amanda's department—so she was pleased to see that it wasn't quite as outdated as she thought it might be. Although the Princess Diana sleeves—an update added by her mother in the '80s—would have to go. The dress had a fitted bodice, a cummerbund made of thick layers of silk on the waist, and a full skirt done in silk faille. Three skirts, actually, if you included the skirt support, silk skirt with ruffled petticoat, and train insert.

"Do you need a pair of shoes to put on?" Greta asked, holding out a pair of sling-backs.

And there it was. She might have looked all right—nice, even—but she didn't look like herself. She never wore dresses, for one, and even if she did, she would never wear white. And the way her mother was holding down the voluminous sleeves of the dress made it clear that she was happy that, at just under elbow length, they would cover up her tattoos. But Rocky was proud of her tattoos. They told her story, one by one. She tugged up the sleeve to reveal one of her favorite tattoos just below the crook of her right elbow. The name of her fiancé, written in script. Drew had a matching one on his arm, in the same spot.

It was the seventh tattoo she ever got, inked on the day they moved in together. Lucky number seven.

Greta's hand went to the inside of her own arm, and ran her fingers over it. She stared at Rocky's tattoo, seemingly transfixed by it. Rocky's mother caught a glimpse of Greta's expression in the full-length mirror and tugged the sleeve back down. Rocky rolled her eyes—Greta, like her mother, could not possibly understand why her tattoos were important to her.

"Give me your phone," Joan said. "I'll take a picture."

"I don't think—" Rocky began.

"The groom must not see his bride in the wedding dress," Greta cut in. "These kids with phones in clouds, nothing stays private."

"Good point." Joan nodded. "We don't want any chance that Drew might see it. Thank you, Greta."

Rocky saw a flash go off; Joan had taken a photo with her own iPhone, an old 6 model that Rocky had begged her to replace. (She made a mental note to get her mother the newest phone for Christmas that year.)

Rocky imagined Drew's reaction to her in the dress. He'd never seen her in a dress, had he? The closest he'd ever come was looking at the old family photo albums Joan kept in her living room, catching a glimpse of the matching dresses Joan would insist that the girls wear for Thanksgiving. (Even though Amanda was two years older, people were always mistaking Rocky and her sister for twins, with their matching dark green eyes and heart-shaped faces.) One year, they even wore white tights with turkeys printed on the ankles. Joan was so proud of finding those tights with the turkeys, each one with a rhinestone for an eye. Amanda loved wearing matching dresses, but Rocky loathed it. Each year, her father would bribe her to go along with it by letting her eat doughnuts for breakfast as they watched the Thanksgiving Day parade on the television.

Maybe Drew would like seeing Rocky in the dress. He loved

the traditions shared by his large Jewish family, even though he, himself, was adopted from South Korea. He kept his father's tallit, gifted to him on his Bar Mitzvah day, in a special velvet bag on the top shelf of their closet. When a neighbor told him of a flood in their apartment, he immediately ran to the Container Store to get a plastic box, in which to keep the prayer shawl even more safe.

So maybe the idea of a dress passed down from grandmother to mother to daughter would appeal to Drew. But aren't you supposed to look like yourself on your wedding day? That's what the bridal magazines Amanda had been buying for her said: a bride should look like the best version of herself on her wedding day. It is the day when you announce to the world that you are becoming part of a team. Shouldn't you be yourself for that?

She didn't look like herself.

"A wedding dress passed down three generations," Greta said, breathless. "How special. It would be my honor to work on the restoration of this dress."

Rocky did *not* want to wear the dress. But what to say?

TWO

The mother of the bride, as a bride herself
Long Island, 1982

She loved the dress. She loved the veil that went with it, too, though she wasn't sure if it could be salvaged. It was showing signs of age, its edges curling and tinged with brown. But that wouldn't dull her excitement.

Today was the day she would be trying on her mother's wedding dress. Even though Joanie had tried it on countless times as a child—it was a favorite rainy-day activity with her mother—today felt different. She was engaged, just like she'd dreamed about ever since she could remember. When she tried the dress on this time, it was for keeps. She was completely in love with the dress.

"Let me help you get it on," Joanie's mother said, her French accent coming through. It was always more pronounced when she was feeling emotional. With her American friends, Joanie noticed, her mother always tried to sound "American," softening her accent and using American expressions. But when they were alone, she could be herself. Let her guard down. Joanie knew exactly who her mother was, and she loved her for it.

Her mother handed Joanie a pair of white cotton gloves and then put on her own set. The first step in trying the dress on, always, so that the oils in their hands wouldn't defile the fabric. She laid the large box on her bed and nodded her head at her husband, her signal to give them privacy. The door closed to Joanie's childhood bedroom, and she and her mother were alone.

The white cotton gloves were cool and smooth on her skin. Joanie opened the box slowly. So slowly. It was sealed with a special plastic that was supposed to keep it airtight so that the dress would not oxidize and turn yellow. She and her mother laughed as they struggled to set the dress free. The last time she tried the dress on was the summer before her sister died. It was after Michele's death that her mother brought the dress into the city so that it might be cleaned properly and preserved for just this day. At the time, Joanie hadn't understood the connection between her sister's sudden death and her mother's tight grip on family heirlooms, but now, a year into her psychology degree at NYC University, she understood. It was so hard to hold on to things that were important to you, things that mattered, and preserving her wedding dress, this memory, was her mother's way of taking control of something. It was something she could save.

The dress was just as beautiful as she'd remembered. Crafted from rose point lace, the same lace used on Grace Kelly's iconic wedding dress, it was delicate and classic and chic and a million other things Joanie couldn't even articulate.

"Go on," her mother said, holding the first part of the dress— the bodice with the attached underbodice, skirt support, and slip—out for her to take. As a child, it had thrilled Joanie to no end that the wedding dress her mother wore was actually made up of four separate pieces. It was like a secret that a bride could have on her special day, something that no one else knew.

"I couldn't," Joanie said, hands at her side. Knowing how

carefully preserved the dress had been, what the dress had meant to her mother, it was hard for Joanie to touch it. She didn't want to get it dirty, sully its memory. "It's just so beautiful."

"It's yours now," her mother said, smiling warmly. "The dress belongs to you. Put it on."

Joanie kicked off her ballet slippers, and her mother helped her ease the bodice on. Joanie stood at attention as her mother snapped the skirt into place and wrapped the cummerbund around her waist. Joanie held her hands high above her head, not wanting to get in the way of her mother's expert hands, hands that knew exactly where to go, fingers that knew exactly what to do.

"You ready in there, Birdie?" her father yelled from the hallway, impatient, his French accent just as strong as the day he left France. Joanie always loved how her father had a special nickname for her mother. When they first married, he would call her mother GracieBird, a nickname of Grace Kelly's, because of the Grace Kelly–inspired wedding gown she wore on their wedding day. Eventually, it was shortened to Bird, and then over time, it became Birdie. What would Joanie's fiancé call her?

Joanie inspected her reflection in the mirror. Her shoulder-length blond hair, recently permed, looked messy. Her pink eye shadow, which had always seemed so grown-up on her sister, made her appear tired and puffy-eyed. But the dress? The dress was perfect.

Her mother opened the door slowly, and her father's face came into view. His expression softened as he saw his daughter in the wedding dress. She walked out into the hallway, towards him, and she could see a tear forming in the corner of his eye.

She turned to her mother, about to tell her that Daddy was crying, when she saw that her mother, too, had teared up. Joanie couldn't help it—seeing her mother and father cry, she began to cry as well. She could never keep a dry eye when someone else was crying, least of all her parents, expats from Europe who hardly ever cried.

Michele's presence floated in the air like a haze, but no one would say it. No one dared mention that she would have worn the dress first. Should have worn the dress first.

"And look at us," her mother said, her hands reaching out and grabbing for her husband and daughter. "All of us crying like little babies."

All three embraced—carefully, of course, so as not to ruin the dress.

Her father kissed the top of her head. "Give us a twirl."

Joanie obliged. The dress moved gracefully as she spun. Joanie curtsied, and her father gently took her hand and kissed it.

"I know what you're thinking," her mother said, her voice a song.

"What?" Joanie asked absentmindedly, while staring at her reflection in the mirror. She knew the first thing she'd change— the sleeves. The dress needed big, voluminous sleeves, just like Princess Diana had worn on her wedding day.

"Or I should say who you're thinking about," her mother said, a gentle tease.

"Who?" Joanie asked, under her breath, twirling from side to side in front of the mirror, watching the dress move.

"Your fiancé," her mother said, furrowing her brow. "Remember him?"

"For sure," Joanie said, spinning around to face her mother. "My fiancé. Yes. I knew that. And, yes. I was." But the truth was, she had completely forgotten.

THREE

The seamstress
Paris, 1958

Rose loved this moment. She relished it. Each and every time, she held her breath when a new bride entered the atelier.

Madame Michel stood in the front of her shop, head up, back straight, hand elegantly resting on her cane. The faint scent of her ylang-ylang perfume drifted up towards the loft where Rose perched.

Watching. Waiting.

Madame Michel was a woman who knew her worth. Since coming back to Paris after an illustrious career in America, creating costumes for Paramount Pictures under the tutelage of Edith Head, she was in high demand. Hundreds of young girls yearned for her to design their wedding dresses, hoping to be dusted with the magic so many others had experienced. It was said that to wear a custom-designed Madame Michel wedding dress was to guarantee a happy marriage.

Madame Michel was a woman who knew how to choose her

clients well. Today, the daughter of a prominent businessman. A man who was well connected in the newly re-formed government. After the coup d'état that had returned Charles de Gaulle to power, Monsieur Phillipe Laurent was a good man to have as a friend. Madame liked nothing more than a powerful man. An influential man. When the guests at his daughter's wedding— the best and brightest of Paris society—saw the dress Madame would create, her business would double overnight. Of course, if she were to fail, her business would dry up completely. Dress orders would be canceled, her waiting list would disappear. But she would not fail.

Madame took a deep breath as Monsieur Laurent opened the door to the atelier. His footsteps reverberated on the hardwood floors, and Madame opened her arms out wide to welcome him. He was tall, so incredibly tall, and had a neatly trimmed mustache. His black hair was slicked back with pomade, and he wore a small smile on his lips. Monsieur Laurent delicately took Madame's hand, kissed it, and then introduced her to his wife.

But that wasn't who Rose was waiting to see. Her favorite part was this: seeing the future bride for the first time. Laying eyes on the girl for whom she'd hand-sew delicate designs, eight hours a day. In that moment, Rose would create a narrative, a story, to fit each girl. And that story would keep her mind busy through the endless hours of labor. Working on Madame's designs until her hands ached, away from the customers, in the tiny upstairs loft.

She shouldn't complain. Rose was lucky to have this job—to train under the tutelage of Madame, to learn from a master, to get a weekly paycheck. An orphan, Rose needed the money to pay for her room at the boarding house where she lived.

The bell chimed again, signaling the arrival of the bride. Rose tiptoed to the edge of the loft—she knew that she was supposed to be at her sewing station, working on the embroidery of a duchess satin gown, but she couldn't help herself. She looked out the tiny window of the loft and watched, waited. Mademoiselle Diana Laurent walked in, and immediately smiled. She turned her head to and fro, taking it all in. Madame's beautifully curated atelier; the dresses on the forms, taking shape; the reams of fabrics, lined up like soldiers; and the impeccable sketches that were tacked to the walls, delicate works of art.

This bride would be a perfect muse for Madame. Like a Degas ballerina, she had a tiny waist and a long, graceful neck. Her dark hair was styled in a poodle cut, with tight curls and short bangs. The girl had a tiny button nose, and full lips, parted slightly, as if she had something to say.

She wore a Pierre Cardin coat, one Rose had seen in the windows of the shops she could not afford. Rose fingered her own dress, a dress she'd made herself from a wool that was on sale at the fabric shop. The first time Madame saw Rose wearing it, she stopped to admire the design, the clean lines of the neckline, the way the embroidery on the waistline enhanced her shape. Rose smiled, bathing in the praise. Then Madame felt the fabric, and a slight frown formed on her lips. Still, Madame often complimented Rose on the clothes she designed for herself, which did not make her very popular with the other seamstresses. Most days, Rose ate lunch by herself on the back door stoop.

"Oh, I'm so delighted to meet you!" the girl cried out.

"Decorum, Diana," her mother said firmly, and Diana lowered her head.

"Yes, of course," she said. "I'm honored that you've agreed to work on my wedding gown."

"Aren't you going to be my most beautiful bride yet?" Madame said.

Diana's face flushed, and she smiled carefully. "Why, thank you," she quietly said.

Madame said this very thing to each and every bride who walked through her doors.

"Come, dear child." Madame ushered Diana to a table already

set with afternoon tea. "You must tell me all about yourself so that I may design the dress of your dreams."

Diana tried to give Madame a sense of who she was, what she wanted. But she didn't need to. Everyone already knew what she wanted. She wanted what every girl wanted that year: the dress that American actress Grace Kelly wore to her wedding to Prince Rainier of Monaco. The Grace Kelly dress.

And Diana Laurent was no different. As she gushed about the rose point lace, the *peau de soie*, and of course, the prince himself, Madame smiled broadly, and her butler furiously took notes.

Rose knew that Madame was conflicted about all of the Grace Kelly dresses she was asked to create. Not because they weren't beautiful, of course they were all beautiful. Each and every one of them. It was because of her loyalty. She'd worked for ten years under Edith Head, and respected her fully. When Grace Kelly became engaged to Prince Rainier, Edith Head had assumed that she would be asked to design the wedding dress. After all, they were friends. But Grace Kelly was contracted to do two more movies with MGM studios, and they weren't about to allow an opportunity for great publicity to pass them by. MGM's head costume designer, Helen Rose, would have the honor of designing the thing that would go down in history: the gown. Edith Head was asked to design the going-away suit for the honeymoon, but of course, no one remembered the suit.

Rose knew what she would design, if given the chance. She'd make the neckline higher, the sleeves shorter, and the skirt, edged with embroidered flowers. She would create a dress that honored the inspiration, but truly belonged to the bride herself. But no one ever asked Rose. And she knew better than to suggest a design element to Madame.

The meeting ended, and Madame walked her new clients to the door. The Laurent family exited, and with that, Madame spun around, looked around her atelier, and dropped to the ground.

FOUR

The bride
Brooklyn, 2020

It was hate at first sight. Was that an awful thing to say? Maybe it was, but that didn't change the fact that it was true. From the second Rocky laid eyes on Drew, she absolutely, positively hated him.

Rocky sat across from him in a meeting about funding for her start-up. She was supposed to be impressing them, Drew and his team, wooing them, but instead she was just angry. Yelling at them, almost. And a bunch of men in finance? They do not like an angry woman.

But she couldn't help it. Drew's firm barely listened to her team's presentation about her video game app and declined to make an offer (his firm was their fourth appointment of the day, and their fourth no of the day). Drew, himself, seemed more interested in the tray of mini muffins than in what she was saying. When he approached her afterward to shake her hand ("No sore feelings, right?"), Rocky instead challenged him with a question: "Do you even know what the game is about?"

Drew furrowed his brow. "Of course I know what the game is about." He shrugged his shoulders and popped another mini muffin into his mouth.

Rocky waited. She stared Drew down until he finished the mini muffin, and then washed it down with a swig of coffee.

"What, are you waiting for me to explain it to you?" Drew asked, stifling the laughter in his voice.

"No," Rocky quickly said, all at once realizing that this was not the way to get funding for her company. She hated this man, hated his company, and hated the way they didn't take the meeting seriously. But challenging him, the only member of the team who was confident enough to shake her hand after saying no to their proposal, wasn't going to change anything. Wasn't going to turn the no into a yes. "Thank you for your time."

That night, Drew downloaded Rocky's app—a game that was a mash-up of *Scrabble*, *Boggle*, and *Rummikub*—and invited her to a game. He was terrible at it, truly terrible, and Rocky stopped playing with him after an hour.

He messaged her in the app's mailbox feature: I'm really more of a math guy.

Rocky did not respond.

He messaged her again an hour later: Drinks?

Rocky didn't respond to that message, either, but she did invite him to play another round on her app. Drew eventually got the hang of the game—it was addictive; Drew's team had made a huge mistake, he would later realize—and the following month, when they bumped into each other at a mutual friend's birthday party, Rocky noticed how handsome he was, what a good dresser, and mostly, how he treated everyone on his team like equals, even the female assistants that most men in Drew's position ignore (or hit on shamelessly, inappropriately). From across the bar, she messaged him: I'll take that drink now. And they spent the rest of that night side by side, inseparable. They didn't notice when Rocky's friends went home. They didn't notice when Drew's team decamped to another bar. And they didn't notice when the birthday girl closed the party down at 11 p.m., when she realized the guy she'd been seeing was a no-show. Rocky and Drew didn't notice any of it as they climbed up to the rooftop deck with a bottle of champagne. Rocky kissed him at midnight and they'd been a thing ever since.

"The couple I've been waiting to see," Rocky's doorman said, as she and Drew came home, walking hand in hand. "Thank you, Rocky."

"It was nothing," Rocky said, smiling, walking past his desk.

"It was hardly nothing," Sal said, coming out from behind his desk, arms thrown out wide. He was a hugger, Sal the doorman. Rocky was not. The faint smell of his cigars enveloped her as Sal embraced her. "Thank you," he whispered.

"You're welcome." Releasing a hand from his embrace, Rocky patted his back awkwardly.

Sal turned to Drew and gave him the bear hug treatment as well.

"You two are the best," Sal called out as Rocky and Drew made their way to the elevator.

"Sal gives too many hugs for no reason." Rocky pressed the button for their floor.

"You're probably the only person in the building who sent something when he had his heart attack, Rock."

"It was just common courtesy. Anyone else would have done the same thing."

"And then paid for the visiting nurse for a month."

"It was nothing."

"Sure," Drew said, but something in the curl of his lip told Rocky that he had her number. He knew the truth. Drew always had a way of seeing through Rocky's tough guy act. Could always see right through her, right down to her soft, gooey center.

Rocky busied herself with the mail so she didn't have to meet Drew's eye.

"So," Drew asked, putting the key into the door. "How was it?"

"I can't even." Rocky threw her work bag down in the entryway. Drew hung his up on the hooks he'd installed to keep the entryway neat and organized.

"I'm sure it wasn't that bad," Drew said, his face open and bright, the perpetual optimist.

"Wasn't that bad?" Rocky asked, the perpetual pessimist (or realist, Rocky would hasten to correct). "I'm sorry, but were you there?"

"I was not."

"The dress is really more Amanda than me." She flung open the refrigerator door and rooted around for a drink. Drew opened the cabinet and grabbed a glass—*"see what a great husband I'll make?"* the subtext that sparkled in his eye—and handed it to Rocky. She was already drinking straight from a bottle of Red Stripe.

"I got you a glass."

"I didn't even look like myself," Rocky said, between sips.

"Well, then, who did you look like?" Drew said, putting the glass back into the cabinet and grabbing a Red Stripe for himself.

"Amanda," she said slowly, overenunciating each letter of her sister's name. "I just told you that. I looked like Amanda. But, like, a less attractive version."

"That's impossible, babe," Drew said, matter-of-factly. "How could you look like Amanda? She's a generic Barbie doll. She looks like half the bland, cookie-cutter women walking around the Upper East Side. You? You are a fucking original."

Rocky tried to hide the smile coming over her lips. But it

was no use. She loved how Drew saw her: fierce, powerful, and just as tough as she pretended to be.

She reached over to Drew and kissed him. It never ceased to amaze her what a good kisser Drew was. He may have looked like the requisite nice boy, with his clean-cut hairstyle, freshly shaven face, and sensible shoes, but he did not kiss like a nice boy. He kissed like one of those bad boys you met at a seedy bar after last call.

Drew's kisses—the perfect balance of soft and strong—made Rocky melt. When she closed her eyes and let their lips meet, the world could be crashing down outside the door, but Rocky wouldn't notice. She could live in those kisses.

No, Drew did not kiss like a nice boy. He didn't do a lot of other things like a nice boy, either. In fact, there were a number of things Drew did to her on a regular basis that might not be considered nice by polite society.

They didn't even make it to the bed. Clothes were off in the hallway, and Drew pressed Rocky against the wall, his hands everywhere. Drew's kisses trailed down her body, and Rocky called out what she wanted him to do next. The nice boy that he was, Drew always listened.

Drew loved how noisy Rocky could be during sex. Advantage of top-floor loft living: no neighbors to complain about how loud you were. In Drew's last apartment, his next-door neighbor had cornered Rocky in the elevator to remind her that there were three children living next door, one of whom shared a bedroom wall with their bedroom wall. Drew and Rocky went apartment hunting the following weekend.

Rocky loved their loft. It was in a brand-new building in Brooklyn, which meant that all of the amenities were state-of-the-art and totally tech friendly. Their loft was what they called "a smart loft": they could control the lights, the HVAC, and the entire sound system from their phones.

In the shower afterwards: "See, now this is why I shouldn't wear a white dress."

Drew laughed. "You're right. I won't wear a white tux, either. Pizza for dinner?"

"Perfect."

They had pizza in bed that night, something that Rocky considered to be the ultimate indulgence, and something you could only do when you were young and in love. Growing up, Rocky hadn't been allowed to eat food in her bedroom. Someday, they'd have kids of their own and set house rules of their own, but for now, it was just Rocky and Drew. Free to do as they pleased.

"I'm still hungry," Rocky said, placing her paper plate on the bedside table.

"Another slice?" Drew asked, ever the dutiful spouse-to-be. He reached over for the pizza box, and opened it.

"Not for pizza."

FIVE

The mother of the bride, as a bride herself
Long Island, 1982

It was love at first sight. That's what Joanie told people. It just
sounded so romantic, didn't it? Like she was in one of those old-
fashioned movies that she watched with her mother on Sunday
afternoons.

But it wasn't true. It was not love at first sight. Truth was,
Joanie couldn't remember the first moment she'd laid eyes on
Matthew. He had always just been there, it seemed, the presi-
dent of her sorority's brother fraternity.

Matthew Ryan was the boy that everyone in her sorority
wanted to date. Already the stuff of legends at NYC University, even though he was still only a junior. When he looked at
you, it felt like you were the only person in the room. When
he smiled at you, it felt like there was a ray of sun shining on
your face. When he held your hand, it felt like your whole body
was on fire. Yes, Matthew Ryan was handsome and smart and
charming and everyone wanted him.

And he wanted Joanie.

The start of school always began with the Back to School Party at Matthew's fraternity house. Fresh back from summer adventures, it was the place to be to reunite with old friends and start the school year off right. Joanie walked into the Theta house with her three best friends, Debbie, Jenny, and Missy, arms linked.

"Who wants a beer?" Debbie asked, and Jenny and Missy's arms flew up in the air. Debbie liked to take charge of any situation she was in, even a fraternity party. Jenny liked to judge. And Missy just liked to drink.

"Don't be a downer," Jenny said to Joanie, who stood primly with her hands folded in front of her. "Have a beer."

"I hate the taste," Joanie said, wrinkling her nose. "I can't help it."

"It's an acquired taste," Missy said. "And it helps you to acquire the lowered inhibitions necessary to have fun. We're sophomores now. Think you can have a little fun this year?"

"I have fun," Joanie said, fingering her pearl necklace, a gift from her mother. She tried very hard not to pout. "I always have fun."

"Joanie's about to become an old married lady," Debbie said, winking at her friend. "Don't be jealous just because she's the only responsible one here."

"Oh, sorry," Jenny said. "Are you Sober Sister tonight?"

Joanie usually took the position of Sober Sister at sorority mixers—the one sister who vowed to stay sober and look out for the well-being of the rest of the sorority members. But she hadn't that night. Amidst the excitement of her recent engagement, she'd completely forgotten. "Yes, I am, as a matter of fact."

"Well, then, I thank you for your service," Jenny said with an overly dramatic military salute.

Matthew caught Joanie's eye across the room and smiled at her. She smiled back, getting a bit lost in his eyes for a moment.

He was handsome, no one could argue that. A dead ringer for Rick Springfield, he was surrounded by a group of four girls as he popped the collar of his white Izod polo shirt and walked over to Joanie.

"Hey, you."

"Hey, back." Matthew leaned into Joanie and kissed her. As he pressed his body against hers, she felt her engagement ring press into her chest. She'd been wearing it on a chain while back at school since she hadn't yet formally announced her engagement to her sorority. Joanie hated that she couldn't properly wear her gorgeous ring. It was a two-carat pear-shaped stone, set on a gold band. Exactly what she'd always wanted. But the sorority announcement was tradition.

"Oh, lovebirds," Missy said, interrupting the kiss, "Matthew is wanted up at the bar."

Joanie looked up and saw five of Matthew's friends chanting his name: "Ry-an! Ry-an! Ry-an!"

"I'm a little busy here, guys," Matthew said, pointing to Joanie.

"You go. Everybody wants you," Joanie said, and it was the truth. "This is good practice for when you become an astronaut. Everyone loves an astronaut. I'll just have to learn to be your long-suffering wife."

"It's just an internship," Matthew said, rubbing the back of his neck. "It doesn't mean I'm going off into space. It's basically just a lot of science and math."

"Well, they don't know that," Joanie said, nodding her head towards the crowd of people.

"No," he said, looking over, then back at Joanie. "They do not. Should we go somewhere else?"

"How about this—you go be with your fan club, and I'll grab us something to eat. Meet back in the front room in twenty minutes?"

"You're the best," Matthew said, and gave her a quick kiss before running off to the bar.

Joanie walked up to the rooftop, and could barely move, it was so packed with people. They'd set up a huge grill, and she got at the end of a long, winding line to order hamburgers.

"Cut-sies!" Debbie yelled out, as she grabbed Joanie and dragged her up to her spot near the front of the line. The crowd groaned.

"I could have waited."

"We're at the Theta Alpha house, which is our brother fraternity, which means it is basically our house, which means you shouldn't have to wait for a hamburger!" Debbie was yelling.

"How many beers have you had?"

"Oh, I did a few shots on my way up," Debbie explained, still yelling. "So, now I need to eat a hamburger so that the grease will soak up the alcohol. It's basic science."

"Should I get you a glass of water?"

"No, Sober Sister! I'm fine."

"You definitely seem fine."

"It's our turn!" Debbie yelled as the brothers manning the grill asked for their order. "If I don't have a cheeseburger with pickles right this very moment, I will literally die."

Joanie laughed. Drunk or sober, Debbie could always bring a smile to her face. "I'll take two cheeseburgers as well," Joanie said.

"Got it. You want something for Ryan, too?" he asked as he flipped a set of burgers.

"Do you think *I'm* eating two cheeseburgers?"

"Ryan hates cheese."

"Oh, right," Joanie said, quickly correcting her gaffe. "I know that. I meant, a hamburger and a cheeseburger."

"I'll take the extra cheeseburger!" Debbie said, raising her hand as if she were in elementary school. "What? You shouldn't waste food."

Joanie laughed as they took their plates and made their way down to the front room. Sorority pledges had commandeered the good tables by the windows for the sisters, and Debbie and Joanie slid into one, setting their plates down.

"Can I get you another beer, Sister Debbie?" a pledge asked.

"Why, yes, you can."

"Beer for you, Sister Joanie?"

"I'll take a soda, please."

"So, what was up with that?" Debbie asked, once the pledge was out of sight. She took a tremendous bite of her cheeseburger.

"What's up with what? I say 'please' to everyone. I hated the way the older sisters treated us last year."

"Not that. I mean, yes, also that. You do not have to say 'please' to a pledge. But I mean the hamburger thing."

"What hamburger thing?"

"You don't know how your fiancé takes his hamburger?"

"Oh, that?"

"How does he take his coffee?"

"Trick question," Matthew said, walking up to the table and sliding next to Joanie. "I don't drink coffee." Matthew kissed Joanie, and she could taste the beer, still on his lips.

"I'll leave you two lovebirds alone," Debbie said, polishing off the last bites of her (second) cheeseburger. "Pledge! I asked for a beer!"

"Alone at last," Matthew said, and leaned in for another kiss. "Stay over tonight."

"I have to be home by midnight," Joanie said, taking a peek at her watch to check the time. It was only nine. Plenty of time to enjoy the night.

"Bet you're regretting that decision not to stay in the dorms this semester, huh?" Matthew gently took her hand in his own. His smile was full and warm. Even his eyes smiled at her. "I mean, your freshman year it makes sense to live at home. I guess. But I told you that you'd want to be in the city for soph-omore year."

"Yeah, totally," Joanie said, but really, she was lying. She liked living at home. Sure, her mother could be overprotective, but there was something so comforting about being home. Starting college at the same school that her sister had attended had done something to her. Walking the same hallways that her older sister Michele had once walked left her feeling unmoored, unsure of who she was, but when she was back home with her parents, it was like she could breathe. She knew everything would be all right when she was back under her mother's roof.

Her mother hadn't always been overprotective like this, of course. But everything had changed when Michele died sud-denly of a heart attack three years ago at age twenty. She could feel her mother's grip even tighter. Her hugs were stronger; she would say "I love you" every time Joanie left the house. It was like she was constantly afraid that each time she said goodbye, it would be the last time.

But Joanie understood. She felt it, too. This feeling that life was so ephemeral, that everything could change in an instant. She wanted to be strong for her mother, let her know that she would never cause her more pain. She would be good. She wouldn't give her mother any reason to stay up at night worrying about her. To do otherwise would just be selfish. She couldn't let her parents suffer more.

The rest of the night went by in a blur—talking, dancing, kissing—and once the clock struck eleven, Joanie's Prince Charming reminded her of her curfew: "We don't want you to turn into a pumpkin, Cinderella."

Joanie checked her watch. "Thank you. I should go."

"I'll take you to the train station."

"You don't have to leave the party. I can make it over there on my own."

Matthew looked at Joanie and smiled. "But I want to."

Out on the street, Matthew hailed a cab. Joanie looked around to the downtown alley. There were three homeless people huddled between two shopping carts, a blanket draped over the two carts to create a sort of roof. Joanie rooted around her clutch and found a five-dollar bill. She walked over to give it to them. They didn't have a can out at this hour, but surely they would take the money?

"What on earth are you doing?" Matthew said, grabbing her arm. "You could get mugged. They're probably on drugs."

"They look hungry," Joanie said, her voice small.

"We can't take the chance," Matthew said, as a cab pulled over. "You know how dangerous the city can be at night. You've got to be careful. Get in."

Joanie got into the cab and slid over for Matthew. She looked out the window and saw the three homeless people getting smaller, and smaller still, as they drove away.

"I need to make sure my future wife stays perfectly safe." Matthew offered her a sweet smile, the sort that always made her melt.

"Future wife," Joanie repeated. She loved the way that sounded. She leaned into him for a kiss.

"Penn Station, Long Island Rail Road," the cab driver announced, and Matthew had his money out, ready to pay.

"Thank you, Matthew," Joanie said, and gave him a peck on the lips.

"I'm coming with you," he said, following her out of the cab. "I'm not letting you wait on that dark platform alone." He held her hand as they rushed into Penn Station and down onto the platform to await Joanie's train.

"I can think of a few things that would be appropriate for a dark platform," Joanie told Matthew.

"Can you now?" He grabbed her close, and kissed her. He tasted sweet, and his kisses made her head feel light. Perhaps she *was* regretting her decision to live at home this semester?

"I love you," Matthew said as the train pulled up. Joanie checked that she had her train ticket, wallet, and keys, and then quickly kissed him goodbye before rushing onto the train. As it pulled away, she looked out the window and waved at Matthew, standing firm and tall on the platform, not walking away until the train left the station safely. She blew a kiss at him and he pretended to catch it and put it in his pocket. It was only later, as the train neared her station on Long Island, that she realized she forgot to tell Matthew that she loved him, too.

SIX

The seamstress
Paris, 1958

Most of the girls who worked in the loft used their lunch breaks to go out onto the city streets, but Rose preferred the quiet. She would sit by the back door of the atelier and eat her home-made sandwich, listening to the sounds of the city, sketching her dress ideas.

Also, no one ever invited Rose to tag along.

Rose was used to being alone. Orphaned at eight years old, she was taken in by an elderly aunt, and she quickly learned how to keep herself out of the way. How to make herself small. Not a bother. Barely noticeable at all.

Her aunt wore a stern expression and seldom smiled. She believed in cleanliness and seriousness and God, and she went to church every morning. (Rose accompanied her on Sundays.) She enrolled Rose in the primary school connected to the church, where Rose was taught by nuns who also believed in cleanliness and seriousness and God. They prayed every morning before their lessons began.

After school each day, Rose often found herself alone in her aunt's garden apartment, endless hours to fill on her own. With her aunt volunteering at the church almost every afternoon, Rose would gaze out the window at the garden that connected the apartment building to the others on the block. She would see kids playing together, but heeded her aunt's warnings to stay safely inside when she wasn't home. Rose did not want to disappoint her. She was desperate not to alienate her only living relative.

For her ninth birthday, her aunt bought her a sketch pad and some charcoals and Rose would sketch pictures from memory of the glamorous storefronts they passed on their walks to school and church. She taught herself how to draft clean lines, and the importance of scale. The next year, her aunt bought her a proper art kit, filled with oil pastels in sixteen different colors. The next year, it was a Little Traveler's sewing kit, complete with a doll for dressing, fabric to make shirts and skirts with, and embroidery thread. The year after that, a Singer Featherweight sewing machine.

Her aunt died when she was sixteen, and Rose was lucky enough to find the job at Madame's atelier, a listing for a seamstress that seemed too good to be true. Rose spent her days at the atelier and, after work, retreated to the boarding house where she rented a room. She often wondered what the other girls did when they left work. She heard them whispering about their plans—double dates, evenings spent at the cinema, parties around town—but she was never invited. Rose may have grown up, but on the inside, she was still the same little girl, face pressed against the window, watching others have fun while she stayed in.

The back door to the atelier opened, and Rose jumped. No one had ever come back here when she was having lunch before.

Things had been even stricter at the atelier since Madame had fallen ill, with Madame's butler keeping an even closer eye on the girls in the loft than usual. Rose looked up and saw the butler, glancing furtively from side to side. She gathered her things— her sketch pad, her sandwich, and her hat—and readied herself to get back to work. He glanced down at her for a moment, and without a word, spun on his heel and reentered the atelier.

Rose wondered if she had done something wrong, if she wasn't allowed to be out on the back stoop of the atelier. But her thoughts were quickly interrupted by the handyman, the young man who did small repairs around the atelier, as he jumped over a fence to make his way into the courtyard. When he looked up and saw Rose, their eyes met. Then, he quickly vaulted himself back over the fence, racing back to wherever he'd come from.

Two men in less than ten minutes. And both had taken one look in her direction and then fled. Was this what the other seamstresses were out chasing in their free time? If so, Rose would happily remain a spinster.

SEVEN

The bride
Brooklyn 2020

The office was perfectly quiet. Rocky liked to be the first to arrive each day, at 7:30 a.m. sharp. She reveled in the silence. Having the office all to herself before the chaos of the day, it felt more sacred than a church. She looked around the space—the company she'd created—and a feeling of pride washed over her. This was all hers.

It wasn't always like this, Rocky being successful, so she tried not to take it for granted. In elementary school, she lived in Amanda's shadow. Teachers expected her to be just like her sister, a good student who always had a smile to spare. The resentment, when they discovered how different Rocky was from her sister, would be palpable, her seventh grade science teacher even going so far as to yell: "How can you be related to Amanda?" once when Rocky didn't have her homework for the third day in a row.

It wasn't until high school that Rocky took her classes seriously. When she saw Amanda thinking about Ivy League schools, she knew that she wanted that, too. She wanted to be successful, if only she could get out of her own way. Rocky finally listened to what her mother had been trying to tell her all along: the things that she thought were weaknesses would be the things that would make her a success. She channeled her anger, her stubbornness, into hard work, and kicked her grades into high gear. She signed up for extracurricular activities, and wrote her college essay about the coding class she'd been taking, how it was a metaphor for life in general: follow the steps in order to get the desired result.

Rocky slipped off her motorcycle boots and socks and pressed her feet to the hardwood floor of her office. It was something her therapist had taught her—not her childhood therapist, and not the one from college, but the therapist she saw now, the one she started seeing when she moved to New York—to begin each day barefoot, grounded. Of course, it was better to do this exercise on the actual ground, on grass or sand or soil, but Rocky liked the idea of doing it in her office. As she walked her open-concept work space, she would do her daily meditation, bringing herself to the present, readying herself for the day. On particularly stressful days she'd keep her shoes off the entire day, trying to bring her energy back to where she started, trying to soothe herself through mindfulness.

Today, she only needed a few minutes. Rocky sat down at her desk, positioned at the back of the loft, underneath an enormous wood sign with the logo for her company—a small black cat over the words Kitten Games. Drew had commissioned a local artist to make the sign, pyrography on reclaimed wood.

Rocky sipped her green tea as she opened her laptop, got her boots back on. She pulled up her calendar and checked her schedule—not bad. Meeting at ten, one of the creatives pitching a new video game, and then an informal Board of Directors meeting at one. Her grandmother would have to Skype in from Paris, where she was helping her uncle recover from a hip replacement surgery. Rocky loved having her grandmother on her company's Board. Her grandmother was smarter than she gave herself credit for, and was always adept at troubleshooting.

Rocky often thought that if her grandmother had been born in a different time (her time, that is), she would have been the CEO of her own company, just like Rocky. But Grand-mère did her one better, becoming the company's angel investor when Rocky couldn't get funding for her app.

Rocky set an intention for the day—peace—and watched as her office filled up with employees. Her employees. She met with each and every prospective hire before giving a job offer. She knew every staff member by name, from her CFO, a classmate from Stanford, to the interns who cycled in and out each semester, to the cleaning crew who came in at eleven each night.

After her 10 a.m. meeting, her phone pinged. Rocky checked her Apple Watch. It was an email from her mother, subject line: Wedding! Rocky felt her heart rate jump, her face heat up. She took a deep breath in, two, three, four, and out, two, three, four. Out loud, she reminded herself of today's intention: peace. Without opening it, she clicked the tiny button on her Apple Watch that read Delete and went on with her day.

EIGHT

The mother of the bride, as a bride herself
Long Island, 1982

Joanie had a ritual: each time she entered the Delta Epsilon Gamma Chapter Room, her sorority's meeting space, she would walk directly to the back wall. It was filled with framed composites, collections of photographs of every girl who was active in the chapter that year. There were composites going back to the 1960s, when the chapter was first established at NYCU, but there was only one picture that Joanie wanted to see. The composite picture of the Delta House from 1979. The last year her sister was alive.

Her eyes would go directly to Michele's picture, and in that moment, it felt more sacred than visiting her grave. Some days, she would talk to her sister in her mind. Tell her what was going on in her life.

Tonight, the room was dark, illuminated only by candlelight. But Joanie knew exactly where the picture was, even in the dark. She took her place in front of her sister's composite.

Joanie looked around the room at the faces of her sisters,

standing in a circle. All there for the Candle Lighting ceremony. All there to find out which sister was engaged. The sorority tradition that would mark her engagement to Matthew. A lit candle would be passed around the circle, and when it came to Joanie, she would blow it out, letting her sisters know that her single days were over. Standing in front of her sister's photograph, it felt like Michele was right there with her.

Debbie stood to her right, then Jenny, and Missy stood on her left. As the candle traveled the circle, Debbie grabbed Joanie's hand and gave it a squeeze. One of the seniors coughed loudly as she held the candle, and the girls all held their breath—would the candle go out? There was no protocol in the Delta Handbook for a Candle Ceremony going awry in quite that manner. But the girls had nothing to fear: the candle stayed alight, and continued to make its way around the room. Finally, the candle passed to Debbie's hand. She held it still for a moment, reflecting on the solemnity of the occasion, and then handed the candle to Joanie. "I'm so happy for you," she quietly said.

Joanie blew out the candle.

The room erupted into a chorus of "Congratulations!" and "I knew it was you!" Sisters lined up to catch a glimpse of Joanie's engagement ring, her two-carat pear-shaped diamond on a gold band. She took the ring off her necklace, where she'd been wearing it for safekeeping, and put it back onto her finger, where it belonged.

"We're not done yet," the sorority president said, trying to regain order over the room. The Pledge Master took out another box of candles, and had the pledges hand them out to the sisters.

The sisters formed a circle again, now each holding a candle, and Joanie stepped into the middle to begin the next part of the ceremony. She was to walk around the circle and blow out the candles of the sisters who would serve as her bridesmaids. She began with her Big Sister in the sorority, a junior named Chrissy, and then blew out the candles of six other friends from her pledge class. Then, making her way to her best friends, smiling as they stood in front of Michele's picture, she blew out the candles of Jenny and Missy. Saving the best for last, she stopped at Debbie.

"You're the best friend a girl could ask for," Joanie said.

"I know, right?"

Joanie blew out Debbie's candle and they hugged. The lights came on and the sorority president approached Joanie. "You did it wrong. You don't blow out the Maid of Honor's candle. You bring her to the center of the circle and then *she* blows out her *own* candle. Now we have to do it again."

"We don't have to do it again," Debbie quickly said. "I know what I mean to Joanie and so does everyone else."

"But it's tradition," she said, as Debbie led her away to the other side of the room.

Joanie knew what Debbie was telling her—that there would be no Maid of Honor at Joanie's wedding. That role should have been filled by her sister. It would have been filled by her sister if not for a heart condition they knew nothing about.

Joanie spun around to her sister's picture. *Would you be my Maid of Honor?* she imagined herself asking.

Of course I will, she imagined Michele saying back.

"That was beautiful," Jenny said, throwing her arm around Joanie's shoulders. "You okay?"

"Yes, of course."

"We're here if you need us," Missy said.

"Thank you."

"Now, let's talk about who Matthew is choosing for his groomsmen. Because I think I would look really great walking down the aisle with Bradley Moore."

"I'll see what I can do about that." Joanie smiled at her friends.

"So, who else is he choosing for his groomsmen?"

Joanie opened her mouth to respond, and then quickly realized something: she had no idea.

NINE

The seamstress
Paris, 1958

There was no denying it—he was staring at her. Madame's butler was staring at her. Rose put her head down, into her work. What could he possibly want? Was he still upset about finding her outside on the back stoop the other day?

He was a short man, with a thin mustache and hair cropped closely to his head. His hair was so short, it could not even be parted. His clothing was always pressed perfectly, his shoes freshly shined. He was a man who took pride in his appearance.

Rose had never spoken a word to him before, in the four years she'd been working there. And he never spoke to any of the seamstresses in the loft.

He spent most of his time by Madame's side, working as her assistant, secretary, and confidant, tending to her every need. Cold as Madame was, they seemed to share a camaraderie, something that tied them together.

Madame's butler approached Rose's workstation. He picked

up a veil that Rose was embroidering and examined it closely. He placed it back down and then fingered a few of the sketches that Rose had done during her lunch break.

"Have I done something wrong?" she asked him. Was it the sketches? Perhaps she shouldn't have done them on her lunch break. She should never have left them out in the open. She should have thrown them away. After all, they were rough and unpolished.

"On the contrary," he said. "Your work is stunning. These sketches are beautiful."

Rose bowed her head. She didn't want him to see how broadly she was smiling from the compliment—her aunt always said that pride was sinful.

"You don't seem to socialize with the other girls here."

"Is that a problem?" she asked, and he regarded her. "I take my work very seriously. I want to learn as much as I can from Madame."

"We appreciate that," he said. "Madame appreciates that. Madame knows your value here. She has taken notice."

"Thank you."

"Would you be so kind as to follow me?"

As the other seamstresses watched curiously, he led her to the stairwell. Rose paused before entering. She knew that Madame owned the entire building, but she had never left the first floor, where the atelier was housed.

They climbed one flight of stairs, and then another. And then, still, another, until they were on the fourth floor. The door opened to a large parlor. Was this Madame's private apartment? As she looked around, she saw photograph after photograph of Madame. On the walls. On the bookshelves. On the piano. Rose knew that she should not be there—she was certain that this was Madame's apartment.

The butler directed her through the parlor to another room. Madame's bedroom? Rose immediately turned to leave.

"I should not be here," Rose said, making her way back towards the front door. It wasn't proper. What would Madame think?

"It's all right. Madame is not here," the butler explained.

Rose knew he was trying to ease her mind, but it had the exact opposite effect.

"I'm not that sort of girl," Rose said quietly, her hand on the door handle.

The butler laughed. "Oh, Rose, I can assure you, I am not that sort of man." He perched himself on the edge of Madame's windowsill and motioned her to sit down on the chaise longue in the opposite corner.

Was Rose losing her job? She couldn't bear the thought. She needed the weekly paycheck from Madame. Her savings were so small, so meager, she would only be able to survive for a few weeks without employment. And what atelier would hire her if they knew she'd been fired by Madame Michel? She would be marked. Unhireable. Sewing was the only thing Rose knew how to do.

"Your work is impeccable," the butler said. "Madame always thought that you were the most talented of all of her girls."

"Madame said that?" Rose asked, her eyes wide.

"Your designs are modern and fresh," he said, handing over the sketches from her workstation. She hadn't even seen him take them.

"I do those on my lunch breaks," Rose quickly said. "Not during work hours."

"They're very good. But we knew that already because we take note of what you wear every day. What you design for yourself. It's very impressive."

"Thank you."

"You are very welcome," he said, clasping his hands together. "Now, would you like to know why you are here?"

TEN

The bride
Brooklyn 2020

"I lied to my mother."

"Sometimes people lie to save the ones they love," Drew told Rocky as he sat down next to her on the couch. He grabbed her hand. "Anyway, you're not really lying to her. You just haven't been able to tell her the truth. That's different, right?"

"It's still lying."

"I suppose," Drew said. "But aren't there levels of lying? Like, a white lie being the most innocuous?"

"A lie is a lie."

"Then tell her the truth," Drew said.

"I mean, she would completely freak out."

"So, white lie?" Drew regarded her.

"White lie." Rocky shook her head in agreement.

"So, you'll wear the dress?"

"I work in tech," Rocky said, getting up from the couch and pacing. "I like things that are new. She should know that."

"This isn't like getting a new phone or computer. It's our wedding. Weddings are steeped in tradition. I think it's special that the dress belonged to your grandmother and your mother."

"I don't have the same relationship with my mother that you do with yours."

"I know."

The silence felt heavy. Rocky didn't know how to respond any more than she knew how to have a closer relationship with her mother. How to be honest with her mother. With her father, it had always been so easy. But her mother? Her mother was hard.

Don't let her appearance fool you—the buttery blond hair, always freshly styled, never a gray hair in sight, the gentle blue eyes, made up with only the slightest bit of mascara, bright and alert. She may have looked soft, angelic even, but Joan was formidable. She always got what she wanted. People usually didn't realize it, though, because she was so busy making them feel comfortable, making them feel heard, making them feel important. She would smile widely and act as if she was easygoing and accommodating. But you don't get a golf handicap of eight by being nice.

"Let's put a pin in that," Rocky said as she walked back, sank into the couch, and turned on the television. "What do you want to order for dinner?" She opened her phone to the Seamless app and waited for Drew's response.

Drew didn't answer. Rocky looked over to him and could have sworn he was sweating. But that couldn't be right. Drew never sweat. Even after he ran a half marathon last year, he didn't sweat. He was cool as a cucumber, always.

"What is it?" Rocky asked, but Drew's eyes didn't leave his phone.

"Nothing," he said, almost under his breath.

"Okay, so then, dinner?"

"I was thinking of inviting my mother to the wedding," he blurted out. And Rocky could see it: sweat on his brow. She

squinted her eyes to be sure, but there it was. Beads of sweat.
"Would that be weird?"

"It would be weird if your mother wasn't at the wedding,"
Rocky said, examining every square inch of his face. What was
she missing here? "She's *your mother.*"

"No, I don't mean my mom-mom," Drew said. He took a
huge gulp of beer and continued: "I mean my birth mother
from South Korea."

Rocky put her phone down. She turned off the TV. She
opened her mouth, as if to say something, but instead just shook
her head, looking for words. "I thought you didn't know who
your birth mother was?"

"I didn't. I don't. It was a terrible idea," Drew quickly said.
He flipped the TV back on. "So, Indian? I kind of feel like
tikka masala."

"I don't think it's a terrible idea," Rocky said, taking the re-
mote control and turning the TV off again. "I'm just processing.
Give me a second here." She rubbed her temples and closed her
eyes. Then, opening them: "Trying to find your birth mother.
I think your mom's feelings—your mom-mom's feelings—could
get hurt. Have you talked to her about this?"

"I haven't talked to anyone about this." He turned to face
Rocky. "I'm talking to you about this."

Rocky put down her beer. "I had no idea you felt this way."

"Me neither," Drew said, suddenly unable to meet Rocky's
eye. "Actually, that's not true. I have thought about it. I think
about it all the time."

"Since we got engaged?" Rocky asked, grabbing Drew's hand.

"Since I was born," Drew said, releasing her grip and running his hands through his hair. "Since I knew I was adopted.
Since forever."

"Oh, honey."

"Sorry," Drew said, throwing his hands up and getting up

from the couch. "I shouldn't have laid this on you. We were talking about your grandmother's wedding dress."

"I think this is a little more important than a stupid dress." Rocky followed Drew into the bedroom. "Talk to me."

"Your grandmother's legacy is important. Tradition is important."

"We can deal with that later. For now, your birth mother. How would we find her?" Rocky asked quietly. "Let's talk this through."

"I already contacted the adoption agency."

"When?"

"Three months ago."

"You've been doing this for three months and you didn't say anything?" Her words poured out slowly, like the honey at the bottom of a jar. Drew always told her everything.

"I'm sorry."

"You don't have to be sorry. You know that I'm there for you no matter what, right?"

"I know that."

"I have your name tattooed on my arm," Rocky said, touching the spot where Drew's name lived on her flesh. "You're a part of me."

"And you're part of me." He pulled his sleeve up to show Rocky his matching tattoo, and then leaned over and gently kissed her on the lips.

She ran her hand over Drew's cheek. He put his hand over hers and then pulled it away from his face to kiss her palm.

"So, do they think they'll be able to find her? Your birth mother?"

Drew held up his phone to show Rocky the email. "They just did."

ELEVEN

The mother of the bride, as a bride herself
Long Island, 1982

Joanie turned the invitation over in her hands. Was this what it was like for her mother, forever getting the mail of a dead girl delivered to your house, no matter how many times you tell people she'd gone? A painful reminder of the past, every day at 1 p.m.

She quickly threw the invite into the trash. No point in leaving it on the kitchen counter with the rest of the mail, where it was destined to upset her mother when she got home later. Joanie felt her anger rising—the invite was for the opening of an art gallery in SoHo, the sort of thing Michele had gone to all the time when she was alive. Surely those friends had noticed that Michele was long gone?

It had been three years. Three long years.

Everyone knew, didn't they? Some days, it was all Joanie could think of, and she knew it was the same for her mother. She could always tell when her mother was thinking about

Michele—she would get that faraway look in her eye, as if she were trying to remember something, some long-forgotten detail that was there, right there, but as soon as she tried to access it, there it went. Gone.

Joanie stacked the rest of the mail neatly on the kitchen counter, and made her way towards her bedroom. She stopped as she passed her sister's room, her fingers grazing the door frame as she looked in. When was the last time she'd entered Michele's room?

Joanie took a tentative step inside. Michele's room still smelled like her. How was that possible? It was as if her essence had seeped into every pore of the room—the wall-to-wall carpet, the light blue curtains that hung around the windows, the white eyelet bedding. Everything was preserved exactly how she'd left it, as if she'd just run out for a moment and would be back at any second—the bulletin board filled with Polaroids and old invitations, a closet full of clothing, bursting at the seams, and her record player, sitting on top of a Lucite cube, hundreds of albums filling the space below. A moment frozen in time.

From the second Michele got the record player for her thirteenth birthday, she'd shared it with her sister. They'd spend lazy Saturday afternoons together at the music store in town, flipping through albums, pooling their allowances to get what they wanted. How many days did they spend side by side in Michele's room, listening to Supertramp, David Bowie, and Queen? Whenever their mother wanted to find them, there was only one place she ever had to look—the floor of Michele's room, where both girls would be lying down, heads together as they passed the album covers back and forth.

Joanie wished she could have one more afternoon with her sister, one more chance to lie down on the plush carpet, their heads touching, and do nothing more than listen to music together.

Joanie picked up the record and dusted it off with her fingers. Michele had tried to get Joanie into the new music she'd discovered while living in the city, but Joanie preferred to stick with pop.

Joanie imagined Michele was there with her as she turned the record over in her hands. The label said: The Runaways. *I'd love to listen with you*, she imagined herself saying to Michele, and Michele would put it onto the turntable. Joanie picked up the needle and set it to play. An aggressive guitar riff blared through the speakers. A sound she'd never heard before. This was the music her sister listened to when she was in college, the music her sister had wanted her to hear, not the Billboard 100 stuff that Joanie and her friends preferred, Hall and Oates, J. Geils Band, Duran Duran.

The singer practically screamed the lyrics, like she was angry. But the lyrics were suggestive, flirty even. Joanie felt the music inside her chest, in her bones. She was transfixed and couldn't turn it off if she'd tried. She picked up the album cover and stared—a young blonde held the mic, and looked at something off in the distance. Her hands were blurry, as if she were in motion. As if she were singing to Joanie right in that very room at that very moment.

The chorus crashed over her: "I'm your ch–ch–ch–ch–cherry bomb!" It was rough, it was dirty. Joanie almost felt like she shouldn't be listening to it. But she couldn't stop.

When the singer started moaning—it was pure sex—Joanie looked around, to check that she was the only one home. But she knew her mother wouldn't be back for hours—she always came home in time to watch *General Hospital* at 3 p.m.—and her father didn't get back from work until well after seven.

By the third repeat of the chorus, Joanie was singing along as she watched herself in the mirror, her lips mouthing the seductive words: "I'm your ch–ch–ch–ch–cherry bomb!"

The next song queued up and Joanie sat down at her sister's dressing table. A clear Lucite organizer held Michele's makeup— dozens of eyeliners in varying shades of blue and gray, too many lipsticks to count. Her lip glosses were lined up like little soldiers in tiny compartments, each one big enough to hold just one tube. She fingered one of the eyeliners—it looked like the shade of blue that Princess Diana wore—and opened it. Still perfectly sharpened, probably never even used before. Joanie carefully pulled her lower eye down and applied the liner to the inside of her lash line, the way Diana did. Then she grabbed a pale pink lipstick and carefully applied it, pressing her lips together to get it evenly distributed.

Michele always favored darker eye makeup, always pushed the boundaries. Even before she moved out of the house to go to college, Michele wore black kohl and dark eye shadow around her almond-shaped eyes. Joanie laughed to herself as she recalled how her mother and Michele would fight over it.

"Less is more," her mother would chide.

"More is more." Michele's constant refrain.

Michele's bottle of Yves Saint Laurent Opium was half full. Joanie carefully removed the cap and inhaled the heady scent, a mixture of rose, sandalwood, and coriander. This was the smell that lingered in Michele's room. This was the smell that reminded Joanie of her sister, and always would, even years later. Joanie brought her wrist to her nose—the faintest remnant of her own Love's Baby Soft remained, but only slightly. She sprayed Michele's perfume, and then instantly remembered how her mother had taught her to apply it—far away from your skin so as not to overpower. If you sprayed the scent too close, it would apply too much to your skin, and it would walk into a room before you did. The point of perfume was to delight the person who you let get close enough to smell it, not to announce your arrival.

But Joanie didn't care. She rubbed her wrists together (*bruising the perfume*, she could hear her mother chastise), and took a deep breath. The scent swirled around her, making Joanie dizzy. She felt hot, so she took off the pastel pink sweater that she'd had draped over her shoulders, and her white button-down top, too, leaving on only a delicate white camisole.

When she looked back at her reflection, she liked what she saw. She didn't look like the preppy good girl. She looked sexier, dangerous. Like someone else entirely.

Was it Michele she looked like? Even though her sister was three years older, people were always mistaking them for twins, the same heart-shaped face. But now, Joanie realized, she couldn't quite recall what her sister looked like. She grabbed a Polaroid off the bulletin board. Michele stared back at her with dark eyes, dangerous eyes. Joanie couldn't quite recall when that photograph had been taken.

"What are you doing in here?" Her mother's voice drowned out the music, shaking Joanie from her trance.

"I didn't think you'd be home until three." Joanie quickly pulled the needle off the record. Silence filled the room.

"Well, I'm home now. And I'd ask you to please put everything back the way you found it."

"I'm sorry," Joanie said, but her mother had already left the room.

TWELVE

The seamstress
Paris, 1958

There was talk around the atelier that Rose was having an affair with Madame's butler. He called for her every day around the midmorning break, and they disappeared into the stairwell. Since no one who worked for Madame would dare come close to her private quarters, it seemed obvious that they left the loft each morning for a rendezvous on the second floor, a guest suite that Madame hadn't used in years. Rose had no friends to speak of, so there was no one to refute the story. No one to defend her honor. She could see how the girls now eyed her suspiciously, looked at her with disdain.

If they only knew the truth.

"Now, would you like to know why you are here?" he had asked her that first day.

Rose hadn't been sure if she wanted to know. But her response didn't matter. He explained: "I am sorry to inform you that Madame died the day she collapsed at the atelier. That evening, to be precise."

Rose gasped. She was losing her job. Without a regular paycheck, she would not be able to afford her room at the boarding house. She would be out on the street in one month's time. Tears sprang to her eyes and she covered her face with her hands. She could not cry in front of this man she did not know, even with what he was telling her.

"It's not possible." She composed herself and looked up at the butler. He had an open face, an honest face.

He spoke quietly: "I'm afraid it is, dear child."

"We've all been conducting business as usual. How could this be?"

"This is what Madame would have wanted," he explained, retrieving a handkerchief from his jacket pocket and handing it to Rose. Despite her best efforts, the tears were slowly streaming down her face. "She left the atelier to me, and I've been running it behind the scenes, as I've always done."

"I had no idea that you and Madame were," Rose began, searching for the words, "...in a relationship."

"We were not in a relationship," he said, laughing under his breath. "Madame was my aunt. My name is Julien Michel."

"I don't understand."

"It's quite simple, really," Julien said, sitting down on the longue next to Rose. "Madame was my aunt, and she took me in after my parents died. When I turned eighteen, she put me to work at the atelier, and I've been here ever since."

"You're an orphan." Rose used his handkerchief to wipe away her tears. "Like me."

"Yes."

"What happens now?"

"Onward," he said, rubbing his temples. "Just as she always wanted. Her plan had been to select a protégé, someone she could train, but life often does not follow a plan. No one could have suspected that she would pass so quickly—we had no idea she had a bad heart. So, we adjust."

"How?"

"Why, you will finish Mademoiselle Laurent's dress," he said, as if it were the most natural thing in the world.

"Finish the dress?" Rose asked. She felt a sinking feeling in her stomach. "It hasn't even been started yet."

"Madame created a few sketches before she passed." He walked over to Madame's desk, and pulled out the drawings. "At the next meeting, you will present these sketches to Mademoiselle Laurent. She will pick one, and that is the dress you will create for her."

"Won't the Laurents wonder where Madame is?"

"Monsieur Laurent will be traveling to London for his work. And I've recently discovered that his wife will accompany him. It will be easier to keep up our ruse with only young Mademoiselle to fool." Julien passed the drawings to Rose.

Rose studied the sketches. They were perfect. Madame's lines were so assured, so clean. Each design was a work of art, truly. "Won't Mademoiselle wonder where Madame Michel is?"

"We shall create an excuse for each meeting," Julien explained. "Florence one week, Monaco the next. The possibilities are endless."

Rose shook her head and looked up at Julien. His words seemed so confident, so sure, but she could see a thin layer of sweat gathering on his brow.

"Mademoiselle mustn't know about Madame, of course," Julien said. "She must not know. The fate of the atelier depends on it. If one bride finds out, the atelier's business would dry up before we had the time to create the illusion that you are her chosen protégé. No one would dare order a wedding dress from our atelier again. No one would take the risk on an unknown designer, someone who Madame has not vouched for. After all, the gown is the most important part of the wedding. And you will create a dress so beautiful that there is no doubt in anyone's mind that you have been trained by Madame. That you were chosen by her to take over the atelier. And then, that is exactly what you will do, while I continue to run things behind the scenes. We'll make the announcement after Mademoiselle Laurent's wedding. After the world sees her wedding dress, you will be the toast of Paris, and the new lead designer of the atelier."

Rose didn't respond. She agreed with Julien's assertion—the gown was the most important part of a wedding—but she was stuck on Julien's words. *Create the illusion.* Because the truth was that Julien had chosen her to play the role of Madame's protégé.

Madame had not.

THIRTEEN

The bride
Brooklyn, 2020

Rocky balanced her laptop on her knees in the car. She had dozens of emails to respond to, and three open projects at work, but none of that mattered today. Today, she was on her way to see her father. She had a million things to tell him, a million things to discuss. First, there was the matter of the dress. Oh, the dress. Then, there was Drew's search for his birth mother. Rocky cringed as she thought about what it would do to Drew's mother. Rocky opened the notes app on her phone and listed the things she needed to tell her father, in order of importance. She looked up and saw that she had at least another twenty minutes in the car. She turned her attention to emails next.

Rocky wanted to get all of her emails cleared before seeing her dad—an empty inbox always had such a calming effect on her, but just as she was making a dent, a ping rang out. She clicked over to Mail and saw her mother's name on the From line, and Wedding! in the subject line. She felt her temples pulse.

Now was not the time for this. She took a deep breath in, two, three, four, and then out, two, three, four, and looked again. She hit Delete.

Her mother was taking over every aspect of wedding planning, bit by bit. The only thing they had agreed upon was the date—both women immediately loved the idea of a June wedding. But that was the only thing they could agree on. Where Rocky wanted a small, casual dinner on the rooftop of her apartment building, her mother was inquiring about a three-hundred-person formal affair at her country club. Where Rocky wanted a local DJ to come spin after the dinner, her mother had an appointment already set with a fourteen-piece band. And, of course, there was the dress. Oh, the dress.

But she wouldn't let this upset her. She was going to see her father. It was her time alone with him, and she wasn't going to let her mother's ideas about the wedding take away from that.

Rocky had always belonged to her father, just as her sister, Amanda, had always belonged to her mother. It wasn't anything specific, there was no particular reason, but ever since she could remember, Rocky had gravitated towards her dad, and Amanda towards her mother. A memory: Rocky going into the office to work with her father on Sunday mornings—armed with dozens of doughnuts for the staff—and coloring on Xerox paper while he punched away furiously on his calculator. And another: getting her first bike with him, the evening before her fifth birthday, at the shop in town. And more still: how he would grab her hand after every school play and tell her that she had been the best one on stage, even when she wasn't. Rocky remembered countless Saturday afternoons at the local park, feeding the ducks in the pond, careful to stay out of their reach. She never knew what Amanda and her mother were doing those days, probably sipping tea out of fine china or shopping for clothes (again), but she didn't care. Rocky reveled in her father's attention. Craved it. Needed it. It was as if Amanda and her mother were a closed set of two. And Rocky didn't mind it. She was happy to be a daddy's girl and leave her sister to her mother.

Rocky looked out the window, watched the trees passing her by, and did a meditation exercise: take note of the world around you without judgment.

The trees are beginning to change color.

The air is cool and crisp.

Email from my mother.

Rocky shook her head, brought herself back to the present.

The sky is perfectly blue, like in a postcard.

The leather seats of the car are soft and smooth.

Email from my mother.

Guilt overcame her. She opened her laptop and rescued her mother's email from the Trash folder.

Hi honey! it read. Are you free to come look at a band with me on Thursday night?

Rocky drafted a response about having a work dinner, but then reconsidered. She didn't want to lie to her mother. She was not a person who lied. She wrote back: Sure, what time?

"Excuse me," the driver said to Rocky. "You'll have to show me which road to take up here."

"Follow the main road and make the third left. It's there on the corner."

The driver did as she said, and pulled up to the spot. "Am I coming back or waiting for you?"

"Drive around and come back for me in an hour," Rocky said, sliding her laptop into its case and grabbing the flowers. "There's a coffee shop around the corner that serves a phenomenal blueberry pie. I'm happy to pay for the wait time. And the pie."

"Okay, be back soon."

The car pulled away and Rocky walked slowly towards her father. She placed the flowers down at his grave and said: "Hi, Dad."

FOURTEEN

The mother of the bride, as a bride herself
Long Island, 1982

Joanie leaned her head against Matthew's chest. She loved how
he was the perfect height for her—even in the heels she was
wearing, her body fit perfectly against his. In high school, she'd
dated a guy who was shorter than her and she'd had nowhere
to rest her head when they slow-danced.

The Theta house was filled to the brim with hay bales and
leaves of every color for the Fall Formal. Joanie had borrowed a
black velvet dress and double strand of pearls from her mother.
The dress was strapless, which at home had made her feel so
adult, but at the Theta house with the windows opened, she
felt freezing cold in the November air. She burrowed closer to
Matthew for warmth.

"Should this be our wedding song?" Matthew asked, holding Joanie tight.

"'Endless Love'?"

"Well, it makes sense. You're *my* endless love."

BRENDA JANOWITZ

Joanie hadn't given much thought to their wedding song. In fact, she hadn't given much thought to wedding planning at all. Her mother was handling most of the planning on her own. She'd picked the date—Labor Day, a long weekend that would give their out-of-town family time to travel. She'd gotten the venue, her country club, and created the guest list, three hundred of their closest friends and family. She'd even taken care of the music, a fourteen-piece band that had a harp player for the ceremony. All Joanie had really cared about was the wedding dress. Oh, the dress.

Matthew sang quietly into Joanie's ear, and she felt his breath travel up her spine. "I have the record in my room. Wanna go listen?"

"We're listening to it now." And then, grasping his meaning: "Oh, yeah. Let's go."

Upstairs. Matthew's hands: everywhere. His lips: trailing down from her mouth to her neck to her collarbone. She fell back onto his bed and he pushed up the bottom of her dress.

"Wait," she said, and sat upright.

"Okay, I'll wait right here," Matthew said, his hands frozen between her thighs.

"I mean it, wait."

"All we do is wait." Matthew sighed and rolled over onto his back. "Let's try not waiting for once and see what happens."

"I'm serious," Joanie said. "I'm not ready."

"Okay," Matthew said. "I understand. We'll wait until you're ready."

Joanie kissed him. "Thank you."

"When, exactly, do you think you'll be ready?" He turned his head towards her and offered a sweet smile.

"Won't it be special if we wait for our wedding night?"

"Our wedding isn't until after the summer. Labor Day weekend," Matthew said, and Joanie regarded him. Then, cupping

70

Joanie's face in his hands: "Yes, that would be special. Should we go back downstairs to the party?"

"No, let's just stay here for a while."

"I know you want to dance with your sisters."

"No, I don't."

"Liar."

But Matthew was right: Joanie was lying to him. She wanted to be downstairs, dancing with her sisters. Half of the Delta House was there for the formal, including seven of her bridesmaids.

"I did put in a song request with the DJ. It wouldn't be right if I wasn't down there when it came on."

The door flung open. "They're playing 'Don't You Want Me, Baby'! We are legally obligated to go downstairs and dance."

"Debbie," Matthew said, "you can't just barge in. What if we were—doing something?"

"You weren't, were you?"

"No."

Debbie grabbed Joanie's hand and they ran down to the dance floor.

"You know there's a line of girls who want to have sex with your fiancé, right?" Debbie asked as she shimmied close. "When are you going to give it up?"

"Keep your voice down!"

"No one can hear me. And besides, I'm right."

"I happen to take it more seriously than you do. And I don't think that there's anything wrong with that."

"There's nothing wrong with it," Debbie said, bumping her hip into Joanie's, "but I just don't want to see you get hurt."

"That's not going to happen." Joanie looked over to the bar, where Matthew stood, surrounded by five different women. Where were their dates?

"You're getting married. Don't you want to sample the merchandise before you commit to buying?"

"I've sampled enough."

"Not as much as me," Debbie said, a devilish look in her eye.

"No," Joanie conceded, smiling widely at her friend. "Not as much as you."

"If you can't have fun in college, when can you have fun?"

"I have fun," Joanie said, just as the DJ cued up "We Are Family" by Sister Sledge. Missy stood next to the DJ with a microphone: "Delta sisters, get your asses on the dance floor!"

Debbie grabbed Joanie's hands as the floor filled with sorority sisters, ready to dance to the Delta House anthem.

The photographer approached. "Joanie, can I get a picture of you and your sweetheart?"

Joanie threw her arm around Debbie's neck and posed. "Say cheese!"

Debbie smiled brightly as the flash went off. Then, turning to Joanie: "I think he meant your fiancé."

FIFTEEN

The seamstress
Paris, 1958

"Stop!" he called after her. "Please don't go!"

"I'm sorry, Julien," Rose said, as she flew down the stairs. "I'm so sorry."

"You cannot say no," he called, as he jumped down the steps and stood next to Rose. "You simply cannot."

They stood face-to-face on the landing between the second and third floors of Madame's atelier. She was so close to her workstation, so close to the atelier, and all she wanted to do was go to her desk, put her head down, and get back to work. Rose wished she could forget everything Julien had just revealed to her: Madame's death, the plan to keep the atelier alive, her role in creating Diana Laurent's wedding dress. She would not do it.

She could not do it.

"You said it yourself," she said to Julien. She found herself staring down at her shoes, unable to look him in the eye. "We would be pretending that I was the one chosen by Madame as her protégé. But that is a lie. She did not actually choose me."

"But I chose you. Is that not enough?"

Rose did not know how to respond. Wasn't the answer clear? No, it was not enough. Madame was the master. Madame's was the only opinion that mattered. And Madame had not chosen her, had not thought she was good enough.

"I see," Julien said, and let out a long breath.

"I think it would be best if you were to approach whichever girl is your second choice," Rose said quietly. "Any girl would be lucky to have this opportunity."

"There is no second choice," Julien said, looking into Rose's eyes and placing his hand on her shoulder. "It is you. You are my choice. My only choice."

"Nicole is quite good," Rose said, shrugging away Julien's touch. "Have you seen the embroidery work she did on Mademoiselle Deon's dress?"

"I have seen it," Julien said, nodding slowly. He regarded her. "No one else's work compares to yours. Don't you know that?"

Rose shook her head furiously. The words simply would not come to her. She stood like that for a few moments, shaking her head, willing herself to speak. Her hands curled into balls as she tried to form a thought. And then, finally: "I can't."

"You can."

"I wasn't chosen by Madame," Rose said quietly. She drew her arms around her body, hugging tightly.

"She didn't know she had to choose!" Julien said, his voice raised, louder than Rose had ever heard it before. He slammed a foot on the floor and then looked surprised that he had done it. That he had lost control, if even for a moment. Then, much softer, with his eyes to the floor: "She thought she had more time. She didn't know she had to choose."

Rose took a small step back. Had she crossed a line? Had she gone too far? It felt like she had. After all, she hadn't considered

Julien's feelings. He was mourning the sudden loss of his aunt, the only family he had left in the world, but also mourning life as it had been. It wasn't so long ago that Rose was doing the very same thing. She knew how he felt: the fear, the loneliness, the uncertainty. The anger. When Rose's aunt died, all she could think was: *What will I do now?*

Neighbors came by in the days surrounding her aunt's death, but after a couple of weeks, the visits stopped. No one checked on Rose. No one brought her food like they'd done in the days right after the funeral. Once she'd depleted the meals that had been left in the icebox, she realized how ill prepared she was for her future. How little thought she'd given to the next step in her life. How little thought her aunt had given to making sure she'd be taken care of. It was all up to Rose. And it felt impossible.

"I'm so sorry," Rose said, her voice barely a whisper.

"Come with me," Julien said, and spun around to return up the stairs. Rose was powerless to say no. She followed Julien back to Madame's apartment, where he quickly disappeared into her bedroom. Rose stood out in the entryway, unsure of what to do.

"I want to give you something," Julien said, emerging from the bedroom with an orange box.

"That's not necessary," Rose said, without thinking. Always having to rely on herself, she had a hard time accepting the kindness of others, and her first instinct was always to say no. Sometimes even before the words were fully out of the other person's mouth.

"I know it's not necessary," Julien said, crossing the room. "That's why it's a present."

"I couldn't possibly," Rose said, a flush taking over her face.

"I haven't even opened the box yet." Laughter rose in his voice. "I have an entire apartment of my aunt's things to take care of. I need to figure out which items I will keep, which items I will give to charity, and which items I want to gift to people who meant something to my aunt."

"I meant something to her?" Rose asked, furrowing her brow. She wondered if that was really true.

Julien opened the box and Rose peered inside.

"Go on," he said, holding the box out.

Rose touched one careful finger to the scarf inside. The silk was so incredibly soft, she immediately reached for the cotton work gloves she kept in her pocket, so that she wouldn't damage the fabric.

"It's yours," Julien said, removing the scarf from the box. "You can touch it. You're not going to ruin it."

He held it up and Rose admired it. She recognized it as Hermès—bold, beautiful colors leaped off the silk twill, hand-stitched on the edges, so nearly perfect you'd swear a machine had made them. It had a bright yellow sun in the middle of an enormous circle, and the sun looked like he was sleeping. Each corner featured a different animal, and they corresponded to the symbols of the zodiac. Numbers and days and months swam around the inside of the circle, creating a calendar, with each zodiac sign represented. It was a piece that would never go out of style.

Julien draped it over her shoulders. Rose fingered the edges, ever so slightly. "My aunt would have wanted you to have it," he said. "This was her favorite one. Just as you were her favorite one in the atelier."

Rose admired her reflection in the full-length mirror on the other side of the room. "Thank you."

"She bought this scarf for herself with the profits from the first wedding dress she ever made."

"It's a family heirloom, then." Rose wanted to take the scarf off and give it back to Julien. How could she possibly accept such a present? But something was holding her back. It was as if the scarf already belonged to her, as if she knew that it was rightfully hers. But then, her aunt's voice rang out in her head, telling her that she mustn't accept such a gift. It wasn't appropriate. "I cannot accept such a gift," Rose said, even as the scarf stayed wrapped around her shoulders.

"I want you to have it," Julien said, his hands up, as if he couldn't possibly take it back. "Simple as that."

Tears threatened to fall from her eyes. She wasn't accustomed to such kindness. Such generosity. "I love it," she finally said.

"So, tell me, Rose," Julien said, grasping her hands in his own. "Will you help me save the atelier?"

SIXTEEN

The bride
Brooklyn, 2020

"I'm basically in love with the dress," Amanda said, as they walked. "Let's go see it."

Rocky immediately regretted asking her sister to come with her for the cake tasting she'd set up on a whim. The real tasting would be next week, with her mother, at the Upper East Side bakery she had carefully selected. Rocky knew that. Of course she did. But a new bakery had popped up in her Brooklyn neighborhood a few weeks prior, so Rocky thought it would be fun to check it out. More casual. Less formal. More like Rocky. Less like her mom.

"I don't think you can see the dress without an appointment," Rocky said. She raised her voice at the end, as if it were a question, but Rocky was certain. You needed an appointment to go see the dress.

"Of course you can," Amanda said. Amanda firmly believed that the rules in life didn't apply to people like her. And they usually did not. Amanda was beautiful and sweet and had an infectious smile. Everywhere she went, men, women, and children alike all fell head over heels in love with her. Animals, too. It simply could not be helped. She had a Marilyn Monroe figure and Brigitte Bardot hair. Even when she was straight-faced, she seemed as if she were laughing, a deep, throaty, sexy laugh like she thought that you were the most fascinating person in the world. She gave off a glow that made everyone around her feel desired and alive; you could feel her presence in a room before you saw her. And she was smart, too, brilliant really, but not in a threatening way. She could speak just as easily about intersectionality in the feminist movement as she could about her favorite cast member of *The Real Housewives of Beverly Hills*. (Which, Rocky felt, had its own feminist problem, but people usually didn't want to talk about that.)

Amanda stopped walking and pulled out her phone and dialed. She held her perfectly manicured finger up to Rocky, as if to say: *Watch me work my magic, this will only take one minute.* Rocky looked up at the trees, changing color for the fall. It would be summer by the time she and Drew got married. Eight months away. Three seasons. She could hardly wait.

"Oh, that's okay," Amanda said sweetly into the phone, though Rocky could tell she was mad as hell. "Next time, then."

"What did they say?" Rocky said as Amanda ended the call.

"You can't go in without an appointment."

Rocky tried not to gloat as they resumed walking towards the bakery. "Oh, really?" she asked, as calm and collected as she could muster.

"Yes. How rude," Amanda said, roughly throwing her phone into her Hermès Kelly bag, a gift their grandmother had bought her when she passed the New York State bar exam. "You're the bride. She shouldn't say no to you."

"She didn't say no to me," Rocky said, swinging her arms

by her side. It really was one of those perfect New York days. "She said no to you."

"I just wanted to see you in it." Amanda stopped at a crosswalk for the red light and pressed the button for the crosswalk furiously, over and over.

"That's sweet," Rocky said. The light changed and they crossed the street. Not looking her sister in the eye: "Can I tell you a secret?"

"Of course."

"But it's a secret."

"Yes," Amanda said. "I gleaned that from when you said 'Can I tell you a secret?' thirty seconds ago."

"I mean, you can't tell Mom."

"I wouldn't tell Mom," Amanda said, her lips thrust out like a petulant child. "I don't run and tell Mom everything, you know."

"You totally do."

"I totally do not."

"You do."

"Are you planning to tell me or are you just torturing me about how often I call our mother?"

Rocky took a deep breath. "I don't really want to wear the dress."

Amanda regarded her sister. She opened her mouth as if to say something, and then looked up, as if the answer were in the sky. She turned to Rocky. "But it's the most beautiful thing I've ever seen in my life."

"I know that it's beautiful," Rocky said carefully. "I'm just not sure that it's me."

"But you're going to wear it, right?" Amanda said, reverently, as if she were discussing something religious, something sacred.

"I don't know."

"Are you trying to give Mom a heart attack?"

"No, I am not trying to give Mom a heart attack."

"This is going to kill Grand-mère. You are literally going to kill our grandmother. She will have a heart attack and die. Her blood will be on your hands."

"I knew I shouldn't have brought this up," Rocky said. "Forget it, forget I even said anything."

Amanda stopped in the middle of the sidewalk, and threw her arms out. "I've got it. I have the solution. If you'd like," Amanda said dramatically, as if she were offering her sister a kidney, "I'll take the heat off and tell Mom that I'll wear the dress."

"You're not even engaged."

Amanda shrugged. "I could be engaged tomorrow."

"To who, exactly?"

"To whom."

"To whom?"

"Anyone I want," Amanda said, as if it were the most natural thing in the world. "You're making it sound like it's hard to find someone. Taking the New York State bar exam, now, that was hard. Finding someone? Not hard."

And Rocky had to laugh. Sure, her sister was being ridiculous, but it was also true. Amanda never had trouble meeting people. She'd probably find someone and fall in love at her and Drew's wedding. Amanda was particularly good at meeting people at weddings.

She'd met Poppy at her work friend's destination wedding in Mexico (after the ceremony, it was so hot they'd all changed into bikinis and Amanda was always at her best when she was flaunting her figure in a barely-there black string two-piece). She'd met Amy at a college friend's civil union downtown (the after-ceremony celebration dinner only lasted two hours, but she dated Amy for three months after that). And she'd met Sloan—oh, poor, sad Sloan—at their cousin Josh's wedding four years ago. (So many tequila shots. Amanda had woken up next to Sloan and from that point on, that they were an item was just a given, living together for nine months, a personal record for Amanda.)

"Turn right here, the bakery is a few blocks that way."

"Sure," Amanda said. "I need some sugar to lighten my mood. Who could be mad with a mouth full of wedding cake?"

Rocky knew of the tradition where the bride smashes wedding cake into the groom's face, after they've cut the cake at the wedding. She wondered if there was a similar tradition of the bride smashing a sample of the wedding cake into the maid of honor's face at the tasting.

"Must you always make everything about you, Amanda? Can anything ever be about me for just a moment?"

They walked into the bakery, and fifteen minutes later, Amanda fainted.

SEVENTEEN

The mother of the bride, as a bride herself
Long Island, 1982

The ghost of her sister surrounded her, enveloped her. She could tell her parents felt it too as they all lingered by the front of the Star Smith gallery, seemingly afraid to walk in. The invite Joanie had thrown away wasn't just any art gallery opening. It was for a group show where Michele's work would be exhibited, curated by one of her former NYCU professors, who'd found Joanie on campus and asked why they hadn't responded to the invite he'd sent.

"Let's find Michele's stuff," Matthew said, grabbing Joanie's hand and pulling her into the exhibit.

Joanie slowly followed. The gallery felt like something out of a movie: a vast space, with fourteen-foot-high shockingly white walls and seemingly no ceiling, pipes and beams completely exposed. The entrance had floor-to-ceiling windows, which enabled you to see everything inside before you even walked in. Every guest looked like they'd come off the runway of a fashion show, and Joanie held on tightly to Matthew's arm as they made their way in. Waiters circled them with glasses of champagne, filled perilously high.

Joanie could hear the sound of her heels clicking on the hard concrete floor. Some of the pieces were enormous sculptures, hovering over her head, and some took up the space of entire walls and looked more like graffiti than art. Joanie walked farther, and when she saw what she was looking for, she didn't need to look at the description. She knew that it had been created by Michele.

On an enormous canvas, she'd printed a map of New York. It was overlaid with something that looked like papier-mâché—delicate, drenched in bold colors—like if it wasn't handled properly, it could tear. And then, over that, were other objects. Items that Joanie had recognized as Michele's—a pink scarf she'd once worn in a grade school production of *Bye Bye Birdie*, an old Barbie doll with most of its hair cut off, and a box of matches from a local Italian restaurant they used to go to all the time as kids. Michele's work was unbelievable, indescribable. Joanie had never seen anything like it. Looking at it made her head swirl—she felt it deep in her bones. It was the story of Michele. The story of her life.

"I don't understand," Matthew said. "What is it?"

"These are all things that belonged to her."

"Oh, I see."

"It's complicated," Joanie said, losing herself in the art for a moment. Then: "And beautiful."

"I love it."

Joanie didn't necessarily understand her sister's work, but it felt like she had her sister back for a moment, like her sister was still with her. She reached out to touch the pink scarf, and a security guard materialized.

"You can't touch the art."

"Oh, it's okay," Matthew said. "Her sister made this."

"You can't touch the art."

"I'm sorry," Joanie said, leading Matthew away, farther into the exhibit. "It won't happen again."

They caught a glimpse of Joanie's parents, staring at a piece of art they'd later purchase and hang in their living room: a free-hand painting of the French flag, colors vivid and bright, with a photograph overlaid in the center—their wedding picture—covered in a blush of pink overlay so that her parents looked ethereal, soft, perfect. Joanie thought of what her wedding picture with Matthew might look like, and squeezed his hand.

"There's a bar set up in the back," Matthew said. "Drinks?"

"Soda, please."

"Your wish is my command." He offered a dopey smile as he walked off. Joanie watched as he walked away.

"Michele?" a stranger with a massive black mohawk said, grabbing Joanie's arm and spinning her around.

"Excuse me?"

The girl's eyes were lined in black kohl and her lips were bloodred. Her ears had tiny silver hoops climbing all the way to the top, too many piercings to count. Even her nose was pierced.

"Oh, shit," the girl said, using her fingers to smooth the top of her mohawk into shape. "I'm sorry. I thought you were someone else."

"My dead sister?"

"I'm sorry," she said, shaking her head.

"It's okay."

"So, you're the little sister," she said tentatively. "Not Michele."

"How do you know I'm not Michele?" Joanie asked defiantly. The girl looked back at her, sadness covering her face. She remembered. She remembered that her friend was dead.

"I'm sorry. I just got confused for a second. Being around so much of Michele's work, it's doing something to me."

"Me too. I'm Joan," she said, extending her hand. "Everyone calls me Joanie."

"I'm Melinda. Everyone calls me Mel."

"Are you an artist, too? Are you showing tonight?"

"Yeah, that's how I knew your sister," Mel explained. She regarded Joanie. "God, you look so much like her."

"I know," Joanie said. "Everyone says we had the same face. But, luckily, I don't have the same heart."

"What's that supposed to mean?"

"You know, because of the heart attack. We have the same face, but thankfully, I don't also have the bad heart."

"Heart attack?"

"Yeah," Joanie said, her words coming out slowly. "That's how she died. She had a heart attack."

Mel regarded her. She furrowed her brow: "But your sister didn't die of a heart attack."

EIGHTEEN

The seamstress
Paris, 1958

"You must be Rose," Mademoiselle Laurent said.

"Please, have a seat." Rose directed her to sit down, just as Julien had instructed. They'd gone over it repeatedly, as if choreographing a dance: what Madame would have said in greeting, how she would begin the meeting, how she would end it. Rose knew exactly what to do. Madame might not have chosen Rose as her protégé, but she would still make her memory proud.

"I'm Diana," she said. "I don't think we met the last time I was here."

"Lovely to make your acquaintance," Rose said.

"I was disappointed when Julien phoned to tell us that Madame would be in Monaco today," she said. The edges of her lips turned down into an impossibly sweet pout.

"I—I'm sorry," Rose stammered, and out of the corner of her eye she saw Julien approaching.

"Yes, we were so sorry about the scheduling," Julien said

fluidly, "but sometimes these things cannot be helped. When Madame learned that her favorite silk merchant would be in Monaco today, she could not pass up the chance to see him. And your dress will be the better for it."

Mademoiselle Laurent smiled broadly at Julien, and when he held out the chair for her, she sat down. Rose marveled at how Julien could lie so easily. Her entire body felt hot, she only hoped it did not show on her face.

Rose looked up to the loft, to where she used to do her sewing, and saw the girls diligently working. So consumed had they been over the gossip about Rose and Julien that they weren't surprised when Rose had been selected as Madame's protégé. Jealous, yes. But not surprised. And they believed Julien when he told them that Madame would be traveling to unearth new fabrics. Believed every word.

The tea was poured, and the meeting began.

"So," Rose said, remembering what Julien taught her, how Madame started every dress consultation, "how did you meet your fiancé?"

"It was love at first sight," Mademoiselle Laurent said, smiling, looking off in the distance as if she were in a dream.

"Love at first sight?" Rose asked, laughter in her voice. Julien threw her a stern look, and she brought her napkin to her lips, as if she had been coughing, not laughing.

"Yes. It was my dear friend Gabrielle's birthday party," Mademoiselle Laurent said. "We were gathered at her house for a party and I saw him from across the room. I was standing in the corner, surrounded by my friends, and when I looked up, I saw Bertram walk into the party. In that moment, our eyes met, and it was as if I'd known him my entire life. He walked straight across the room, took my hand, and asked me to dance. I didn't even know his name."

Rose smiled, thinking of the moving pictures she liked to see at the theater, an indulgence she allowed herself once a month.

Love at first sight. Just like when William Holden sees Audrey Hepburn for the first time, upon her return home from Paris in *Sabrina*.

It was a lovely idea. Perfect for the movies. But she didn't believe it actually happened in real life.

Rose passed Mademoiselle Laurent the sketches Madame had created after their first meeting. But Mademoiselle Laurent gently rejected each and every one. An elbow-length sleeve? Mademoiselle Laurent was horrified. No cummerbund? Mademoiselle Laurent looked offended. A shorter train so that the bride might dance at her reception without a bustle? Mademoiselle Laurent wouldn't hear of it.

Rose was in disbelief. She thought that everything Madame had sketched was above reproach. After all, she was the master.

"What else do you have?" Mademoiselle Laurent asked.

Rose didn't know how to respond. Julien had assured her that the meeting would be short—Rose would show Mademoiselle Laurent the sketches, and Mademoiselle Laurent would pick her favorite parts from each one. From there, Rose would draw a sketch that incorporated all of these ideas and create the dress from there.

This was not something they had planned for—Rose carefully sipped her tea as she considered what to do next.

"I rather like the sleeve on your dress," Mademoiselle Laurent said.

Rose hesitated. It was as if her breath was caught in her throat. Was Mademoiselle Laurent asking for a bracelet length sleeve? Rose could easily sketch that. But how dare she change the design work of the great Madame Michel? What would Madame think? She could hear Madame's disapproving voice in her head: *No, no, dear child. That simply would not do.*

But then Rose remembered—Madame was no longer there.

Her fingers moving quickly, Rose sketched out a dress and passed the paper to Mademoiselle Laurent. Bracelet sleeves, a higher neckline, button details down the back instead of the front, and a delicate lace border on the bottom. Mademoiselle Laurent looked carefully at the sketch. The edges of her lips curled ever so slightly, and her face lit up.

"Why, it's perfect."

Rose was so relieved that her eyes teared. She looked over to Julien and he beamed with approval.

The door to the atelier opened, and as Rose turned, she was blinded by the afternoon sun streaming through the windows. She saw his silhouette first: tall, impossibly tall, and trim, like Paul Newman. As he got closer, his eyes caught Rose's eyes. She froze, unable to look away. He looked at her like he knew her, like they'd met before. But Rose had never seen this man before. Surely, if they'd met previously, she'd have remembered.

A small smile played on the man's lips as Julien shook his hand to greet him. "I am Robert Laurent," he said. "I'm here to walk my sister home. If, of course, you have concluded your work for the day."

"I think we're ready," Mademoiselle Laurent said, looking to Rose for confirmation.

"Of course," Rose said. "Let me see you out."

"Thank you for taking such good care of my sister," Robert said. "I didn't catch your name."

Rose looked up at him and got lost in his eyes, once again. Now that she was closer to him, she could see that they were a royal blue, striking and bold. His hair was a dark blond, as were his eyelashes. He crinkled the sides of his eyes, waiting for Rose to respond, but she could not speak.

"This is Rose," Mademoiselle Laurent said. "She'll be helping Madame design my dress."

Rose shook her head in agreement, but again, no words came out of her mouth. She willed herself to speak, but she could not. She simply could not.

"She's incredibly talented," Mademoiselle Laurent added.

"Well, thank you, Rose," Robert said. "A beautiful name for a beautiful girl." And with that, they left.

"Thank you," Rose whispered back, minutes too late.

Love at first sight. Rose hadn't believed her, hadn't believed that such a thing could exist.

But if love at first sight did not exist, what was this feeling in her chest, in her heart? This feeling that left her woozy, as if she were floating? If love at first sight did not exist, how could one explain how Rose felt she knew this man, knew him completely, even though they'd never met before?

"Oh, dear child," Julien said, walking over to Rose, whose feet were still firmly planted at the front door. "I know that look. You mustn't fall in love with Robert Laurent. There's something you don't know about him."

NINETEEN

The bride
Brooklyn, 2020

"I think you could have been a little bit more understanding with your sister," Joan said, and Rocky's entire body tensed up. They were at Joan's country club for Sunday brunch, so Rocky was already feeling out of her element. It was as if everyone there had gotten the memo about the dress code, except for Rocky. Weren't Sunday brunches supposed to be casual? Whatever happened to casual? Her mother had specifically said that you could wear jeans for brunch at the club. Drew fit in seamlessly, knew the right thing to wear, with his expensive dark-wash jeans and Zegna button-down shirt. Rocky had the jeans part right, but it was as if she'd put the pieces together wrong. She shifted uncomfortably in her seat in her ripped jeans and silk camo blouse. Must they also discuss her sister?

Of course everything was still about Amanda. Everything was always about Amanda. Even Rocky's wedding planning.

"I was very understanding," Rocky said, her voice clipped. "I called the ambulance."

"I don't even understand what you were doing at that cake shop anyway," her mother said. "We have an appointment with the best bakery in the city next week."

What Rocky heard was: *This was your fault. If you hadn't taken your sister to a bakery in Brooklyn, she would never have fainted and ended up with a concussion.* Rocky didn't respond. She put her fork into her omelet and carefully cut it into pieces. It was a trick her childhood therapist had taught her to manage her anger—focus on something small that you can do methodically as you come back to your breath. Breathe in, two, three, four, and out, two, three, four.

A waiter came by with a coffee refill, but Rocky kept her eyes firmly planted on her plate.

"How's your omelet?" Joan asked.

Rocky closed her eyes—why couldn't her mother allow the silence to sit for even a second? Breathe in, two, three, four, and out, two, three, four.

"Mine's great," Drew said, and made a big show of taking another big bite. "I'm so glad they had green peppers this week."

"I got the peppers, too," Joan said, delighting in their similar tastes. Joan got along far better with Drew than she did with Rocky. Sometimes Rocky was left to wonder if Joan would rather have had Drew as her son than Rocky as her daughter.

"What did you get, Rocky?" Joan asked, and Rocky looked down again at her omelet. She couldn't remember what she'd put inside.

"Rocky always gets the broccoli and mushroom," Drew said, and he was right. Rocky was a creature of habit, though she wouldn't admit it.

"Yes, I did," Rocky said, and struggled with what to say next. If she didn't talk fast, her mother would bring the conversation back to—

"Amanda's feeling much better," her mother said.

"That's good to hear," Rocky said, her mouth full of food. Joan hated it when Rocky spoke with her mouth full, and Rocky liked doing it, simply to get a rise out of her.

"Don't speak with your—" Joan began, and then seemed to catch herself. "Yes, it is. The doctor wasn't too concerned about it."

"I know," Rocky said. "I was at the hospital with her."

"Well, she went to her internist, too, just to make sure everything checked out."

"Was it a panic attack?" Drew asked. Rocky shot him a look. *Do not encourage her*, it said. *We've spent enough time on Amanda*, it said. *Eat your damn omelet so we can get out of here*, it said.

"They don't think it was." Joan motioned to a nearby waiter for a refill on her coffee. Rocky motioned for a refill on her mimosa. There was not enough champagne in all of Fairfield County to get her through this brunch. And then, sotto voce, Joan said: "I think it was just the shock of seeing Sloan again."

"She tore that poor girl's heart out," Rocky said, matter-of-factly, downing her mimosa just as fast as it had been poured. "Twice."

"I don't think that's fair," Joan said, shaking her head, as if trying to get the bad sentiments about Amanda right out of her brain. "That's not a fair assessment at all."

"I would have liked to have met Sloan," Drew piped in. "You know, after hearing all of the stories."

Rocky shot Drew another look. *Do not feed the animals*, it said. He carefully sipped his water; he knew he'd be hearing an earful about this later. "It *is* a fair assessment. Sloan was madly in love with her and Amanda literally ripped her heart right out of her chest."

"I doubt it was literal, babe," Drew said, laughter in his voice.

"What did you just say?" Rocky said, through clenched teeth.

Drew threw his hand up and ordered a Bloody Mary from a

passing waiter. "Nothing," he said. And then, under his breath: "I mean, you can't literally rip someone's heart out of their chest. And even if you could, then they'd be dead."

"I, for one, think it's great that Amanda saw Sloan again," Joan said. "Maybe they'll get back together. I really liked Sloan."

"You only liked her because she actually got Amanda to settle down," Rocky said. And then quickly added: "For nine months. A record."

"That's not the only reason that I liked her." Joan brushed something nonexistent off her nose.

"You only liked Sloan because she's the only woman Amanda ever dated who actually wanted to get married."

"Not true."

"And I don't think it bodes well for a future relationship if the moment you see a person, it causes you to literally lose consciousness."

"See, now, that's how you use *literally* correctly," Drew said, and grabbed one of the scones from the center of the table. Rocky turned towards Drew and glared at him. He smiled back, lips parted, mouth full of chocolate chip scone, and Rocky couldn't help but laugh. This is the kind of person you marry— someone who loves the worst parts of you, someone who knows how to make you laugh even when you're mad as hell.

"Maybe it's all part of their cute story," Joan said, waving her hand around for dramatic effect. "After all, I've noticed that you delight in telling people that you and Drew were hate at first sight."

"I do not delight in telling them that," Rocky said. "Every freaking vendor asks me how I met Drew. Do you want me to lie?"

"Don't say *freaking*," Joan said to Rocky. And then to Drew: "Are you aware that your intended tells everyone that it was hate at first sight?"

"I've heard the story," Drew said, wiping his mouth with a napkin. "I think it's cute."

"It's not cute."

"Can we just talk about something else here?" Rocky asked. Her mimosa was refilled. She downed it again. "Anything else? Surely there is something else to talk about."

"Ah, our bride and groom!" Rocky heard a voice call out from over her shoulder. She spun around and saw the club's mâitre d' approaching their table.

"What did you do?" Rocky asked her mother. Joan shrugged in response, feigning innocence.

"I'd love to give you a tour of our ballroom," the mâitre d' said, more to Drew than to Rocky. "I think it's the perfect venue for your upcoming nuptials."

"Don't look at me," Drew said, his hands up as if in surrender. He pointed to Rocky. "Rocky's the one planning the wedding."

Rocky had desperately wanted to change the conversation. But this was not what she had in mind.

"Would you excuse me for a moment?" Rocky got up from the table and rushed to the bathroom. It was her best trick for cocktail parties and weddings—when you want to avoid an awkward social interaction, retreat to the bathroom. She'd been doing it since she was thirteen years old, always the odd man out at the countless bar and bat mitzvahs she got invited to. Rocky ducked into the last bathroom stall and sat down, head in her hands.

A country club wedding. That was the farthest thing from what Rocky wanted. A traditional ceremony, only Rocky didn't have a father to walk her down the aisle. She needed something that was more like her—less traditional, less of a reminder that her dad wasn't there to give her away.

"It's lovely for Joan, don't you think?" Rocky held her breath. Two women had walked into the bathroom and they were talking about her mother.

"Oh, I think it's wonderful. And she deserves something nice, doesn't she? Poor Joan."

"I just hope the wedding is here at the club so we don't have to drive all the way into Brooklyn."

Both women laughed. "Oh, I know. But maybe Joan's daughter has someone nice for your Chelsea to meet? Is she still single?"

A pause: "Yes."

"Weddings are great places to meet someone!"

"Well, Chelsea won't be invited. The girls haven't been friends since they were little."

"Joan's younger daughter is a strange one, isn't she?"

"Has been since she was little."

"Well, Joan is over the moon that she'll be wearing her wedding dress. That's special, isn't it?"

"It really is. I wish I had saved my wedding dress. Did you save yours?"

"I did, but with two sons..."

"I, for one, am happy for Joan. All she has in her life are those girls. To be honored like that on her daughter's wedding day? I couldn't think of anything more wonderful."

"Let's go over and say hello. I think the fiancé is a venture capitalist. Maybe there's someone in his office for your Chelsea?"

Rocky heard the door close and waited a few moments to make sure she was alone. She closed her eyes and tried to think what her father would say.

Seems you're in a bit of a pickle, she imagined him telling her.

Indeed.

Well, Kitten, you can either wear the dress or tell your mother you won't wear it. But you need to do something. Can't walk down the aisle naked.

I can't break Mom's heart, Rocky imagined herself saying back to her dad. She could almost see his kind eyes staring back at her. *I just can't.*

Then you wear the dress, I suppose. Can you do that?
Rocky didn't know.

She opened her eyes and found herself alone in the bathroom. She walked out to the sink, splashed some water onto her face. She looked at herself in the mirror. It was decided. Her mother cared about the wedding dress. Rocky did not. Rocky didn't really care much about what she wore down the aisle, as long as Drew was standing at the end of it. She would make her mother happy. She would wear the dress.

TWENTY

The mother of the bride, as a bride herself
Long Island, 1982

"We're heading out in a few minutes," Joanie's mother said, poking her head into her daughter's room.

"You look beautiful," Joanie said. Her mother did a little spin in the doorway—she wore a navy Diane von Furstenberg wrap dress and gold wedge sandals. Delicate gold jewelry and a small gold clutch. She was dressed perfectly for the holiday party at the country club. Fashion had always been her mother's strong suit.

"Enjoy yourself in the city tonight," her mother said, and gave her a kiss goodbye.

Joanie examined her mother closely. Had everything changed? Had the way she looked at her mother changed? After Mel told Joanie that Michele didn't die of a heart attack, Joanie had pressed her for more information. But Mel quickly backtracked, clamming up and saying that she'd made a mistake. Who was lying—Mel or Joanie's mother?

She would find out that night. She was going back to the gallery to see Mel again. This time, Mel would tell her the truth.

Being at the gallery by herself felt different. The security blanket of her parents and her fiancé gone, Joanie felt untethered, unsure of herself. For starters, her outfit was all wrong. Joanie thought that shopping in her sister's closet would have ensured that she'd be dressed the part for a gallery opening in SoHo, but she had put the pieces together all wrong. She caught a glimpse of her reflection in the floor-to-ceiling glass wall of the gallery. The black short-sleeved button-down that had looked so edgy in Michele's closet somehow looked like her usual preppy white shirts, only dipped in another color. And the black cigarette pants that Joanie was sure screamed hip and downtown looked anything but. She had thought she was Audrey Hepburn in *Funny Face*, all hip and cool, but she now realized that she was actually Audrey in *Roman Holiday*, a princess pretending to be someone else.

Joanie spun on her heel—the faster she found Mel, the faster she could leave—and smashed right into a man standing behind her.

"My goodness!" she cried out as her drink flew out of her hand and spilled all over the person in front of her. "I'm so sorry!"

"It's cool," the man said, laughing, and wiped the front of his ripped black T-shirt with a flick of his wrist. His arms were covered in black leather bracelets, all detailed with silver grommets of varying shapes and sizes, and he wore painted-on black leather jeans. "I was actually kind of hot, so thank you for cooling me down."

"I really am sorry," Joanie said, and took the cocktail napkin wrapped around her drink and attempted to dry his shirt with it.

"Nothing to be sorry about." He grabbed her hand as it frantically dabbed at the spill. With their hands entwined, he looked up, and their eyes met. His eyes glowed violet—they weren't blue, they were a definite shade of purple—and they seemed to be smiling at her. Joanie felt a jolt—a frisson of energy that went from her belly right up to her head, making her feel like she was outside of her body, looking down at herself.

"I'm Jesse."

"Me too."

"Your name is Jesse?" he asked.

"Oh, no," Joanie said, laughing nervously. She felt her hands start to get hot, and she pulled hers away from his. "I'm—"

"Who are you supposed to be?" a voice called out from over her shoulder. She spun around and saw another man, similarly attired in an old gray T-shirt, filled with holes, and ripped jeans. He looked like a clone of Jesse. A copy. But he wasn't as handsome. His outfit wasn't as cool. And his eyes? Just plain old brown.

"Oh, hi, I'm Joan," Joanie said, partially to him, partially to Jesse, trying to make her name sound more grown-up, cooler, by dropping the suffix. And then, to fill the empty space: "As in Joan Jett."

"More like Joan," the other guy responded, now standing next to her, "as in Joanie Cunningham from *Happy Days*."

"Lay off her, Danny," Jesse said, and playfully punched his arm.

"Where's Chachi?" the clone asked, smirking at her. Joanie furrowed her brow and turned to Jesse.

Jesse threw his arm over her shoulder and whispered: "Ignore him. It's what we all do."

"Who's we?" Joanie asked.

"We're Dead Dream," Danny said, as if it were obvious. But Joanie had no idea what he was referring to.

"The band," Jesse said, though it was more like a question. Joanie shrugged her shoulders.

"You've never heard of us?" Danny asked. "Then why are you talking to this loser?" He pointed at Jesse.

"I'm actually looking for my friend Mel. Have you seen her? She's one of the artists exhibiting here tonight."

"My sister?" Jesse said, furrowing his brow. "You don't look like the sort of girl who's friends with my sister."

"Well, I am."

"Well, then, you just missed her. On Tuesdays at eight, she visits her friends Bill W. and Dr. Bob."

"Oh, I didn't meet them."

Jesse stifled a laugh. "She'll probably be at our show this weekend. We're playing at the Rooster. You should come."

"Oh, I don't—"

"You have to come," Jesse said. "Friday night at midnight. You can see your friend Mel. I'll put your name on the list. You can walk right in. Don't have to wait in line."

"That's so nice," Joanie said, feeling the weight of Jesse's arm around her shoulders. "I'm not sure—"

"Don't break my heart," Jesse said, leaning into her ear. Joanie could feel his sweet breath on her cheek, and she turned to look up at him.

"We need to go," Danny said, and Jesse's arm flew off Joanie's as he checked his watch.

"Yeah, we've gotta go," Jesse said. "Joan-as-in-Joan-Jett, will I see you this weekend?"

"Yes." She didn't mean to say yes. There was no way she'd be able to make it—her curfew would be up before the show even began, for starters. And even if she could convince her mother to allow her to stay out past midnight, she had no one to go with. She couldn't take the Long Island Rail Road by herself after midnight. Not to mention the fact that she had no idea what the Rooster was, or where.

But still, she had said yes. She was powerless to say anything else.

TWENTY-ONE

The seamstress
Paris, 1958

Engaged. Robert Laurent was engaged.

When Julien told her, Rose pretended that she didn't care, that she barely even knew what he was going on about, but it wasn't true. Of course it wasn't true. In those few moments between Robert's goodbye and Julien's warning, Rose had already created an entire narrative for herself, for her life with this man.

She would dress carefully the next time she saw him, setting her hair slowly the night before and wrapping it in a silk scarf so that it would look its best come morning. She would let Marion, the girl who lived in the room next to hers at the boarding house, apply her makeup. (Marion worked at Galeries Lafayette in the makeup department and was always inviting Rose to stop into the store for a makeover.) Then, she would pick out her favorite dress, one that Madame had approved of, and wear her best stockings and shoes. And then, her most prized possession: earrings that had belonged to her aunt, large pearl studs that brightened her face.

Robert would see her and they would lock eyes. Rose would know, in that moment, that they were meant to be, and when he asked her to accompany him to a late supper, Rose would say yes. Even though it was last minute. Even though they'd just met. Even though she barely knew this man at all.

And after dinner, he would walk her home slowly. He would want to savor every moment with Rose, and she, with him. When they arrived at her front door, he would gently kiss her hand, like a gentleman, and Rose would know—even though they hadn't even kissed yet—that he was the man she would marry.

But none of that was meant to be. He was engaged. Betrothed to another. So, on the day of Mademoiselle Laurent's next appointment at the atelier, Rose did not wear her best dress. She did not take extra time to style her hair, and she did not take special care on her makeup. She convinced herself that it was just another day, like any other before it, and when Mademoiselle Laurent came in with her brother accompanying her, Rose barely looked his way.

"Rose," Robert said, walking over to her and gently taking her hand. "It's lovely to see you."

"It's lovely to be seen." Rose imagined herself as the ingenue of one of the films she liked to see on Saturdays. Debbie Reynolds in *Singing in the Rain*. She smiled coyly, and then caught Julien gazing at her from the corner of her eye. She quickly took her hand from his and sat down at the worktable with Mademoiselle Laurent.

"I was so sorry to hear that Madame would be traveling again today," said Mademoiselle Laurent.

"Yes," Julien said, not even giving Rose a moment to respond. "When Madame heard about a new lace maker in Florence, she couldn't resist the chance to meet him. And since lace will make up such a large part of your dress, well, there was simply no question."

"How wonderful," Mademoiselle Laurent said, her eyes dancing with glee. "I can't wait to see what she brings back."

"Ah, yes," Julien said.

Once again, Rose marveled at how Julien was so easily able to lie to Mademoiselle Laurent. It was as if he believed every word he was saying as gospel truth. It was as if he was used to deception, was comfortable with it. Rose, herself, couldn't bear to lie. She hated the feeling she got in her chest when she wasn't being completely honest. She knew this was why Julien took the lead in telling Mademoiselle Laurent about Madame—he didn't want her to feel uncomfortable. Or perhaps it was simply because he didn't want her to make a mistake and give up the ruse. Either way, Rose couldn't imagine what was going on inside his head. Did he mind the subterfuge? Or was it all a game to him, like Cary Grant's cat burglar in *To Catch a Thief*?

Rose took a deep breath. She was nervous for the day. Nervous to see Robert again, knowing what she knew, but also nervous to show Mademoiselle Laurent her work. This was the first time that a bride would be looking at a wedding dress sketch she had designed. Rose had cleaned up the draft she had done on the fly during the first appointment and had created a final vision for the dress.

Mademoiselle Laurent was there to approve the sketch of the dress. If she liked it, they would put the dress into production. From there, Rose would create a muslin for Mademoiselle Laurent to try on, and if all went well, they would then move on to fabric selection.

Rose took out her sketch and hesitated. She'd worked on this drawing longer than she'd ever worked on a design in her life. First, she'd consulted Madame's old books—pages upon pages of dress designs she'd created for former clients. Then, Rose had pored over all of her own old work, all of her old ideas. She considered which design elements would work with Mademoiselle Laurent's vision, while staying close to the inspiration: the Grace Kelly dress. She experimented with different styles and patterns, only to start over again the next day. She had drawn eleven sketches before finally settling on the one that she would be presenting to Mademoiselle Laurent. Would Mademoiselle Laurent be able to tell how much work had gone into her design?

Would Mademoiselle Laurent believe that what she was looking at was created by the protégé of the most celebrated wedding dress designer in Paris? That it was designed with her guiding hand? That it held the blessing of the great Madame Michel herself? It seemed unimaginable. Perhaps she was fooling herself. Her work could never hold up to the impossible standards Madame had set. There was simply no way.

Rose slid the delicate paper over to Mademoiselle Laurent. She had meant to infuse the moment with more confidence, more importance, but instead found herself holding her breath as the girl examined the drawing.

"Why, it's the most beautiful thing I've ever seen." Mademoiselle Laurent wiped a tear from her eye. "Thank you, Rose. I love it."

"Thank you, Mademoiselle Laurent," Rose said, bowing her head. She felt a flush come over her face, and she didn't want Mademoiselle Laurent to see it. She wanted to keep up the ruse that she created wedding dresses every day under the guidance of Madame Michel, and that today was no different, no more special than any other day.

"Oh, please, Rose," Mademoiselle Laurent said. "You must call me Diana. After all, you're designing my wedding dress!"

"Diana," Rose said, trying the word out in her mouth. She looked up to Julien to see if it was all right for her to call an esteemed client by her first name. Julien nodded his head imperceptibly, and Rose got the message.

"Yes," Diana said, smiling broadly. When she smiled, Rose felt like she could tell all of her secrets to her.

"It's the most important dress you'll ever wear," Rose said, echoing a statement she'd heard Madame say to her brides countless times. It never failed to impress. Sometimes it even brought brides to tears.

A slight laugh escaped Diana's lips. Rose had no idea what was so funny. No bride had ever laughed at Madame when she'd said that.

"I'm so sorry," Diana said. "I hope you won't find me rude."

"I don't understand."

"It's just a wedding dress," Diana said plainly, and Rose could not respond. She furrowed her brow. Why, a girl's wedding dress was the most important garment in the world. Every bride who walked into Madame Michel's atelier spent their entire lives dreaming about it. And now Diana didn't think it was important?

"It's your wedding dress," Rose said, barely getting the words out. She looked down at the sketch of Diana's dress. She thought of how tirelessly she had worked on it. Always with the thought in her head: this will be the most important dress this woman will ever wear in her life.

And then, leaning in, Diana said: "Do you want to hear a secret?"

PART TWO:
PICK YOUR FABRIC

"The importance of this step cannot be understated. If you pick the wrong fabric, your dress is doomed from the start. Pick a fabric that has the right weight, that will flatter the design. And the figure of the bride who will wear it. Once you pick your fabric, the die is cast. There is no going back."

—Excerpted from *Creating the Illusion* by Madame Michel,
Paris, 1954

TWENTY-TWO

The bride
Brooklyn, 2020

She should not be there. She should not be there at all. It was totally inappropriate, like seeing your grandmother in her underwear.

Rocky felt an overwhelming sense that this was a huge mistake. It was personal, for one, too personal, and Drew and his mother should be alone for this. Drew and his adoptive mother, she should say. She now had to clarify between the mother who raised him and the birth mother he was trying to track down.

"I completely understand," she was saying to Drew. She kept running her hand through her hair, trying to pat it down into place, as if the act of getting her hair to behave would change the conversation. "Of course I understand."

"I don't want to do anything without your blessing," Drew said. He took his mother's hand in his and held it. Steadied it. Rocky noticed that Drew's mother, while smiling, would not meet his eye.

"You have our blessing," his father said, shaking his head side to side, furiously. "Of course you do."

Rocky wanted to melt into the couch cushions. This overly accepting display of mixed message blessing-giving was making her feel ill. Therapist or not, having a child tell you that they want to set off and find their birth mother could not be easy. And then the added bonus that said child also wanted to invite said birth mother to his wedding? Impossible.

And Drew's mother had to pretend that everything was okay, that this decision was fine with her, even though it had to be difficult. When Rocky and Drew left, what would his parents say about it? Would Drew's mother discuss it with her own therapist?

It was something Rocky had always wondered—did her therapist see a therapist? Or was he just perfect? Just followed all of his own advice? Having asked Drew's therapist mother this very question, she now knew the answer: an unequivocal yes. Every therapist has a therapist of his or her own.

What, then, would Drew's mother be telling her therapist this week? How she had to pretend that she was totally fine with Drew's decision to track down his birth mother before his wedding? That her son suddenly felt as if he didn't belong to their family anymore, as if some other mother was pulling him away? Rocky knew how much this wedding meant to Drew's mother—she basically told her that very thing every time they saw each other—so, this couldn't be easy. And then, having to pretend that all of this didn't bother you? Even harder.

Rocky knew what she'd be telling her own therapist that week—that she wished she hadn't come for this. Hadn't been forced to witness it. And then her therapist would ask her: *Why do you think you felt that way?*

Rocky had been in therapy for so long, she could always anticipate what her therapist would say to her. Sometimes she even made it a game. She'd tell her therapist what was going on that week, and then tell the therapist: *I know what you're going to say.* Eight times out of ten, she was right.

Rocky went to her first child psychologist when she was five years old. Her kindergarten teacher had "expressed concern" about how Rocky had outbursts of anger. How she didn't play well with other children. How she didn't share. Her mother pulled her out of school once a week for the next five weeks to see a dizzying array of experts to weigh in on what was going on with her daughter. There were IQ tests, cognitive tests, and skills tests. There were group play settings, there was observation of solitary play. And there were interviews. So, so many interviews.

Joan didn't like the first doctor's opinion, so it was on to a second doctor and his team. And then a third. While each doctor was very different, had a very different way of doing things, they each came to the same conclusion: Rocky had explosive anger disorder, a behavioral disorder that was characterized by uncontrollable outbursts of anger, usually to the point of rage, that were—more often than not—disproportionate to the situation that triggered it. And they each recommended the same treatment: medication that would regulate Rocky's serotonin levels. Joan was adamant that she would not allow her child to be medicated, it was not up for discussion, so it was on to the next best thing: therapy. So many types of therapy. Individual therapy, group therapy, family therapy.

Every time she came out of a meeting or a therapy session, her father would shrug his shoulders and say: "Well, I think you're perfect, Kitten. But we all have things to work on, right?" When they got home, her mother would usually disappear into the master bedroom to "lie down," but Rocky knew that she went there so she could cry in the bathtub. She would emerge an hour later, as if nothing had happened.

Drew's mother seemed like the type who could appreciate a good midafternoon cry in the bathtub. Their Upper West Side townhouse was pre-war, but had modern finishes. The style was bohemian, but expensive. So, you might sit down on a couch that was soft and comfortable, looked like it had been purchased in the 1970s with its mismatched fabrics and wild color scheme, but then you'd later learn that the couch came from Roche Bobois and cost over forty thousand dollars.

Drew's mother looked much the same way—bohemian, but expensive. The enormous scarves that were always draped over her shoulders? Hermès. Her many sweater vests? They were cashmere. And they were from Loro Piana. The wide-leg trousers? Silk. Armani.

Rocky sat with Drew's parents on the first floor, the parlor level. One floor up was the kitchen, living room, and dining room. Drew's childhood bedroom was on the third floor, the master was on the fourth, and the basement, ahem, garden level, had been converted into an office for Drew's mother to see patients. It had its own separate entrance, making it function perfectly as a place of business. Drew's parents always entertained on the parlor level, and Rocky puzzled over how there were no television sets on the entire floor.

"What are we supposed to do?" Rocky asked Drew the first time he brought her home to meet his parents.

"Talk to each other," Drew said, laughter rising in his voice.

"Well, I know that," Rocky had said quickly, defensively, in response. She wondered, but did not say: *What are we supposed to eat if the kitchen is upstairs?*

Rocky crossed her legs on the couch and checked her phone. Drew hated when Rocky took her phone out when she was at his parents' house (*We try to be present* was a thing Drew's mother often said), but she didn't think he would notice.

He had noticed. "Rocky?" Drew said, his voice carrying across the room. Rocky looked up from her phone. "Would you like that?"

Rocky had no idea what they had just been talking about. She considered this a special skill of hers—the ability to drown out noise and retreat into her own world—and it served her well at work, where her loft-style offices were set up as an open concept workspace. She had to code and run the company all from a desk in the corner of the room. If she didn't tune out the noise, she could hear seventeen different conversations happening at the same time, twenty-two different people slurping their morning coffees at the same time, and fifty-four different keyboards typing away furiously at the same time. She would never get any work done. But here, in this situation, it hadn't served her well. She had no idea what Drew and his parents had just been discussing, and now she had only one option: she had to come clean and ask Drew to repeat the question, admit that she hadn't been listening. After all, if she didn't, who knew what she might be agreeing to? But then she thought of how disappointed Drew would be—she was supposed to be there supporting him, and instead, she'd completely zoned out into her own little world. (We try to be present.) This would never have happened if the Goodmans just had a goddamned television down here.

"I think it's a great idea, babe." Rocky had no idea what she'd just agreed to, but Drew and his parents seemed pleased, so she chalked it up as a win.

TWENTY-THREE

The mother of the bride, as a bride herself
Long Island, 1982

The ruse: Joanie told her mother that she'd be attending a late-night party at the Theta House, and she'd sleep in the dorms with Jenny, so as to avoid taking the Long Island Rail Road too late at night. Her mother had agreed. Easily, without question. Normally Joanie would feel guilty about lying to her mother. But not this time. She was on a mission. She would find Mel at Jesse's show and learn the truth about what happened to her sister.

Time to get dressed. Joanie walked to her sister's record player, as if it was beckoning her. She put the needle down on The Runaways record, and set it to top volume. She shook her head from side to side, letting the music fill her up, seep into her pores, get her ready. She knew she needed the right clothes, the right outfit tonight.

Joanie surveyed her sister's closet. She grabbed a black leather mini skirt and shimmied out of her jeans. The skirt fit like a glove, but what to match with it?

Joanie pulled out an army-green jacket and slipped it on. Then a black silk blouse. And then an old black T-shirt. Nothing looked right. She grabbed an old Polaroid off Michele's bulletin board and tried putting on the exact same outfit. But somehow it looked entirely different on her.

She thumbed through Michele's albums for inspiration. On The Runaways album, the lead singer wore a sequin jacket, sleeves pushed up. Her hair was feathered, and Joanie ran her hands through her own hair to try to get it into a similar shape.

Next she pulled out an album called *Parallel Lines*. Joanie took the record out and set it to play. A telephone rang, and then the lead singer's voice called out with the opening lyrics to the first track, a song Joanie had never heard before. She flipped the cover over to see what the song was called: "Hanging on the telephone."

Joanie examined the front of the album cover—the sleek black-and-white stripes in the background, contrasted with the name of the band in a bold red. The guys, all in black suits with black ties. And then, the one thing you couldn't take your eyes off, the girl. Debbie Harry, standing defiant in front of the group, hands firmly planted on hips, looking gorgeous in a slinky white dress with spaghetti straps. Joanie instantly thought two things: first, that she wanted to look just like that. And second, that she easily could. Her mother had an identical dress hanging in her closet.

Joanie made a beeline for her mother's room. As a little girl, Joanie had loved getting lost in her mother's walk-in closet, running her hands along the lush fabrics, putting her tiny feet into her mother's high-heeled shoes, and draping herself in soft scarves made of silk. But if Joanie wanted to make her train into the city, she had to be quick. She found what she was looking for at the very back of the closet, still in a plastic bag from the dry cleaner's. The dress was Halston, and it was perfect. She hung it on her bedroom door and set off to Michele's room to put her makeup on.

Joanie threw all of her clothing off and sprayed herself with Michele's Opium, recalling the famous line by Coco Chanel: *Where should one use perfume? Wherever one wants to be kissed.* Her neck, the crook of her arm, the backs of her knees. The room filled with the heady scent. Joanie thought of Matthew, how he would smell like her Love's Baby Soft after they'd been making out. Smelling herself on her fiancé always gave her a thrill. She thought about what he'd say about the aggressive scent she'd just put on. There's no way he'd like it. But then she remembered: she wasn't seeing Matthew that night.

Next, makeup. Joanie carefully examined each of the shades of eyeliner in her sister's collection and realized it was organized by color. On the farthest end, the shades were light, and then moved to medium colors, finally ending with various sticks of black. Joanie's fingers went to the darker shades. This time she wouldn't choose the medium blue that Princess Diana favored. Tonight, she would use black.

"Mel?" Joanie called out as she got out of the cab at the Rooster, a rock club in the East Village. The massive black mohawk had been the tip-off—Mel would always be easy to spot in a crowd. But when the person turned around, it most certainly was not Mel.

"Oh, sorry. I thought you were someone else." Joanie choked on the cigarette smoke that enveloped the air outside of the club. She tried to wave it away, but there was no use. It was everywhere. She wrapped her arms around herself—she was freezing cold in the skimpy halter dress she'd worn. She was dressed all wrong yet again.

"You in or out?" the bouncer asked, lifting the velvet rope up for Joanie. She walked through, unsure of what she would do once she was inside. Fraternity parties were easy—everywhere she went on the NYCU campus, she was sure to be greeted by the friendly face of a sorority sister. But here? In a smoke-filled rock club in the East Village? This was farther downtown than any Delta sister had traveled before. She was on her own.

Joanie coughed again as she walked down the steps, through the haze of cigarette smoke, into the club. She would definitely have to get her mother's dress dry-cleaned before sneaking it back into her closet. And she would definitely have to wash her hair before getting into bed that night.

At the base of the steps, the room looked pitch-black. It took Joanie a second for her eyes to adjust, to make out the bar in front of her, which ran the entire length of the club. All the way to her left, she saw the stage and a small dance floor. There was a band onstage and the music was so loud, it hurt her ears just to stand there. A couple next to her were etching their names into the wood frame of the doorway, and she took a step to the side, to give them some space. She smelled something funny, the faint scent of a skunk, and as she tried to place the smell, the guy standing next to her held out a fat cigarette and asked: "You want some?"

"Oh, no thank you," Joanie said, as politely as she could muster, realizing a beat too late that it was pot. He was smoking marijuana right out in the open, where anyone could see him. Wasn't that illegal? Hadn't Nancy Reagan said something about a contact high? She would need to make her way into the club, and not just hover at the doorway.

In front of her: a mass of sweaty bodies. They didn't look like the students she was used to socializing with at NYCU. They were punk all the way, with more tattoos than she could count, hair dyed every color of the rainbow (one guy's mohawk was actually dyed to look like a rainbow), and piercings as far as the eye could see. Joanie had to laugh—at the Delta house, they called her sister Michele the "punk" sister, but the sisters had no idea what punk truly was.

"Joanie Cunningham," she heard a voice call out from the bar, and she realized that she was still standing dumbly at the entrance to the club. "How's Chachi?"

Joanie knew the voice before she saw his face. He was at the end of the bar over on the right, smiling like the Cheshire Cat, taking shots with a guy who had a pair of drumsticks in his back pocket. They chased the shots with beer, and then motioned for the bartender to pour another round of shots.

"Hey, so have you seen Mel?"

Danny didn't respond. He took another shot, washed it down with his beer, and then pointed his bottle towards the other side of the bar. Joanie's eyes traveled all the way to the other side, at the opposite end of the club, close to where the stage was set up. And there she was, the woman Joanie came to see.

It wasn't easy, teetering in her mother's three-inch heels, but Joanie moved as quickly as she could through the crowds of people trying to get a drink at the bar. Despite her calls of "Excuse me!" and "Pardon me!", no one budged. Joanie hugged the wall, trying to find some empty space to squeeze by.

She couldn't take her mind off the task at hand. She would find Mel. She would find out the truth about her sister.

But by the time she reached the end of the bar, Mel was already gone.

TWENTY-FOUR

The seamstress
Paris, 1958

Her voice barely a whisper, Rose said: "Yes." She put her hands around the arms of the chair and got ready to hear Diana's big secret. What could it possibly be?

Perhaps this was it. The moment she and Julien had feared all along. Perhaps Diana knew that Madame was not helming the design of her wedding dress. Diana would out Rose and Julien as liars, and the atelier would be forced to close down in scandal.

But they'd been careful, hadn't they? If Rose didn't know the truth herself, she wouldn't doubt Julien when the words came off his lips, smooth as silk. And Rose's work was good. Very good. Insecure as she was, even she had to admit that. It wasn't at the level of a master like Madame Michel—that took a life-time of practice to achieve—but still, she felt that the design she had created for Mademoiselle Laurent would have made Madame proud.

"Come closer," Diana said, as Rose shifted her chair towards her. "I don't want my brother to hear." Diana nodded her head in the direction of Robert, who sat on a longue in the front of the atelier, reading the newspaper.

Rose looked in Robert's direction and felt a pull in her chest. He was handsome, so incredibly handsome, but it wasn't just that. There was something about him, something in the way that he held himself, that drew Rose to him. It was as if they'd known each other, as if they'd been made for each other, and it was merely fate holding them apart. She was meant to be with him, she felt sure of it, but how could that be the case when he was engaged to another woman?

Robert looked up from the newspaper and smiled at Rose. The edges of his eyes crinkled, and his entire face lit up. Rose quickly looked back down at the table. She grabbed a charcoal pencil and held it over the wedding dress sketch, busying her hands so that her mind might follow.

"Well," Diana began, careful to be sure that she had Rose's full attention. "I don't even want this big wedding that my family is planning. My fiancé, Bertram, doesn't either."

"I don't understand," Rose said, and she truly did not. How could any girl not want a big, beautiful wedding? Surely she was misunderstanding Mademoiselle Laurent's intent.

"My dream, my secret dream, is that Bertram and I run away together and elope. He wants the same thing, you know. All we want is each other. The marriage. The relationship. This big wedding is all for our fathers. For their political allies."

Diana went on about her father's political career, and the importance of appearances, but Rose was in disbelief.

Rose would give anything to have a wedding like what was being planned for Diana. And Diana didn't even want it. If the gossip papers were to be believed, there would be over four hundred guests, a fourteen-piece orchestra, a dinner with five courses. Who wouldn't want such an affair thrown in her honor? To be surrounded by four hundred people who wanted to celebrate her happiness. A family who loved her enough to throw such a thing. Love. Money. Security.

Rose looked to Robert. Perhaps she had underestimated this family. Perhaps the money and the political connections had blinded her to who these people truly were. People who were spoiled. Who didn't appreciate what they had in life. Who took their lives and their luck for granted. Maybe she was destined to surround herself with people like Julien, people who'd been abandoned. Who could understand where Rose came from. Because from what she was hearing, the girl who sat before her didn't appreciate a thing.

"I would never do it, of course," Diana said, taking a careful sip of tea. "I could never do that to my mother. Or my father, either, but mostly my mother. It is her dream to dance at my wedding. You see, Bertram and I both believe that family is everything. Do you agree?"

"I don't have any family," Rose admitted, too taken off guard to realize that she'd revealed too much. Her eyes flickered to Julien, who was pretending to busy himself with paperwork, even though Rose knew that he'd been listening to every word. He offered a small smile to Rose, and she continued. "I'm an orphan. I lived with my aunt, but she died when I was sixteen."

"Oh, that's simply too awful," Diana said, drawing Rose towards her for a hug. Even though Diana was thin as a twig, her hug was still warm and soft. "My friends are just like family to me," Diana whispered in her ear.

"You are very kind."

"You know," Diana said, "I may not want the big, fancy wedding, but I do want the dress!"

"I should hope so," Rose said, smiling back at Diana, laughing nervously.

"And the groom, of course. That's what I want more than anything. I'm completely, utterly, and madly in love. I suppose that's why we're in such a rush to get married. Have you ever been in love like that?"

"I have not." Rose's eyes drifted across the room to Diana's brother. And then, just as quickly, she brought her attention back to Diana. "I suppose love isn't for people like me. Let's get back to the dress, shall we?"

TWENTY-FIVE

The bride
Brooklyn, 2020

All eyes were on Amanda.

All eyes were always on Amanda. Sweet, beautiful Amanda. Girly, flirty Amanda. Rocky was used to it, really. Anytime she was with Amanda, it was as if she, herself, became invisible. But Rocky learned to use it to her advantage. In fact, growing up in Amanda's shadow had taught her to relish it. *Underestimate me,* she often thought. *That's when I do my best work.*

"I love the lace," Amanda said, and Rocky could have sworn she saw two different salespeople fight over who would start a fitting room for her.

"Pretty."

"This is fun, isn't it?" Amanda said to Rocky. "Just the two of us."

Rocky could not think of anything less fun. She would rather be a million other places than dress shopping with her sister. Maid of honor dress shopping, that is. Amanda was acting as if she was shopping for her own wedding gown (as if she would ever settle down and get married), the way she was giving this such an air of importance. Amanda would later tell her that it was all for her benefit, that she was taking dress shopping so seriously because of the love and deep respect she had for her sister, because of the love and deep respect she had for this solemn occasion, but Rocky would not believe that for one second. (She would laugh in her face as she said it.) Because everything in Amanda's world was always all about Amanda. The girl couldn't help herself.

"So, seeing as how you now embrace pink," Amanda said over her shoulder, motioning to Rocky's hair, newly dyed baby pink, to clarify. "What do you think of this one?" She held out a very, very shiny, very, very sparkly bright pink gown.

"I think I need a pair of those glasses you wear when there's an eclipse," Rocky said. "That dress is hurting my eyes."

Amanda laughed and went back to the rack. Rocky caught a glimpse of herself in a mirror—it was nearly impossible not to, as almost every surface in the store seemed to be reflective, which was, perhaps, why Amanda liked it there so much—and couldn't help but compare herself to her sister, the way they'd been compared all their lives. Even with the pink hair Rocky was sporting that week, Amanda was still the princess. But if Amanda was the fairest one of all, where did that leave Rocky?

A memory: sitting in Dr. Kind's office, family therapy. Rocky in first grade, Amanda in third. Her mother on edge, always on edge when discussing Rocky's anger issues. Dr. Kind was focusing on Amanda that day, the central conceit of the whole thing being that it was family therapy, and not just therapy for Rocky, even though that was exactly what it was. Amanda was talking about an incident at school, how she had yelled at her teacher when she received a punishment.

"And why do you think you got so upset with your teacher?" Dr. Kind asked Amanda.

"Because I shouldn't have gotten in trouble," Amanda said, her lower lip thrust out, as if to prove her case.

"And why not?" Dr. Kind asked her.

"Because I'm the good one," she said, as if the answer were obvious.

"In the class?" His brow furrowed as he snuck a furtive glance at Joan.

"In the family," Amanda explained, matter-of-factly. "Rocky's the bad one and I'm the good one."

"There's no good one and bad one in our family," Rocky's father quickly said. "We all have things we need to work on. For Rocky, it's her anger. And for you, dear Amanda, it's your vanity."

"What's vanity?" Amanda asked, only to be interrupted by her mother.

"It's the dressing table in your bathroom," Joan said, throwing a dirty look in her husband's direction. "Now, what were you saying about that mean teacher of yours?"

When the appointment was just about over, as Rocky and Amanda picked out their prizes from the treasure chest for having a good session, Rocky overheard Dr. Kind explain to her parents: "It's common for children to try to fit themselves into roles, to define things in black and white."

I'm the good one. Rocky had never forgotten that. Never fully got over it. If Amanda was the good one, then what, exactly, did that make her?

"What's your color scheme?" a well-meaning sales associate asked Rocky.

"I'm not sure I really have one yet," Rocky said, her mind still fuzzy from the memory.

"She likes black." Amanda ran her hands along Rocky's outfit of the day as proof of concept: black skinny jeans, black leather bolero blazer, with a dark gray T-shirt underneath.

"I love this one," the sales associate said, pulling a dress out from the rack.

"Oh," Rocky said, wondering what a dress like that was doing in the bridesmaid selections. She could not think of one bride who would want her bridesmaid wearing such a dress. If you could even call it that. It looked more like a slip, with its delicate spaghetti straps and bra-like detailing on the bodice. It was cut on the bias, which meant it would hug Amanda's curves even more than a regular dress would. And the best part (or worst part, depending on your view of things) was the waistline, which had triangular cutouts with lace insets.

"It would look amazing on your figure," the sales associate said suggestively to Amanda. Flirting or just doing a hard sell? Rocky wasn't sure.

"It looks cheap," Amanda said under her breath. And then out loud: "I don't think our mother would approve of that."

"She most definitely would not," Rocky agreed, laughter in her voice. She could just imagine her mother's reaction to a dress like that. *I'm not sure that's appropriate*, she would gently remark, and the girls would immediately know how she truly felt about it: that it should be set on fire and never mentioned again. Rocky felt a pull in her chest at the thought of her mother. All the things she couldn't say. That she didn't say.

"Penny for your thoughts," Amanda asked gently. Rocky could tell she was feigning nonchalance, looking at the dresses instead of looking her in the eye. Casual. Like an animal trainer at the zoo—*Do not challenge the animal, do not assert dominance.*

"Didn't you once date a girl named Penny?" Rocky flipped through the dresses, too. She would feign nonchalance like her sister.

"I can always tell when something's on your mind. If you want to talk," she said, bumping her hip into Rocky's, "I'm here."

"I'll keep that in mind," Rocky said. "Same goes for you, you know."

"I don't know what you mean."

"Seeing Slo—"

"I'm good," Amanda said, tugging another black dress off the rack and showing it to Rocky.

"You know, just because I wear a lot of black doesn't mean that I want the color scheme of my wedding to be black."

Amanda laughed in her face. "Yes, you do. You just know that Mom wouldn't approve of it."

Rocky felt a flush cross her face. Amanda was probably right. And it made her angry—Amanda had no right to know her that well. "Okay, fine," Rocky conceded. "But Drew wouldn't like it, either."

"Middle ground: what about charcoal gray? It's sort of like black, but it's black's impossibly chic cousin," Amanda said, grabbing a dress from the rack. It was strapless with a lace overlay and the skirt was tea length, A-line. As Amanda held it up to her body, it fell perfectly, just a few inches above her ankle.

"I love it," Rocky said, without thinking. "Try it on."

Amanda reached over and enveloped Rocky in a hug. Rocky hadn't quite been expecting that, so she stumbled as Amanda grabbed for her. It was barely detectable, but they both heard it at once: the sound of the fabric ripping as Rocky stepped on the hem.

Rocky held her breath—did this mean they had to buy the dress? Surely a salon like this had one of those *you break it, you buy it* policies? Or perhaps the fact that they had an on-site seamstress meant that a little rip didn't really mean a thing. They could have it repaired by the time Amanda had her clothes off, ready to try it on. Rocky puzzled over what to do: Tell the truth? Or try to get out of it? But before she could gather her thoughts, she heard Amanda addressing the salesperson in her honey-sweet voice. She would later tell Rocky that she didn't lie—not outright anyway—because what she said had actually been the truth.

"We love this one," she said, which was true, "but it appears to be damaged?" Also true, but not the whole truth.

Not like Amanda cared.

TWENTY-SIX

The mother of the bride, as a bride herself
Long Island, 1982

Gone. How could she already be gone? Joanie sank down onto a bar stool. She'd missed her chance. Her chance to see Mel again. To find out what really happened to her sister. Her chance to learn the truth.

Joanie put a hand up to get the bartender's attention, but it was no use. It was as if she was invisible.

When the bartender finally walked over, it was not to take Joanie's drink order. She pointed to the stage. "The singer is totally singing to you."

Joanie had completely forgotten about the band. She spun around to see Jesse's band, Dead Dream, on stage. Their music was loud, but were they good? Joanie couldn't tell. It wasn't exactly her type of music. "No, he's not."

"He is."

Joanie brushed it off. "Soda water, please," she said, but the bartender was still staring past Joanie. Joanie turned again to see what she was looking at.

The music got louder. And the bartender was right. Jesse had jumped off the stage and was walking towards the bar. He made his way through the crowd—which parted for him like the Red Sea—and made his way towards Joanie.

"He is singing to you."

"No, he's not." But it was undeniable. He was singing to her. He made a beeline towards Joanie and perched himself on the bar stool next to her. The spotlight blinded her, and she squinted to make out Jesse's face. Joanie could feel the eyes of all of the girls in the bar burn into her. The music was so loud, Joanie could barely make out the words to the song.

"We're Dead Dream," Jesse said into the mic as the song finished up. "We're going to take a quick break and be back in ten."

Someone materialized from out of nowhere to grab the mic, and Jesse turned to face Joanie.

"We meet again."

"So we do." Joanie didn't mean to be flirting. "You guys were great."

He grabbed at his chest, to where his heart would be. "You mean that? Man, thank you."

"You're welcome." Joanie fingered her single strand of pearls. Her neck was hot to the touch, sticky. She twirled her engagement ring around her finger, as if to remind herself that it was there.

"What are you drinking?" With a flick of the wrist, the bartender came to their side of the bar.

"Soda water, please."

"She'll take one of these, too," Jesse said, as the bartender poured him a shot of whiskey.

"I don't drink."

"Would you like a glass of milk, then?"

"Are you making fun of me for not drinking?"

"I'm just messing around with you. You like to mess around?"
He wrapped a finger around one of Joanie's curls. Joanie lost her
breath for a moment, and then remembered herself.

"I'm engaged."

"I don't care."

"I said I'm engaged," Joanie repeated, this time flashing her
two-carat engagement ring as proof.

"I said I don't care," Jesse said, offering a devilish smile. "Do
you?" Joanie couldn't help herself from smiling. Her smile gave
way to a giggle, and she found she couldn't quite stop. She covered her mouth with her hand.

"She's trying to tell you that she's not interested, Jesse," said
a voice behind him. "Gimme your seat, you're back on in five
minutes anyway."

"Have you seen my sister?"

"She's in the, uh, bathroom."

"Sure she is," he said, his face falling. And then, to Joanie,
plastering a smile back on: "I'll be seeing you soon."

"I apologize for my friend's brother," the girl said, taking the
seat next to Joanie. She had bleached white hair with red tips.
"He's used to girls falling at his feet."

"It's fine. This night is a total disaster anyway."

"Do I know you?"

"I don't think so. I've never been here before."

"You just look so familiar."

"Joanie?"

Joanie turned around and there she was. The unmistakable
black mohawk. The ear full of piercings, the delicate silver hoop
at the end of her nose. The girl she'd come here to see. Mel.

"Mel. I was looking for you."

"Jem, this is Michele's sister, Joanie." Mel was speaking fast,
as if she were a record set to the wrong speed. "We met at the
art exhibit the other night. The one where Michele and I were

both showing? You couldn't come, but it was awesome. Truly awesome."

"Nice to meet you, Jen," Joanie said, as Mel continued on her tangent.

"Jem."

"Jen?"

"Jem, with an *m*."

Mel was still talking: "And Joanie, this is Mikki."

Joanie smiled at the girl standing next to Mel, a dark-haired girl with a tattoo covering her entire right arm. "Nice to meet you."

"This is Michele's sister," Mel said again, and Jem told her that she'd already said that. "She wants to know more about her sister."

"You look just like her," Mikki said, bringing her ink-colored arm up to Joanie's face. "It's eerie."

"I get that a lot," Joanie said. "It's actually how I met Mel. I was hoping we could continue our conversation from the other night."

Mel stared back at her blankly.

"About my sister."

Mel looked to Jem and Mikki. And then to Joanie, she spoke even quicker than before: "She was amazing, you know. Ridiculously talented. The most talented one in the class, always. A true artist. An *artiste*. Michele could have been teaching the class, that's how good she was. She was the one most likely to make a name for herself in the art world, you know? Well, I guess you don't know. I mean—"

Jem cut in: "I think maybe you've had one too many. Let's get you home."

"No, I'm fine. I'm totally fine. I can't miss my brother's show. Joanie, you met my brother, Jesse, right? He thinks you're cute. He said you were looking for me at the gallery the other night? Well, here I am!"

Mikki: "Yeah, we should go."

"But, wait," Joanie said, reaching out to touch Mel's arm. As if to hold on to her. "I want to know more. Why did you say that Michele didn't die of a heart attack?"

Mel's face fell. Jem jumped in: "Okay, we really should go."

"Can I have your number? Can I call you?"

"She works at Trash and Vaudeville," Mikki said. "You can call her at the store. She'll be more herself tomorrow."

And then, just as quickly as Mel had reappeared, she was gone.

TWENTY-SEVEN

The seamstress
Paris, 1958

"Have you ever been in love before?"

"You sound like Mademoiselle Laurent," Julien said playfully. "Your new best friend." They were in the office of the atelier, Rose's new private office, where she would work exclusively on Diana's dress. If the other seamstresses were upset about this new development, Rose wouldn't know it. She now used the back entrance to the atelier, and walked directly into her office each day. Working closely with Julien, she found that she didn't much mind what they thought anymore.

Rose laughed at the gentle teasing. "I guess that was a silly question."

Julien took his reading glasses off and regarded Rose. "There is something lighter about you since you've been working on Mademoiselle Laurent's wedding dress, almost as if you were the one getting married."

"Nonsense," Rose said with a laugh. But he was right. Rose

came to work with a smile each day. She laughed often. She hummed to herself while she worked.

"Then what's all this talk about being in love?"

"I shouldn't have asked," Rose said. "Forgive me."

"You must not fall in love with him," Julien said, as if it were something he'd been holding in for a long time.

"I don't know who you are—"

"He will break your heart," Julien said, raising his voice. And then, more quietly: "You mustn't let him break your heart."

"I won't," Rose said, looking Julien directly in the eye. Her aunt had always taught her to look a person in the eye, especially when you wanted them to understand that you were speaking the truth. Julien shook his head and Rose quietly slipped the white cotton gloves back onto her fingers and picked up where she had left off. The construction on Diana's muslin was giving her problems—she could not figure out how to get the bodice connected to the skirt without creating needless volume on the cummerbund. Even as thin as Diana was, no woman wants extra volume around her waist. She had to get it right.

"I'm just trying to protect you," Julien said. His tone more gentle. "You understand that, don't you?"

"I know," Rose quickly said, not looking up. "But you needn't worry. I'm not at all in love."

"With her, either," Julien said, pushing his chair back from the desk and standing at attention.

"I'm not in love with her," Rose said, laughter rising from her throat, as if such an idea were preposterous.

"She's a client," Julien said. "She's not your friend."

"I know that," Rose said quietly, feeling her face flush red with shame. "Of course I know that."

"She's not your family."

"I know that, too."

"What utter nonsense, friends who are family."

"You don't think friends can become family?" Rose asked,

taking a break from the muslin to look at Julien. She took off her white cotton gloves again and set them down on the desk. Julien looked comfortable sitting at Madame's large wood desk, like he'd belonged there all along. He had his dress shoes off under the desk and his sleeves were rolled up to his elbows. He'd even undone his vest, something he never did in front of the other seamstresses.

"I haven't had much experience with either one."

"Me neither," Rose admitted.

They were quiet for a moment. Rose puzzled over what to say next. Oh, how she wanted to tell him that she felt a kinship with him, one that went beyond the fact that they were both orphans, both alone in the world.

Before she could formulate the words, Julien interrupted her thoughts. "You need to create two separate pieces here," he said, walking over to the dress form. "Two separate pieces, and then the cummerbund attaches over them."

"But then it's not a dress," Rose said, shaking her head, ever so slightly. "I'm making a dress, not a mere blouse and skirt. This is the most important garment a woman will wear in her life. It needs to be done perfectly."

"Now where have I heard that sentiment before?" He looked up at Rose and winked. He ran his hand over the gathered fabric in the middle of the garment. He fingered the part where it puckered. "The purpose of a cummerbund is to cover the working parts of a man's formalwear. The button on the pants. The gap where the shirt is tucked into them. Grace Kelly's dress was constructed in four parts: the bodice, the skirt, a tulle insert, and the cummerbund. You must perfect the pieces before they can come together."

"How would you know that?" Rose asked, as she unpinned the skirt from the bodice.

"I have friends in high places," he said with a coy smile, and they both laughed.

"Must be nice," Rose mumbled, as she held the pins between her lips, careful to keep them all in place so as to not poke herself.

"Thirty-five people worked on that dress," Julien said. "And people talk."

Julien handed her the pin cushion doll that had been sitting on the mantel. Rose immediately recognized it as one of Madame's. On work days, days when Madame didn't have client visits on her schedule, she would walk around the workroom, critiquing the work of the seamstresses. She always carried her pin cushion doll, always ready to show a seamstress how to do something, not just tell her. Even though her hands were old, they worked quicker and more efficiently than those of any of the young seamstresses. It was as if her fingers simply moved without Madame having to think about it first.

Rose smiled at the memory. But she couldn't accept another gift from Julien, she simply could not. These items of Madame's were gems. Priceless heirlooms. They should be handed down to family. She gently shook her head in Julien's direction. But then she remembered: Julien had no family, just as she had none, so she let him place the doll into her hand.

"Thank you," she said, and he smiled back, as if to say: *It was nothing*, even though they both knew that it was certainly not nothing.

"Would you like to know my secret?" Rose asked Julien.

"I would," he said, as his eyes searched hers.

"You made a joke before that Diana was my best friend. But she's not," Rose said carefully. She took a deep breath. "You are."

"Oh, my dear child," Julien said, grasping both of Rose's hands in his. His hands were soft and smooth to the touch. "That's so lovely of you to say."

"You've changed my life," Rose said. "What we're doing here, this. It will change my life. Thank you for believing in me."

"Now, if only we could get you to believe in yourself."

"I mean it," Rose said. "You are my best friend and I value your friendship."

"Thank you for sharing your secret with me." Julien ran his hands along Rose's arms, the way her aunt sometimes used to do when they were at church. Not quite a hug, but affection nonetheless. "Would you like to know mine?"

"Let me guess," Rose said playfully. "I'm your best friend, too."

"No," Julien said. "Well, yes, you are my best friend. My closest confidante. Which is why I trust you with my real secret. Would you like to know what it is?"

TWENTY-EIGHT

The bride
Brooklyn, 2020

Rocky busied her hands with the wedding album her mother had brought. Rocky didn't know why she had brought it. All she knew was she didn't want to be at this appointment today ("So, how did you and your fiancé meet?" she was asked for seemingly the millionth time), at a cake shop on Madison Avenue on the Upper East Side. *It's okay to leave Brooklyn*, her mother would say, but it wasn't just the fact of leaving her beloved borough. It was more than that. The Upper East Side wasn't where she belonged. Girls with blond hair and perfect figures belonged on the Upper East Side. Girls who carried Birkins (or at least wanted to carry Birkins), girls who had tiny dogs that would fit into said Birkins, belonged on the Upper East Side. The Upper East Side was for women like her mother, who had regular weekly blowouts. For women like Amanda. (Who, ironically, lived downtown in SoHo.)

So, the wedding album gave her something to do while her

mother held court at the exclusive bakery. The album felt delicate, like if it was handled too roughly it might break apart. The cover was an ivory white, and the names of her parents and their wedding date were embossed on the bottom right corner in gold foil. Rocky traced their names with her finger.

The first picture: her mother, in the dress. Rocky could hardly bear to look at it. Her mother beaming, proud of the changes she'd made to it—the Princess Diana sleeves and nine-foot train. Her hair was a true testament to '80s style. It was teased and sprayed and gave her an additional four inches of height.

Rocky quickly turned the page.

Her father looked handsome in his wedding tuxedo. She held the album up, closer to her eyes, so that she wouldn't miss a single detail. He wore an ivory dinner jacket with one button and peaked lapels. Black silk bow tie and black trousers with a black silk stripe going down the side. His shoes were black patent loafers. He looked elegant and timeless, like he could hop right out of the wedding album and wear the same ensemble today.

But he wouldn't be wearing anything to Rocky's wedding. Only his memory would be at her wedding. Rocky felt her breath catch in her chest and she took a deep breath in, two, three, four, and out, two, three, four. It was fine. She was fine.

On the next page, Rocky found a picture of bride and groom, surrounded by their parents. What Rocky noticed about the picture was that her father stood proudly next to his best man, but that her mother stood alone, in front of her parents. Rocky tried to remember how old her mother had been when her sister died. She knew that her mother had ten bridesmaids walk down the aisle, but refused to fill the spot of maid of honor that her older sister should have held.

"What do you think of this one?" her mother asked hopefully. Rocky looked up and saw her oohing and aahing over a six-tiered cake. It had sugar flowers separating each of its tiers, in delicate shades of pink, lavender, and yellow.

"It's too big."

Joan furrowed her brow and went back to the showroom of cakes. Rocky found it funny that this shop had samples of their most famous cakes done in cardboard and clay. Beautiful things that weren't real. Rocky had preferred Sloan's place, where they brought out samples first, and then sketched out what they had in mind while you sat there with the pastry chef, eating.

Sloan. Poor sad Sloan. It had pained Rocky just to look at her, see the way she looked at Amanda, still. Sloan shook their hands, as if they were strangers, and then made small talk ("Yes, it's been so long!") as if they barely knew each other. As if she and Amanda hadn't been madly in love. Hadn't lived together for nine months, broken up for two, only to get back together again for one last ill-fated month.

And then, because Amanda must always be the center of attention, she'd fainted. It took Rocky and Sloan so much by surprise that neither of them was able to react quickly enough to catch her. One second, Sloan was telling Rocky about her rash decision to enroll in culinary school, and the next, Amanda was crumpled on the floor. She hit her head on the table on her way down and lost consciousness for thirty seconds. Rocky fell to her sister's side, ordered Siri to call for an ambulance, and felt her sister's forehead. She was burning up, but all of the color had left her face. Her skin was gray, covered in beads of sweat. Before Rocky could even ask, Sloan came running over with a cloth filled with ice, and Rocky put it to Amanda's face. Her eyes fluttered as she regained consciousness.

"What happened?" Amanda asked, disoriented. She opened her eyes and saw Sloan hovering over her, an angel dressed in starched chef's whites.

"You're all right," Sloan said, stroking Amanda's forehead. "Everything is okay."

"I love you."

"I love you, too," Sloan said quickly, before the words were even fully out of Amanda's mouth.

But Rocky didn't tell her mother that part of the story.

"Maybe we should consider something smaller," Joan said, pointing at a pink cake—pink!—that had five tiers of cake— five!—with cupcakes surrounding the bottom layer. She drummed her fingers across her lips as she waited for Rocky to respond.

Rocky looked up from the album. "Smaller."

"Smaller!" she called back to the chef. "She wants smaller. I assume you can do an extra cake that we keep back in the kitchen. I mean, if we're going to have upwards of three hundred people…"

Rocky focused her attention back on the album. A picture of her mother and her mother's mother. Grand-mère. She was elegantly attired in a navy dress. Although the rest of the album seemed like a time capsule of the '80s, her grandmother was dressed impeccably, ladylike, in a timeless outfit that would be fashionable in any decade. Bracelet-length sleeves, a modest neckline, and a straight skirt with a hem that hit just below the knee. Her mother had always attributed Grand-mère's style to being French, to being rich, but it was more than that. Classic style like that could not be taught. Either you had it or you did not. And her grandmother certainly had it. She had it in spades.

"Maybe a tasting would get her in the mood," Rocky heard her mother tell the pastry chef with a wink.

The pastry chef smiled back warmly. "Coming right up."

"Let's eat," Joan told Rocky, motioning with her hands for Rocky to put the album away.

"Yes," Rocky said. "Let's." Rocky carefully placed her mother's wedding album in the silk bag Joan had been storing it in.

"I know how important these memories are to you, especially the ones that connect you to your father."

Rocky regarded her mother. These memories *were* important to her. Was her mother trying to manipulate her? Rocky imagined asking this question to her therapist. Then, she sat in his seat and offered herself an answer: *How can she be manipulating you when she has no idea that you don't want to wear the dress?*

Rocky didn't know what to say. She decided to stick with what she did know: "I'm sad that Dad won't be there to walk me down the aisle. That's why I don't want a traditional ceremony like you're imagining. Who will walk me down the aisle?"

"Oh, honey," her mother said, enveloping her in a warm hug. "I had no idea you felt that way. I just thought you wanted to be nontraditional. But you know that I'll be there to proudly walk you down the aisle, right?"

"It's not the same."

"No," Joan said solemnly. "It is not."

"I'll forever be the girl with no dad."

"I know," Joan said, dabbing at her eyes. "I'll forever be the girl with no sister."

Rocky buried her face in her mother's shoulder. She felt the tears brewing, tears she didn't even know she had, and she did not want to be the crying bride in the Upper East Side wedding cake bakery. She would not.

"Yes, I know it's emotional," the pastry chef said as she walked out, her arms draped in small plates filled with cake. "I cried at every appointment I went to when I got married."

Rocky immediately wanted to punch this woman in the face.

"Could you give us a moment?" Joan asked in a tone that was both sweet and no-nonsense.

"Of course," the pastry chef said, as she quickly arranged the little flags on each cake and then ran off. The tiny flags signaled which cakes were which: red velvet, vanilla, chocolate, coconut...the list was endless.

"Sweetheart, this is why I wanted you to wear my wedding dress," Joan said. "He would be so pleased to see you wearing it."

Rocky didn't know what to say. Would her father have been

pleased to see her wearing the dress? Would she feel her father's presence with her on her wedding day?

"I just want everything to be as perfect for your wedding as it was for mine," Joan said. "This is such a special time in your life."

Joan reached for her wedding album, and they paged through it as they took tastes of each cake. (Rocky was shocked to discover that her favorite flavor was vanilla. Plain, old, boring vanilla. Joan, on the other hand, preferred the coconut with basil sweet cream.)

They ate cake, and they looked at pictures. And they laughed. A lot. They laughed over the bridesmaids' dresses, they laughed over the baby-blue tuxedo one distant cousin chose to wear, they laughed over the absurdity of it all—the massive planning for one night that was over in the blink of an eye. Rocky felt closer to her mother than she had in years. It was just the two of them, enjoying each other's company, bonding over sugar and laughter and bad fashion choices.

"I have Daddy's wedding tuxedo preserved, you know," Joan said after the appointment was over, as they walked around the corner to get espressos. "Perhaps we should take a piece of that and incorporate it into the dress."

"I don't want to ruin your dress."

"It's your dress now," Joan said, looking deeply into Rocky's eyes. "It belongs to you."

"But what about Amanda?" At that moment, Rocky realized that her mother hadn't brought up Amanda today. Not even once.

"What about Amanda?" her mother asked, shrugging her shoulders. "The dress is yours. If she ever decides to get married, you can decide if you will hand the dress down to her, but that will be your choice."

"But I—"

"The dress belongs to you."

Rocky wished she wanted it.

TWENTY-NINE

The mother of the bride, as a bride herself
Long Island, 1982

"How was the party?" her mother asked as Joanie walked into the house the next morning, and Joanie didn't have the heart to tell her the truth. Not about Mel, not about the band, not even about the borrowed dress that now smelled like smoke, desperate for a dry cleaning. She didn't say a word about any of it.

She couldn't.

After Michele died, Joanie had to be enough for her mother. She had to be enough for two. For the daughter she was, for the daughter that Birdie lost. She had to be the good girl, the girl who didn't cause trouble. Most of the time, Joanie didn't even think about it, but then there were other times, times like these, when the weight threatened to crush her.

"It was great," Joanie lied. She gave her mother a smile and Birdie regarded her. From the furrow of her brow, Joanie could tell that her mother wasn't convinced. She set a plate of crepes

down in front of her daughter and then got the strawberry preserves from the refrigerator.

"Was it?" she quietly asked, going back to the dishes in the
sink. Joanie's mother had used this same trick since she was six
years old. She'd pretend she wasn't interested, or that she was
preoccupied with something else, and it usually worked like a
charm—Joanie would spill her guts. But the difference now was
that Joanie didn't want to spill her guts. The trick used to work
because she secretly wanted to tell her mother everything, she
just didn't know how to find the words. But now, overnight,
things had changed. Her relationship with her mother was different. What was Birdie hiding? What wouldn't Mel tell her
about Michele?

"It was a great night," Joanie repeated. She picked up the jar
of strawberry preserves, distractedly spooning generous amounts
on top of her crepes. She watched as the gooey mess oozed all
over her crepes, filling her plate, threatening to spill over onto
the table.

"Well, then, I'm glad," her mother said. She finished up with
the dishes and wiped her hands dry on a dish towel. "So, have
you given any thought to the wedding dress?"

"I can't wait to wear it," Joanie said, her face brightening at
the thought. Of all of the confusion she'd experienced over the
past few weeks, there was one thing she had no questions about:
her mother's wedding dress.

"Well, in that case, we should go about getting it fitted," her
mother said. "And we can add a few little flourishes here and
there to make it your own."

"I did have a few ideas," Joanie said, taking an enormous
forkful of crepes and strawberry preserves. With her mouth full:
"Just to make the dress a little more my style."

Her mother smiled widely back at her. "The dress is utter
perfection. It's everyone's style."

"Be that as it may," Joanie said, with a little laughter in her voice, taking a sip of milk to wash down the crepes she was devouring, "I also loved Princess Diana's wedding gown. I know that you were inspired by Princess Grace, but surely there's a little room for Diana?"

"Of course," her mother said, but Joanie could tell her smile was forced. "What, exactly, did you have in mind? Are you thinking a longer veil? Princess Diana's long veil and long train were legendary."

"Not the veil—" Joanie began, but her mother wasn't done speaking.

"Most people don't know this, but Diana's veil was actually longer than her train. Did you know that?"

"Really?" Joanie asked. She had not noticed that. She tried to recall the many newspaper cutouts that she kept in a box underneath her bed, but the veil did not come to mind.

"I think we can add another layer to my veil and make yours the length of Diana's—it was 153 yards, longer than the dress's 25-foot train—quite easily. That would really enhance the dress."

"I was thinking that I might want to change the sleeves," Joanie said. "I loved how Diana's dress had those wonderful fairy-tale sleeves."

"The sleeves," her mother repeated. "I see."

"Oh, have I upset you?" Joanie quickly asked. "We don't have to change anything. The dress is perfect the way it is."

"You haven't upset me," Birdie said, carefully. "I was just surprised. After all, this dress is a piece of art, a piece of our heritage."

"So, you don't want me to change it," Joanie said, under her breath, as if realizing it for the very first time.

"I want you to make the dress yours." Birdie rubbed her forehead. "You can change it, if that's what you want."

Joanie could tell what her mother was really saying—*Don't*

change the dress, please. So, Joanie would do what her mother wanted. She would not upset her mother.

After all, she had to be enough. And the dress belonged to her mother, anyway. Who was she to make a change to something that wasn't truly hers?

THIRTY

The seamstress
Paris, 1958

He was the same person as before. That was what she had to keep reminding herself. Nothing had changed. If anything, she felt even closer to Julien. Sharing confidences, Rose now knew that there was nothing that could break their friendship apart. Still, she couldn't help staring at him when she thought he wasn't looking. How hadn't she known? How could it be that she hadn't suspected a thing? Not that there was anything to suspect. There was nothing wrong with him.

Diana walked into the atelier, fifteen minutes early for her appointment, and immediately, the air shifted. It was as if Rose could feel the presence of Robert in the atelier before she even saw him. She could feel his essence as he entered the building.

"Rose," Diana said, as she walked over to her friend without even taking her coat off.

"It's lovely to see you." Out of the corner of her eye, Rose could see Robert removing his overcoat and placing it on the coatrack. He made his way towards the two women and took his sister's coat. Rose was careful to keep her eyes firmly on Diana. She would not meet his eye. She could not.

"Nice to see you, Rose," Robert said. "You're looking well."

"Thank you," Rose said, her voice so small she wasn't even sure she'd said the words aloud. She could feel his eyes on her, burning into her. But she didn't dare look at him. If she did, she was sure he would know how she felt about him. And he mustn't know. The work was what was important. A paycheck. Not some silly crush.

Diana looked to her brother and then at Rose. She seemed to be waiting for her brother to speak again, and when he didn't, she grabbed Rose by the hand and asked her where the muslin was. "I simply cannot wait to try it on."

"It's in the dressing room," Rose explained, regaining her composure. "We very well couldn't have you take off all of your clothing in the middle of the atelier, could we?"

"Of course we could," Diana said, with a devilish look in her eye. Rose gasped at her impudence. "I can't wait to see it. I would gladly take off all my clothes if that meant I didn't have to wait a moment longer."

"Well, you don't have to wait," Rose said, directing Diana to the dressing room. "We have everything set up and ready for you."

Rose walked Diana down the hall. She opened the door, and waited. She hoped that when Diana saw the muslin, the design of the dress, she would instantly fall in love.

"It's beautiful," Diana said, quietly. Reverently. She carefully removed her scarf, and folded it four times, until it was small enough to fit into her purse.

Rose turned towards the door to give Diana privacy while she undressed. "Let's start with the skirt," she said.

"The skirt?"

"Well, yes," Rose said. "Grace Kelly's wedding dress was

made up of four separate components, so I'll construct yours in a similar fashion. And for the final dress, it will all be seamless, just like Princess Grace's was."

Rose looked to Diana for her reaction. She wanted Diana to be as excited about the dress as she was.

"You don't have to explain, Rose," Diana said, smiling warmly. "I was just curious, was all."

Rose felt a swell of relief come over her body. She had been nervous. Of course she was. Every time she met with Diana, she was scared that the ruse would be discovered. That she and Julien would be outed as frauds, and that all of their work would have been for nothing.

"I thought that maybe you were interested in dress design," Rose said, trying to keep her voice level. She had told Julien that she could handle the dress fitting without reservations, but perhaps she had underestimated how much she needed him. How much his gentle nods of affirmation had given her the courage to go on.

"I am very interested in how things are made, yes," Diana said as Rose helped her into the bodice. Diana tried to catch Rose's eye, but she had already busied herself with the cummerbund. "I'm interested in what's going on under the surface."

But Rose wasn't paying attention to what Diana was saying anymore. She put the cummerbund onto Diana's waist, and realized there was a problem. The entire fit of the garment was off. It swam on Diana's lithe frame, which made it pucker all over.

Diana didn't notice. She began twirling in front of the mirror. "I love it!" she said, as she swayed her hips to and fro.

How had Rose made such an error? She prided herself on her attention to detail. She had been so careful with her measurements. What could have possibly gone wrong? And in an instant, she knew. As she'd constructed each separate piece of the garment, she'd been using herself as a fit model. She and Diana had the same proportions, only Diana was much smaller. She had planned to take the entire garment in before this appointment. How could she have forgotten?

She had initially tried on the bodice only to make sure it sat properly on her bustline, but she found it hard to take off. She adored admiring her reflection in the mirror as she wore it. Naturally, when it came time to create the skirt, she just knew that she had to try that on, too. She held off on tailoring the bodice until the skirt was done. And then once the skirt was done—oh, how she had twirled around in front of the mirror in it then, just as Diana was doing now—it didn't make sense to tailor the pieces until the cummerbund was done. So, she waited. And waited. And then it slipped her mind until this very moment. She had been too prideful, which her aunt had always said was a sin. But there was no use denying it—Rose simply loved the dress.

Diana could hear Madame's voice in her head: *Oh, what have you done, dear child? How could you have made such an error? You're going to ruin everything.*

Luckily, Diana was none the wiser. "May I show it to my brother? I'm simply bursting with excitement."

"Of course," Rose said, shaking her head to clear her thoughts. "Let me put a few pins in it for you first."

Rose grabbed Madame's pin cushion and worked quickly. She pinned the entire garment while Diana admired her reflection in the mirror.

"Even better," Diana said, and Rose couldn't help but agree. Diana was a vision, truly.

She walked towards the door, and Rose carefully gathered the excess fabric of the dress so that it wouldn't drag along the atelier floor as she walked.

"You look like a dream, dear sister," Robert said, as Diana situated herself in front of the dressing room mirror.

"It's utter perfection, isn't it?" Diana said, her hands gliding along the fabric dreamily.

"It is said that to wear a custom-designed Madame Michel wedding dress is to guarantee a happy marriage," Robert told his sister.

"Is that what they say?" Diana asked, lost in her own reflection in the mirror. "What about a dress by Rose?"

"This is a dress by Madame Michel," Rose quickly said. If she'd taken a moment to think, she might have said something more graceful, less awkward. But Diana didn't seem to notice.

"I simply meant that I feel lucky that you are working on my wedding gown as well." Diana smiled at Rose.

"You are so incredibly talented," Robert said to Rose. "I've never seen anything like it."

Rose wouldn't remember the rest of the appointment. She wouldn't recall Diana changing back into her own clothing, or saying goodbye to Diana and Robert. As she dressed for bed that evening, only one thought would remain: how Robert called her talented. How he'd never seen anything like the dress she'd designed.

Rose would go to bed that evening with his name on her lips.

THIRTY-ONE

The bride
Brooklyn, 2020

"Send me a picture of you wearing the dress," she said, and Rocky froze. The dress. The wedding dress that Rocky didn't want to wear. She hadn't been back to the bridal salon to try it on, and she certainly didn't have a picture of herself wearing it. "Are you still there?" her grandmother asked, and the Face-Time screen shook as her grandmother rattled her phone, trying to get a better connection. When it settled back down, the camera was pointed at her grandmother's forehead.

"I'm here, Grand-mère. Tilt your phone so that I can see your face. There's a tiny window at the bottom where you can see yourself," Rocky said, holding her own phone steady.

"How's that?" Her grandmother righted the screen, and her beautiful face came into view. After all these years, her grandmother's voice still had a slight French lilt to it, which Rocky adored. (And at one point, from ages fifteen to sixteen, unsuccessfully tried to emulate.) The accent was always more pronounced when Grand-mère was spending time in Europe. And her grandmother was there for an extended trip, while she tended to Rocky's uncle after his hip replacement surgery.

"Perfect. How's Paris?"

"How is the dress?" her grandmother asked, fingering her sixteen-inch double strand of pearls, her signature piece that Amanda had already laid claim to. Rocky couldn't tell if her grandmother was purposely avoiding the question, or if her grandmother simply hadn't heard her inquire about her favorite city in the world. Grand-mère had been born and raised in Paris, and Rocky knew how much her annual trips back home meant to her.

"We didn't take pictures," Rocky said, and even though it was the truth, she still felt as if she were holding something back from her beloved grandmother. The whole truth. The only part of the truth that mattered: the fact that she didn't really want to wear the dress.

"She didn't take pictures," Rocky heard her grandmother say, but not to her. Her face was turned to the side, and she was speaking to someone else. Then, he came into view—her great-uncle.

"Why not?" he asked her, putting his glasses on so that he could get a better look at the tiny phone screen. He patted his hair down—still a full head of thick hair at eighty-four years old—and turned his head from side to side, as if to offer his grandniece a better view. "Don't you kids take pictures of everything?"

It was true. Rocky took pictures of everything. Her Instagram was a Technicolor dream, filled with images of her workplace, her Brooklyn neighborhood, and most of what she ate. There were pictures of her apartment, pictures of her friends, and pictures of her fiancé. But alas, no pictures of the dress.

"We were afraid that Drew might see it in the cloud," Rocky

said, using Greta's excuse as her own. Rocky hated being dishonest with her grandmother. But what could she say?

"My genius *petite fille*," her grandmother said, her beautiful face filling the screen again. "Always five steps ahead of the rest of us."

"Genie!" Rocky heard her uncle say in his native French in the background, and her face flushed with pride.

"Thank you, *mon oncle*," Rocky said quietly.

"We cannot wait to see you in the dress," her grandmother said, positioning her phone so that she and Rocky's uncle were both in view at the same time. "You are going to look like a dream."

"Even more beautiful than your grandmother," her uncle said. "And she was the most beautiful bride I had ever seen in my life."

"She was," Rocky agreed. After all, she'd seen the pictures. And while she would never say it in front of her mother, Grand-mère was the most beautiful bride she had ever laid eyes on, too. Even more beautiful, she thought, than Grace Kelly herself, whose own wedding dress was the inspiration for the dress her grandmother wore. Even more beautiful than her own mother, when she wore the same dress, years later.

"And you will be, too," her great-uncle assured her, his smile warm and open.

"I'm not so sure about that," Rocky said.

"Nonsense," her grandmother said, bringing the phone closer to her face. "I won't hear such talk. You will be exquisite. You have a distinct personal style, and you will be a stunning bride."

Was this her chance? Here was her grandmother, referencing her personal style. Maybe this was the escape she'd been looking for. This was the opportunity to get out of wearing the dress. Surely her grandmother would understand. Her great-uncle, too. And then Grand-mère would be back in the States in time to help her pick out a different wedding outfit. It didn't even have to be a dress, did it?

This was it. This was the moment. She would come clean. She would tell her grandmother that she did not want to wear the dress.

After all, Grand-mère was the one Rocky could talk to. After her father died, it was Grand-mère who became Rocky's closest confidante, the one she could speak her truth to. Grand-mère was always there, always listening. Always a source of inspiration and strength. Rocky never bored of her grandmother's stories of growing up in Paris, how she moved to America to start a new life here. Grand-mère was creative. She was smart. She was totally and completely ahead of her time, always, and she was still the person who Rocky went to when she had something that needed fixing, a problem that needed to be discussed.

When she was the only girl in the sixth grade not invited to Olivia Redstone's slumber party, it was her grandmother she called first. Her grandmother arranged for a driver to take them into the city for high tea at the Plaza, seventh-row center seats for *Rent,* and a sleepover at the Pierre hotel. When Rocky decided that she didn't want to attend nearby Yale for college, and wanted to accept an offer across the country at Stanford instead, it was her grandmother she talked it out with. (And who softened the blow by coming to dinner the night Rocky was set to break the news to her mother.) When Rocky dreamed of leaving her comfortable job at Google and starting her own company, it was her grandmother who told her to dream big. (She may not have understood the video game app at first, but she had since figured it out and always had a running game with Rocky.)

"That's the thing, Grand-mère," Rocky said, treading carefully. "The dress isn't really my style."

Her grandmother smiled widely back into the phone. "The dress is utter perfection. It's everyone's style."

THIRTY-TWO

The mother of the bride, as a bride herself
Long Island, 1982

She slowly opened the door to the store, so slowly, as if she were afraid to walk in, and a gentle chime rang out. Joanie felt like Dorothy, walking into Oz and seeing things in color for the first time. It was as if the streets of Long Island, where she lived, were sepia tones, and Trash and Vaudeville, a store she'd walked by hundreds of times without noticing, was in full Technicolor. Bright spotlights bounced off the studded belts hanging on the wall and onto the mannequins wearing platform shoes and neon dresses in fluorescent shades of pink, green, and yellow. There were leather, and grommets, and vinyl, oh my!

"Can I help you?" a man wearing a tartan skirt and Doc Martens asked her. His hair was dyed purple and he had a stud through his bottom lip.

"No," Joanie said without thinking, putting her head down into the racks.

"Okay, well, if you see anything you like," he said cheerfully, "just let me know."

"Actually," Joanie said, something catching her eye on the back wall, "I'd like to try on these combat boots."

"Those are motorcycle boots," he corrected her. "What size?"

"Eight." Joanie wanted to ask what the difference was between motorcycle boots and combat boots—weren't they the same thing?—but she was too embarrassed.

"Be right back," he said, and disappeared into the back of the store.

She sat down on the couch and slid off her ballet slippers.

"Do you have a pair of peds?" she asked when the guy came out with the boots.

"What are peds?"

"Tiny little stockings you can use to try on shoes?" Joanie phrased it like a question, even though she knew exactly what she was talking about. She felt so unsure of herself here, in this store. NYCU was only a few blocks away, but in some ways, it felt like another world entirely. "You know what, forget it."

"I think these might be a little more your speed," Mel said, walking out from the back room.

"Mel."

"Joanie. Sorry I was so out of it the other night."

"I was glad to have found you again."

"My brother's never going to forgive me." Mel's words were clear, not jumbled like they'd been the last time she'd seen her. "I shouldn't have gotten so messed up at his show."

"Oh, I've seen many a Delta sister much drunker than you were that night," Joanie said, offering a warm smile. "Anyway, I'm sure he'll forgive you. Siblings have to forgive each other. It's, like, a rule or something."

"He thinks you're cute, you know."

"He does?" Joanie's face flushed. She thought of the way Jesse held her hand the first night they'd met. The way he sang to her at the club. How every girl there had wanted him, but he only had eyes for her.

"He does," Mel said, pulling a pair of fluorescent pink pointy-toed pumps from the shelf. "You guys should go out."

"I'm engaged." Joanie took a deep breath. She held up her left hand to show Mel her ring.

"Oh, sorry." Mel handed her the shoes to try on.

Joanie slid the shoes onto her feet. Perfect fit. "I love them. I'll take them."

"You'll need something to wear with them," Mel said, already thumbing through the racks, picking out things for Joanie to try on. "Can't wear your mother's dress every time you come out with me, you know."

"How did you know that was my mother's dress?"

Mel responded with a look. Joanie smiled back.

"Tell me more about what happened to my sister."

"Michele. Oh, Michele. Where would I even begin?"

"Begin at the beginning."

"The beginning," Mel said, sighing. She closed her eyes for a moment, as if going somewhere else for a moment. Then, opening them: "Okay, well, we all envied her."

"Me too." Joanie smiled. She picked up a belt and put it around her waist. She looked at herself in the mirror and liked the way the white leather with silver grommets caught the light as she moved to and fro.

"We all wanted to be her."

"Me too."

"And I loved her."

"Me too."

Mel stopped flipping through the racks and looked up at Joanie. Slowly: "No, I mean, I was in love with her."

"I didn't know she was—"

"She wasn't," Mel said. "I am."

"Did she know that you were in love with her?"

"Yeah."

Joanie didn't know what to say.

"Try this on." Mel held out a bracelet for Joanie—a white leather cuff, covered with silver grommets and pyramid studs. Joanie slipped it onto her wrist. The leather was stiff, it barely moved on her arm, but Joanie knew that with wear, it would loosen up. She looked at herself in the full-length mirror and was surprised to see that the bracelet was a perfect match to the belt she'd just picked out. In fact, with their matching silver studs and grommets, they looked like they'd been made for each other. A matched set.

"I love it. I'll take it."

"On the house."

"I couldn't possibly. Please let me pay for it."

"Actually, it was on hold for your sister when she died. I think she already paid for it. So, think of it as a gift to you from your sister."

Joanie looked down at the bracelet. She tried to summon a vision of her sister in her mind, but she couldn't. "Why did you say that she didn't die of a heart attack?"

Mel regarded her. She took a deep breath. "Are you free next Tuesday?"

THIRTY-THREE

The seamstress
Paris, 1958

Rose pressed her palms to the sides of her skirt, but it was no use. Her hands were damp and hot and entirely unbecoming of a lady. She checked her watch for the fourth time. He was late.

Rose wasn't accustomed to going to the movie theater with a date. Going to see a film was her one indulgence, something she treated herself to once a month, and she liked doing it alone. (Or was used to it that way, she would hasten to correct.) Would Julien talk to her during the film, the way she'd seen other couples do? Why, she would hate that. Rose liked to take in the full experience of seeing a moving picture—the scenery, the dialogue, and the costumes. Oh, the costumes! If Julien had an opinion on any of it, she hoped that he would save it for after the film. They were planning on an early supper after the matinee, so the movie would give them plenty of things to talk about. Even though they'd never run out of conversation before. But today might be different. Of course it would. Because it wasn't just

Julien who was accompanying her on this date. He was bringing a date for himself as well.

Rose checked her watch—they only had fifteen minutes until
the film would begin. This was not how Rose usually did things.
When she was on her own, she'd arrive a full half hour before
the start. That way, she could settle into her seat and enjoy the
newsreel before the main show.

She felt a set of hands around her waist, and let out a scream.
She spun around to hit her assailant with her purse, but found
herself face-to-face with Julien. He held his hands up, as if in
surrender, and Rose couldn't help but laugh.

Outside of the atelier, Julien looked different. His face was
more relaxed. More joyful. He wore his usual uniform of dress
pants, dress shirt, and a vest, but he didn't have on a tie. And
the top two buttons of his shirt were undone.

"Julien!" she cried. "You startled me."

"Sorry we're late." Julien introduced his date—well, they'd
be pretending that he was Rose's date, but he was really there
for Julien—and he took her hand.

"It's nice to meet you, Charles," Rose said. "I've heard so
much about you." And she had—since revealing his secret to
her, Julien talked about him all the time. He was a physician
from a wealthy family. He loved cats, loathed dogs, and dreamed
of one day running off to America. What Julien hadn't said was
this: he was handsome, so very handsome. Movie star handsome.
He was taller than Julien, and broader, too. His eyes sparkled
and his teeth gleamed. He was dressed smartly in a three-piece
suit. It was easy to see why Julien had fallen for him. He ex-
uded warmth.

"I'll leave you two to get acquainted while I get tickets," Julien said.

Before Rose could even answer Charles's first question about
the atelier ("So, what is Julien like at work?"), she heard her
name being called from across the street. Rose had few friends

165

to speak of, so she searched the crowd, wondering whose voice it could possibly be.

"I didn't realize you had a beau," Diana said, breathlessly, as she and her fiancé crossed the street. Diana's hair was perfect, as if she'd just visited the salon, and she was wearing a stunning trapeze dress, one that Rose immediately recognized as being from Yves Saint Laurent's first collection for Christian Dior, following the master's death.

"Yes," Rose said, quickly grabbing Charles's hand. He smiled brightly at her and she at him. "My beau."

Rose knew that she had to convince Diana. Julien had entrusted her with his most guarded secret—that he preferred men to women—and there was no way she would reveal it. Pretending Charles was her date was a breeze. She simply pretended that she was with Robert. When Charles held her hand, she imagined that it was Robert's strong hand in hers. When he looked at her and smiled, she was smiling back at Robert.

"Shall we?" Julien said, spinning around with tickets.

"Look who's here, Julien," Rose said. "It's Diana Laurent and her fiancé."

Julien startled, and then quickly regained his composure. "Why, Mademoiselle Laurent, what a lovely surprise." He took her hand and gently kissed it, and then waited to be introduced to her fiancé.

"Julien is your chaperone," Diana said. "I could tell you two were good friends even outside of the atelier."

"Diana!" a throaty voice called out, and Rose looked up to see an impossibly sexy woman crossing the street, holding hands with Robert. As startled as she was to see Robert appear, Rose was even more taken with the woman. She was beautiful, with hair as black as Liz Taylor's, and a figure to match. She wore a sheath dress that closely followed the dangerous curves of her figure, and when she walked it looked like she was on a tightrope, her feet carefully following each other in a line, her hips swaying to and fro.

"Elisabeth! Robert!" Diana called out.

Introductions were made and Rose could barely look Elisabeth in the eye. Shame overwhelmed her. Here she'd been, lusting over this woman's fiancé, and all the while, he was perfectly matched with his soul mate. Elisabeth was gorgeous, rich, and sexy. Rose never had a chance.

"Robert simply cannot stop talking about you," Elisabeth said, breathlessly.

"Me?" Rose asked, her hand instinctively flying to her chest.

"You." Elisabeth pointed a red lacquered finger in Rose's direction. "The famous Rose, protégé of the esteemed Madame Michel. He said that you are simply the most talented dressmaker he's ever seen."

Rose looked to Julien and he smiled blankly back. *Keep your composure*, he telegraphed to Rose. She rubbed her hands on the sides of her dress. They were drenched in sweat.

"It's easy when you work at the foot of a master," Rose said.

"Perhaps I should have Madame Michel design my wedding dress, too," Elisabeth said. "But I've heard it's nearly impossible to secure an appointment with Madame." Elisabeth's ruby-red lips curved into a pout.

All eyes were on Julien. Rose had no idea what he would say—how could he possibly offer her an appointment with Madame when Madame was no longer alive?

"I think you should have Rose do it," Robert suggested. "When everyone sees the work that Rose did on my sister's wedding gown, people will be clamoring for an appointment with Madame's protégé."

"It was all done under Madame's guidance," Rose quickly covered.

"Then it's settled," Elisabeth said.

"How wonderful," Julien said. His mouth smiled at Elisabeth, but his eyes did not follow.

"We should probably go inside," Diana's fiancé said. "The show's about to begin."

"Indeed." Julien held the door open for both couples to enter.

Rose let Diana and Elisabeth pass through the door first. She was trying to create as much distance between them as she could, without letting them know. Rose took Julien's words to heart—she was not Diana's friend, she was merely a client. And she must not fall in love with Robert Laurent. Especially since Elisabeth would soon become a client, as well. Those worlds must be kept separate so that nothing might threaten the fate of the atelier.

But it was no use. When Rose got to their seats, she found that the Laurents were seated right next to them.

PART THREE:
MAKE THE FIRST CUT

"This step is not for the faint of heart. There is no going back. It is time to make the first cut. Are you sure you have made all the right choices? Are you pleased with your plan? Do not make your first cut until you are absolutely, positively sure."

—Excerpted from *Creating the Illusion* by Madame Michel, Paris, 1954

THIRTY-FOUR

The bride
Brooklyn, 2020

"Mexican?" Rocky asked, holding up the Seamless app on her iPhone.

"Whatever you want," Drew said, his eyes glued to his own phone. He'd walked into the apartment that way—glued to his phone. Rocky knew not to press; Drew often brought his work home with him, but this seemed different. Usually he could answer emails on his phone while holding a conversation with Rocky, but today, he was distracted.

"Thai?"

"Whatever you want," Drew said again, agitation rising in his voice.

"I'm sorry, am I bothering you?" Rocky had meant it to sound flirty, the way Amanda could get away with things by smiling and tilting her head just so, but it didn't work. When Rocky said it, it came out entirely differently. From her lips, it wasn't flirtatious banter—it was a challenge.

Drew looked up from his phone and regarded Rocky. "No," he said, his voice even, "you're not. But would you mind picking what we have for dinner for tonight? I can't think about that right now."

"So, we'll do Mexican," Rocky said. "Your usual?"

"That's fine." Drew's face already back in his phone. He was sitting right there on the couch, but he was in another place entirely.

Rocky considered what Amanda would do in this situation. Well, that was easy. She'd slink right next to Drew and shower him with kisses until he was interested in another activity altogether.

Bad comparison. What would her mother do? Joan would probably ditch the Seamless app and set about cooking a delicious dinner from scratch, counting on the seductive smells of roasted garlic and browned onions to bring Drew back to the present. Back to her. Back home.

Rocky opened the fridge to see what ingredients they had. But it didn't matter. Rocky couldn't cook. What would her Grand-mère do? That one was a little tougher. She wasn't sure what her grandmother would do here, really. Her grandmother was always filled with surprises. But there was one thing she knew about her grandmother—she always acted with kindness and with honesty. Perhaps that was the right tack here?

Rocky put her phone down on the kitchen counter and slowly walked over to the couch. She perched down next to Drew and took a deep, calming breath. "Is there something you want to talk about?" she asked him.

"I don't really want to talk."

Rocky didn't know how to respond. Without thinking: "But I'm your fiancée."

"I know that," he quietly said. He did not look up to meet her eyes.

"Is it the Macdonell deal again?" She tried to keep her voice light, upbeat. "I can take a peek at the memo and give some thoughts."

"It's not the Macdonell deal," Drew said.

"Talk to me." She took a deep breath in. "Tell me what's going on with you."

"Everyone has a different way of dealing with things, you know," Drew said, his eyes darkening. "Things are not always black and white, like they are in your world. There's a lot of gray. That's what you can't see, Rocky."

"So tell me."

"I don't have to spit everything out to you the second it happens to me. Sometimes I need a second to process things on my own. The entire world does not revolve around you."

Drew's words landed on Rocky's chest like a dagger. She took a deep breath in, two, three, four. Out, two, three, four.

"I just want to help," Rocky said, putting her hand on Drew's shoulder. "Let me help."

"You can't."

"Of course I can." Rocky rubbed small circles on his back. "Just tell me the problem and we'll fix it."

"I called the number the agency found for my birth mother," Drew said. "She's dead."

THIRTY-FIVE

The mother of the bride, as a bride herself
Long Island, 1982

It had to be the wrong address. Joanie was sure of it. Why would
Mel ask Joanie to meet her at a church? It didn't make sense.

A guy who looked like David Bowie walked into the church,
and Joanie realized. This must be one of those underground
clubs. Places where you need a password to get in. She was so
happy she'd worn the dress, shoes, and bracelet she'd bought at
Trash and Vaudeville. Finally, she'd be out downtown in the
right outfit. Joanie slowly ascended the church steps.

Once inside, her new high heels reverberated off the marble
floors. A man dressed in a power suit rushed by her, and then a
woman who looked like she could be homeless followed closely
behind. *Where am I?* Her feeling of confidence was slowly fad-
ing. Maybe she didn't belong here. There was a sign pointing
to the right. It read: Friends of Bill W. and Dr. Bob. Joanie had
been sure she'd heard those names before. But where?

"You made it!" Mel said, coming up from behind.

"Where are we?"

"I think it's better if I just show you."

Mel led the way through the corridor. They went down a set of steps and Joanie figured she'd been right—underground club. But it was so quiet you could hear a pin drop.

Mel walked past another sign announcing "Friends of Bill W. and Dr. Bob." Joanie glanced back. The building seemed empty. Like they were the only ones there. Had it been a mistake to come down to the basement of an abandoned church with someone she'd just met?

Mel reached the door at the end of the hallway and held it open for Joanie to pass through first. Joanie entered slowly.

It was a small room, with chairs set up in a circle. It looked like a classroom. Or perhaps a room for Bible study—there were Bible verses written on a portable blackboard. There was an old table set up against the back wall, filled with coffee and dough-nuts, but most of the people were already seated. Waiting.

Across the room, Joanie saw Jesse, sitting behind the circle. Mel motioned for Joanie to sit down next to him. She folded herself into the chair, careful not to let her leg touch Jesse's. He awkwardly tried to hug her, and their heads crashed into each other.

"Sorry," Joanie said. "I didn't know you'd be here."

"Do you know why you're here?"

"No. What is this place?"

"Maybe it's better if you just experience it."

Mel walked into the center of the circle. "Hi, my name is Melinda. And I'm an alcoholic and a drug addict."

"That was really brave," Joanie told Mel, as the meeting broke an hour later.

"Thank you for coming," Mel said, stirring three teaspoons of sugar into her coffee. In the corner, Jesse talked to the guy who had been leading the meeting. They clearly knew each other—Jesse had accompanied his sister to these meetings before.

"But I don't understand, why did you bring me here?" Joanie asked Mel.

"I wanted you to know the truth."

"So, when I saw you at Jesse's show, you were high?"

"Yeah." Mel's eyes were fixed on the floor.

"When you said you were messed up, I thought you meant that you were drunk."

"I know. And I was. I was really drunk, and when I went to the bathroom, someone offered me a bump. I'd just found out that I'd been passed up for this group show I really wanted, and I just figured, why not, you know?"

"I'm so sorry."

"Oh, you don't have to be sorry. It means a lot. You coming here with me."

"Of course."

"Your sister used to come with me to a lot of these."

Joanie smiled. That was the sort of person her sister was. A good friend. Someone you could trust. Supportive, just like Mel's brother, Jesse. All the Deltas still talked about how she would go out of her way to help a fellow sister. "I'm glad she helped you."

"She didn't just help me."

"Oh, right. I mean, I'm glad she could help everyone here. Be a good influence."

Mel looked down at her feet again. She stirred her coffee slowly, methodically. "Joanie, I have to tell you something about your sister."

"That's why I'm here. I want to know more."

"Even if you won't like it?" Mel's eyes began to tear up, and she used the cuff of her jean jacket to wipe them away.

"Anything."

"I don't want to hurt you," Mel said.

"You won't," Joanie said, putting her hand on Mel's arm. "Just tell me."

"Your sister didn't die of a heart attack. She died of an overdose."

THIRTY-SIX

The seamstress
Paris, 1958

"Tell me everything," Diana said. She smiled and giggled like a schoolgirl.

"Well, this lace is handcrafted by—" Rose said, but she was cut off.

"Not about the lace, silly girl." Diana pushed the fabric swatches aside. "About the beau."

"The beau?" Rose asked, before realizing her error and righting herself. "Yes, of course, my new beau. Well, he's very handsome."

"I noticed," Diana said. "I don't think there was a girl in the movie theater who didn't notice that."

"And he's a physician." Rose carefully picked up a piece of lace, trying to draw Diana's attention back to the reason she was there. To pick out fabrics for her wedding gown.

"Very impressive," Diana said, eyes focused on Rose, ignoring the beautiful fabrics draped all over the worktable. "But tell me about the good stuff. What is he really like? Is he kind? Funny? A good kisser?"

"Oh," Rose said as she struggled to formulate a thought. "Goodness."

"Now, don't be modest."

Rose didn't know how to respond. She certainly couldn't tell Diana that she didn't consider her a friend, but instead merely a client, and she wasn't sure how to speak about a kiss that had never happened. She looked up to Julien for guidance, but he simply shook his head. *You can do this*, he telegraphed with a nod of his head.

"Well, he's very kind. And very funny," Rose said. "And, ahem, a very good kisser."

"You don't seem convinced." Diana furrowed her brow, and Rose felt as if Diana could see inside her mind, could tell that she was fibbing. "Are you sure?"

"Oh, yes," Rose said, trying to command the same confidence that Julien had when he was telling a lie. "I'm very sure. I'm also sure that this alençon lace is very special." Rose passed the fabric swatch of needlepoint lace to Diana.

"I know exactly what this is. I've seen it before," Diana said, putting the lace back down on the table. Rose could not tell whether she was talking about the lace or the man. "There's nothing wrong with him." Of course. She was still talking about the man.

"Nothing!" Rose picked up a swatch of Chantilly lace and handed it to Diana. "There's nothing wrong with him, I assure you." Diana didn't take the swatch of lace. Her eyes stayed focused on Rose.

"But there's nothing quite right, either," Diana said, shaking her head, as if she already knew the answer to her question. "Are you in love with someone else?"

Across the room, Julien dropped his cup of tea. The sound punctured the quiet buzz of the atelier, reverberated off its walls, and it seemed as if time stood still as everyone stared at Julien. The sewing machines stopped running, and the seamstresses up in the workroom remained perfectly quiet. Even Robert, from across the room, put his newspaper down and looked up.

"My goodness!" Rose exclaimed as she rushed across the room to his aid. "Are you all right? You didn't burn yourself, did you?"

"I'm fine," Julien said, under his breath, as he wiped hot tea off his pants with a handkerchief. "It seemed as though you could use a little help, though."

"I'm fine, too," Rose fibbed. She made a show of picking up the broken pieces of fine china and depositing them into a nearby trash can.

"Can I be of assistance?" Robert said, and Rose didn't look up from where she was kneeling on the ground.

"Please do not trouble yourself," Julien said.

"It's no trouble." Robert kneeled next to Rose to help her pick up the broken pieces of Julien's teacup.

"Please, let me," Rose said, without looking Robert's way. She could feel the heat coming off Robert's body.

"This is my mess. I can take care of it myself," Julien said, shooing both Rose and Robert away. And then, to Rose: "You just take care of our client."

Robert extended his hand for Rose to take, and he guided her up from the floor.

"Thank you," Rose said quietly, her eyes trained on her feet.

"I know what we need," Diana said, once Rose had settled herself back at the table. "The rose point lace used on Princess Grace's gown."

"I have a sample of that right here," Rose said, her fingers recalling exactly where the swatch was. "It's beautiful."

"No," Diana said, mischief in her eyes, "I mean the actual rose point lace."

"I don't understand." Worry filled Rose's head—had she made her first mistake? Were the lace samples she'd collected insufficient? She had been so careful. She'd presented Diana with a number of choices, but not too many. She found rose point lace, the same type of lace used on Grace Kelly's dress, and then she found other varieties, samples that would reference the famous gown they'd be using as an influence, but not directly copy it.

"My brother's fiancée has a friend who knows the lace maker who procured the actual rose point lace that was used on Princess Grace's gown."

"The lace that was used on her gown was one hundred and twenty-five years old," Rose said carefully. "How will you get the exact same lace?"

"The lace you are looking for no longer exists," Julien said, getting up from his desk. "The bolt of fabric was completely used. There is none left."

"Elisabeth knows someone who says otherwise," Diana said gleefully. "When I told her about my inspiration for the dress, she said she'd help me find it."

"Mademoiselle, she must be mistaken," Julien said. "There is no more of the actual lace that was used on the Grace Kelly wedding gown. The only remaining piece had been sent to the shoemaker, David Evins. When it was stretched over the shoes, it ripped. He used a matching antique lace on Princess Grace's wedding shoes."

"Then that must have been what she was referring to," Diana quickly said. "We will find the matching antique lace that was used."

"Why don't you allow me to make some phone calls on your behalf?" Julien pled. "I'm sure that if the matching lace can be found, we will be able to find it."

"I wouldn't want to waste Madame's time with silly telephone calls. Especially with how much she's been traveling lately, on my behalf. I know how hard she is working on my dress."

"That she is," he said.

"Don't you think Madame would prefer to have the correct lace for the gown?" Was Diana challenging Julien?

"I do," Julien said, his voice measured. "Madame wants your dress to be the most special dress she's ever created. And it will be."

"Then it's decided," Diana announced. "I will get hold of the rose point lace."

"You wouldn't mind if I left you on your own, would you?" Diana asked Rose.

"Of course not. But we—"

"And, Robert," Diana called across the atelier, "you wouldn't mind if I borrowed your fiancée for a little while? Just to make the dress perfect. It won't take long at all, I promise."

"I suppose—" Robert began.

"Then it's settled! I will travel to New York with Elisabeth and bring back the rose point lace."

"Mademoiselle Laurent," Julien said. "I urge you to reconsider."

"My mind is made up. It must be done."

It had all happened so quickly that Rose hadn't had time to think. Time to speak.

"Whatever you like, Mademoiselle," Julien said. "I only want you to be happy."

"This is what will make me happy," Diana said. And then, turning to Robert: "While I'm away, I'll need you to bring over the progress payment for the dress and to make sure the dress is progressing on schedule. Can I leave the two of you on your own?"

THIRTY-SEVEN

The bride
Brooklyn, 2020

Drew stood up and ripped his shirt.

Rocky didn't know what he was doing, or why he was doing it. First, he told her that his birth mother was dead, and then next, he got up from the couch, looked at himself in the mirror, and tore the shirt he was wearing.

"Drew?" Rocky said tentatively. She stood behind him at the mirror. Softly, she put her hand on his shoulder. A show of support. "What can I do?"

"In the Jewish faith," Drew explained, still looking in the mirror, "mourners rip their clothing when a loved one dies."

Rocky immediately thought of the one Jewish funeral she'd attended—the grandmother of a friend from college—and how the mourners wore torn bits of fabric attached to their clothing.

She stood next to Drew and pulled at the fabric of her shirt. But it had no give. She tried again, and then again. "Dammit."

"You're not in mourning," Drew said, looking at Rocky, his

eyes soft. Sad. "It's the immediate family who does the rend-ing of the clothing. You don't have to do it. You're not sup-posed to do it."

"I want to," Rocky said, and got a good grip on the but-ton side of her shirt. She pulled once again and the fabric gave way. *Rip.* The sound was so satisfying. She did it again. Ripped harder. "I love you. You're a part of me."

Drew took her face in his hands and looked deeply into Rocky's eyes. She could see the tears beginning to form just as he kissed her.

"I love you," he said back to her. "You're a part of me."

"What can I do?" Rocky asked. "How can I help?"

"I don't know," Drew said. "I don't even know how to feel. This person, this person I never met, is dead, and I don't know how to feel about it."

"I don't think there's a wrong way and a right way to feel. It's a lot to process."

"She was my mother," he said quietly.

"She was."

"And I never got to meet her," he said, even softer now. "Never got to know her."

"I know," Rocky said. "I'm sorry. I'm so, so sorry." Rocky tried to remember what it had been like when her father died—What had she needed at the time? What could she do to help Drew?—but she'd been so young when it happened. There was nothing anyone could have said to her that would have helped. Nothing anyone could have done. Her whole world collapsed in on itself that day. And life was never really the same since then.

Drew shook his head solemnly. "I just remembered. You're not supposed to look in the mirror if you're mourning."

"Oh," Rocky said, and looked around for something with which to cover it.

Drew grabbed a throw blanket off the couch and draped it

across the mirror. It was too heavy—in the coming days, they'd replace it with a sheet—but for now, it would do.

"What else do we need to do?" Rocky asked, glancing across the living room, as if the answers were there, if only she looked hard enough.

"I don't know," Drew said, shaking his head. "My mom would know."

"Do you want me to call your mom?"

"I don't know," Drew repeated, a faraway look washing over his face.

Rocky considered Drew's words from earlier—everyone has a different way of dealing with things, life was not always black and white, and sometimes you just need a minute to process. He might not always deal with things the way that Rocky did, and that was okay.

"Let's sit down," Rocky said, and guided Drew to the couch. "Why don't you take a few minutes to yourself. Do you want me here, or should I give you space? Just tell me what you need."

"Stay," Drew said, and grabbed Rocky's hand. He hugged her deeply, and then as the tears began to fall, he sank lower. He rested his head on her lap, and they sat silently like that, Rocky running her hands through Drew's hair, for the whole night.

THIRTY-EIGHT

The mother of the bride, as a bride herself
Long Island, 1982

"I'm sorry," Joanie's mother said as she turned on the coffee maker the following morning. Joanie was taken aback—it was as if her mother was reading her mind. Did she know that Joanie had discovered the truth about her sister just hours before?

"I can't believe you didn't tell me the truth," Joanie said quietly, her voice barely a whisper.

"I should never have made you feel as if you couldn't change my wedding dress. Matthew will be standing at the end of that aisle, waiting for you in his brand-new tuxedo. You should have a dress that feels new."

"Oh," Joanie said, understanding that she and her mother were having two separate conversations. "The dress."

"Yes," her mother continued, impatient to get her point across. "It belongs to you now. I gave it to you. You can do with it whatever you please."

"I wasn't talking about the dress."

"Well, be that as it may, you can change the sleeves if you'd like. You can change anything. I shouldn't have made you feel otherwise."

"I don't want to talk about the dress!" Joanie slammed a hand down onto the table. She was surprised at how forcefully the words had come out. She never raised her voice to her mother.

"Oh?" Birdie regarded her.

"Michele," Joanie said, careful to keep her voice calm, measured. "You didn't tell me the truth about Michele."

"I'm afraid I don't understand."

"I know how Michele really died. I know the truth now. What I don't know is why I had to find out from someone else."

"I did tell you the truth. Your sister had a heart attack." Birdie looked down at her hands. She brought them together and squeezed tightly.

"She had a heart attack because she overdosed on drugs."

Her mother cleared her throat but didn't say a word. Joanie's voice punctured the silence: "Didn't she?"

"Yes." Her voice barely a whisper.

"So, you told me the truth. But you didn't tell me the important part."

"I told you the truth."

"You didn't tell me the whole truth."

"Your father and I decided to keep the part about the drugs quiet. It was bad enough that we'd lost your sister. We didn't want to sully your sister's memory. We didn't want to compound our grief with judgment."

"Did you know that she was doing drugs?"

"Of course not," Birdie said. "How could you ask me that? If we'd known, we could have gotten her help."

Joanie considered this. "I think people would have understood. I don't think you had to hide the truth."

"You cannot possibly think that."

Joanie shook her head. She had gotten off track. It wasn't important when Michele had started the drugs or whether or not her parents had known about it. It wasn't important what they told people about how she died. "But I'm not the neighbors. I'm not Daddy's work colleagues. I'm not some 'people' that you can't tell. I'm your daughter. I had a right to know."

Birdie remained silent, and Joanie glared at her. Demanded that she respond. Joanie raised her voice: "How could you hide something like that from me? She was my sister."

"I told you what I thought you could handle," Birdie answered quietly.

"What's that supposed to mean?" Joanie's voice was loud, out of control. But she didn't want to control it. She wanted to yell. She wanted to scream. She wanted to hurt her mother as much as she'd hurt her.

"You were too young to understand. It was too much."

"I may have been too young three years ago, but I'm now twenty years old. I'm an adult. There were a million different times you could have told me the truth."

"You may be twenty years old, but you are still not a grown-up." Birdie spoke softly, quietly. She walked over to the sink and ran cold water over her hands, pressed them to her neck, to her forehead.

"I *am* a grown-up. I'm engaged. You can't get any more grown-up than that."

"You are a woman, engaged to be married. But in many ways, I'm afraid, you're just a girl."

THIRTY-NINE

The seamstress
Paris, 1958

The atelier was perfectly quiet. Julien had left work to have an
early dinner with Charles, and the last seamstress had just gone
home for the evening. Rose reveled in the silence. She'd never
had the atelier all to herself before, and it felt more sacred than
a church. She looked around the space—the reams of fabric, the
dress forms tacked with works in progress, and Madame's delicate drawings, all across the walls.

If Julien's plan worked out, this would belong to her. As long
as she stayed the course and delivered a perfect wedding gown
to Diana, then they would announce her as Madame's protégé,
that she would be taking over the atelier. They would stay in
business and Rose would have the thing that had always eluded
her: security. In moments like these, they seemed so close to
saving the business. But in others, it was like in a dream, where
you reach and reach, but cannot grasp the thing you want, until
finally, it disappears.

A slight knock on the door drew her back from her reverie.

"Am I too late?" he asked, as the chime rang out. Rose could barely believe her eyes. It was as if the universe knew her most secret desire and delivered it to her: Robert. "I've brought the check for Julien. You'll have to accept my apologies—my mother called this afternoon and was horrified that I hadn't brought it sooner. Apparently, it was due once Diana approved the sketch as final."

"That's all right," Rose said, running a hand through her hair to smooth it down. "Julien's not here right now. I can leave it on his desk."

"I don't want to keep you, if you're trying to get home. Or if you have plans for the evening."

"It's no trouble at all," Rose said. "I assure you."

Their fingertips touched as Robert handed her the check. Rose quickly drew her hand back. As she rushed off to Julien's office to leave it on his desk, she reminded herself that she mustn't think about Robert. The only thing that was important was the money he'd just given her. Keeping the atelier afloat.

Rose placed the check on the center of Julien's desk and grabbed her coat. She should leave for the evening and stop dreaming. Perhaps the fresh air was just what she needed, would help to clear her head.

Rose walked back into the main room of the atelier and was surprised to find Robert still standing there. "You're still here."

"Well, you mentioned that Julien wasn't here," he said. "I thought you might need someone to walk you home."

"Why, thank you," Rose said, struggling to keep her composure. "But I assure you, that's hardly necessary."

"I know it's not necessary," Robert said.

Rose looked in his eyes to parse his meaning. Did he feel the same way that she did? That would be impossible. After all, Rose had seen his fiancée, and she was the very picture of what every man wanted in a woman. She mustn't read into things. He was simply being a gentleman, nothing more.

"I'm on my way home," Robert explained. "And I would be happy to have the company."

Without thinking: "Yes."

Robert opened the door for Rose to leave first, and then waited patiently as she locked up for the evening. He placed his hand on the small of her back as she stepped onto the sidewalk. The night air was warm, and Rose took a deep breath in so as to enjoy the moment, memorize it.

"I'm this way," Rose said, pointing in the direction of her usual walk home.

"Lead the way."

"I don't want to take you too far off your course."

"Why don't you let me worry about that?" Robert smiled warmly at her.

They crossed the street and made their way towards Rose's boarding house. Rose noticed that Robert walked on the outer part of the sidewalk, with Rose on the inside of the sidewalk, the true mark of a gentleman. If a car veered off the road and onto the sidewalk, he could protect her.

"Elisabeth cannot wait to meet Madame," Robert said. "That was very kind of Julien to get an appointment for her."

"Of course," Rose replied, and immediately felt her hands get hot at the mention of Madame's name. She quickly changed the subject: "How did the two of you meet?"

"It wasn't so much a meeting," Robert said. "Elisabeth and I have known each other our whole lives. Our families were always close, and our fathers always worked together. I can't recall a time when I didn't know Elisabeth. And I can't recall a time when it wasn't a foregone conclusion that we'd get married."

"You were soul mates. How utterly romantic." Of course they had the perfect how-we-met story. Of course they were meant to be.

Lost in her thoughts, Rose stepped out into the street without looking. It all happened so quickly. Before she knew it, she felt Robert's strong hands around her body, quickly drawing her back to the curb. Rose gasped as the realization of what had happened slowly came over her—Robert had saved her from a car driving down the street. She fell into his arms as he held on tight.

"I've got you, Rose. You're all right."

"I beg your pardon," Rose said, regaining her footing and releasing her grip on his arms. "I should have been more careful."

"You've got nothing to apologize for. I'm just concerned about you."

Rose looked up at Robert. "I'm perfectly fine now."

"Seems you do need someone to walk you home, after all," Robert teased, as they resumed walking.

"I can take care of myself," Rose said, straightening her back.

"All evidence to the contrary."

Rose couldn't help but laugh. Robert laughed, too, the timbre of his voice deep and throaty. It was a laugh Rose wanted to hear again and again. They walked in silence for a few more blocks, Rose's skin still alight from the feel of Robert's hands on her body.

"This is me," she said, pointing towards her boarding house.

"I'll see you to the door," Robert said, placing his hand on the small of Rose's back protectively as they crossed the street. "If I were to let anything happen to the woman responsible for my sister's wedding dress, I'd truly never hear the end of it."

"Is that the only reason why you saved me?"

Their eyes met. Rose quickly turned towards the front door. "Well, you can let your sister know, I'm perfectly safe." Rose took the key out of her pocket and turned the lock. "Thank you for walking me home."

"You are very welcome," Robert said, standing back on the sidewalk, waiting for her to get inside safely.

Just before the door closed, Rose heard Robert say quietly: "Until next time."

Rose knew that there wouldn't be a next time. The only person he would be walking home in the future would be his beautiful fiancée. But still, she went to sleep that night replaying the walk home over and over again in her mind.

FORTY

The bride
Brooklyn, 2020

She should never have left them alone. In the six minutes since she excused herself from the table, all hell had broken loose. They were at her office, in her conference room, so Rocky had assumed that she'd have the home court advantage. That she'd be in control. She was wrong. Very, very wrong. The meeting was totally and completely out of her control.

Rocky needed to be back in control. The last week had gone by in a blur—they hadn't sat shiva for the week, not exactly, but both Drew and Rocky took short days at work and met at home each afternoon to be together. Rocky stayed by Drew's side, talking things out, letting him yell, letting him cry, letting him deal with the trauma of what he'd learned. It was going to take a lot longer than a week to heal, but it was a start.

"We've got your hashtag," Amanda gushed. She took a big swig of champagne and passed a flute to Rocky.

"My what?" Rocky asked. She set her champagne glass down

on the conference room table. She would not be drinking at this meeting. She had a full afternoon of work meetings to get through. Of course, her sister had no such strains on her time or attention. Amanda had taken a personal day.

"Your hashtag," Amanda said, as if it were obvious. "Every wedding needs a hashtag."

"I don't think my wedding needs a hashtag," Rocky said. "Maybe we should slow down on the champagne." Rocky reached over to grab her sister's glass, but Amanda was quicker than she was and had the glass away from Rocky's hand before she could get close.

"It's prosecco," Amanda said, and then took a big swig of it, as if to prove her point.

"You totally need a hashtag," the wedding coordinator, Emily, said with a deep vocal fry. Rocky regarded her. She was twenty years old and barely ever looked up from her phone. Rocky felt an overwhelming sense that she should never have hired her. Half of her coding staff at the office was twenty years old, true, but this wedding coordinator seemed different. More twenty. Twenty-er. Twenty going on twelve.

Amanda cleared her throat. "I was thinking, it's all good, man."

"Cute," Emily said, eyes on her phone.

"Are you quoting from *Breaking Bad* right now?" Rocky asked her sister. How had this meeting gone so off the rails? How long had she actually been in the bathroom? "The TV show about meth dealers?"

"Technically," Amanda said slowly, "I'm quoting from *Better Call Saul*, the show about the meth dealer's lawyer, but poh-tay-toh, poh-tah-toh."

"Cute," the wedding coordinator repeated. "But, that's not a hashtag. This is a hashtag—"

Emily put her iPhone down and picked her iPad up. She

smiled as she slowly turned the iPad screen around for the big reveal: #FoundAGoodMan.

"You cannot be serious," Rocky said.

"Get it?" she asked. "Because Drew's last name is Goodman?"

"Oh, I get it, all right," Rocky said, her voice drifting off. She looked at her sister, hoping they were thinking the same thing: that this wedding coordinator must be fired. Immediately. As she puzzled over a nice way to say *Don't call us, we'll call you*, Amanda jumped in.

"Oh, that's a winner," Amanda said, and then dramatically grabbed the iPad from the wedding planner's hands. She gave it a hug and smiled. Why? Rocky did not know.

"Let's put a pin in that," Rocky said, reaching for Emily's iPad. But Amanda would not let go. "Where are we on getting the permits to throw the party on our rooftop?"

The wedding coordinator put up her index finger and then pointed at her iPhone. "Give me one sec," she said, before flying out of the room.

"She's incredible, right?" Amanda said, her face still flushed with excitement.

"That's one word for it."

Amanda could never admit when she was wrong, and she had been the one to hire Emily. Rocky peeked out the door of the conference room and saw the wedding coordinator pacing the hallways, speaking so quickly Rocky could barely make out what she was saying.

"I know it's hard for you to say thank you," Amanda said, polishing off her glass of prosecco in one gulp. "But I know. You're welcome."

"Excuse me?"

"The wedding planner." She blew a kiss in Rocky's direction.

"This wedding planner that you hired is horrible. Calm down."

"She's fabulous," Amanda said, shaking her head furiously.

"She's accomplished nothing but create a stupid hashtag that I don't even want."

"That hashtag is gold." Amanda pointed her index finger at Rocky. "We're using it. And as for your other problem, I'm happy to help with that, too."

"What other problem?" Rocky asked. She honestly didn't know. It seemed as if her problems had been rapidly multiplying as of late.

"The dress," Amanda said. "My offer still stands. I'll take the heat off and tell Mom that I'll wear the dress."

"You're going to wear a wedding dress to my wedding?"

"No, silly," Amanda said. "I'll wear it when I get married."

"You're marrying Sloan now?" Rocky asked. "I didn't even realize you got back together."

"Who?" Amanda said, trying for nonchalance, but Rocky was not fooled.

"You're back together now, aren't you? Just admit it."

"I only meant I'll promise Mom that I'll wear the dress *when* I get married."

This was ridiculous. She was supposed to be running a company and instead she was in a conference room, fighting with her sister. It was time to end this meeting and send Amanda and the twenty-year-old on their way.

Seemingly on cue: "Sorry about that, girls!" Emily announced as she walked back into the room. "Now, let's—"

"Let's discuss the *actual* wedding," Rocky said, taking control. "First things first, we'll need a permit to have a party on my building's rooftop—"

"Done," the wedding planner said to her iPhone.

"What do you mean, done?" Rocky said. "I was told it could take months."

"I know a guy," Emily said, looking up at Rocky and winking at her. "I also handled the noise permits, which you'll need for the band to play until midnight, and I hooked up some street parking permits, too, since you said your mom and her peeps are in Connecticut?" She said it all like a question, but it was anything but.

"Yeah," Rocky said. "That's right."

"I also made a few calls and got quotes from three caterers, two table and linen rentals, and four invitation companies. Sending them now."

Rocky's phone pinged as emails filled her screen. Amanda looked over her shoulder and smiled.

"And that band you mentioned?" the planner said. "The one that you and Drew saw on the Lower East Side on your fourth date? They're holding your wedding date open. They said that they could either play the whole party or just do a featured artist thing around eleven, before they serve dessert. They're ridiculously expensive, but it seemed like the sort of sentimental thing Drew would be into. Sending you those quotes now, along with a few other bands for frame of reference."

Rocky's phone buzzed before she could respond.

"And you didn't mention lighting," she said, "but I toured the roof space a few days ago—your doorman Sal is so nice!—and I think we need to discuss lighting. I did a party last year with these round paper lanterns. It could really work for that space."

"She loves paper lanterns!" Amanda said and Rocky eked out: "I do love them."

"Cool, cool, cool," the wedding planner said. "I have a ton of other quotes I need to send over to you, so I'm going to create a Google doc so that we can all stay organized and on the same page. That way, we can also send notes back and forth to each other. Sound good?"

"That sounds great, actually," Rocky said, despite herself.

"It's all good, man," Amanda said, smiling from ear to ear.

"Never say that again." Rocky swiped Amanda's champagne glass without her noticing.

"I'll have my guy mock up a few bathrobe designs with the new hashtag," the wedding planner said. "And I assume you'll want to cover hair and makeup on your own? Although I've got a killer team. I'll pop the quotes into the Google doc, you can think about it later."

"I need a bathrobe?" Rocky asked.

"Can we approve #FoundAGoodMan?" Emily asked.

At the same exact time, Amanda said yes, while Rocky said no.

"No worries," Emily said. "It's the winner, I know it is, but I'll still have my staff create a few other contenders."

What Rocky wanted to say was *I don't need a hashtag*, but she instead couldn't help herself from saying: "You have a staff?"

"You were right," Emily said to Amanda. "Your sister is so, so cute!" And then to Rocky: "So, with your in-laws handling flowers, all that's left is photographer, videographer, and cake."

"I think we have the wedding cake covered," Amanda said, looking out the window. Rocky couldn't decide if she should let her sister get away with it or just blow the whole thing open.

Rocky looked at Amanda, and Amanda suddenly became very interested in her fingernails.

"You've decided on cake?" Emily asked. She looked down at her iPhone for confirmation and furrowed her brow.

"I guess we have," Rocky said. "We really liked Sloan at Big City Bakery."

"Oh, cool," Emily said. "Everyone's completely obsessed with Sloan lately. This is totally hush-hush, but she's getting a write-up in next month's *Brides* magazine. She does great work. Love her!"

"We love her, too," Rocky said, trying to catch Amanda's eye. But her sister refused to look up.

FORTY-ONE

The mother of the bride, as a bride herself
Long Island, 1982

"Now, *this* is how we should have started the school year. This is how it was supposed to be all along," Debbie said, leaning back onto her dorm room bed. Joanie busied herself getting her own side of the room ready. They were already into the spring semester, but after her fight with her mother, she couldn't get out of the house fast enough.

Joanie smiled as she continued unpacking her bags. Debbie was right—this was where she should have been all along. In the dorms. In the city. With her sisters.

It was kismet. Debbie's roommate was spending the semester abroad in Spain and Student Housing hadn't yet given her a new roommate. Joanie was ready to start the next phase of her life, and moving into the city was the way to do it.

She slowly unpacked her things, careful to cut scented contact paper into squares for her drawers. She didn't want her clothes to touch the shelves and drawers that countless other students had used before. Everything in the dorms seemed to have the faint scent of wet dog. She'd brought wood hangers from home, even though Debbie had only left less than half of the closet for her. And she had yet to come up with a plan for the communal showers. Debbie had bought her a pair of shower shoes as a welcome gift, but Joanie didn't know what bothered her more: that you needed a pair of shoes to shower, or that the bathrooms were completely co-ed.

Debbie went into the minifridge and offered Joanie a beer. When Joanie shook her head no, Debbie pulled out a soda water instead.

"I just can't believe there was a whole part of my sister's life that I knew nothing about," Joanie said.

"I'm so sorry, Joanie. What can I do?"

"Nothing, really. There's nothing to do. I guess I just have to process it."

"Everyone has secrets, Joanie." Debbie took a stack of Joanie's sweaters and placed them into a drawer. She reached out for another piece of contact paper and then moved Joanie's T-shirts into the other drawer.

"I'm an open book. Aren't you an open book?"

"We all have things we hide from the rest of the world, don't we? That's what makes life interesting." Debbie picked up a silk bag filled with bras and panties. She held it up to Joanie as proof.

"I have nothing to hide," Joanie said, snatching the bag away from her friend with a smile. She put the bag carefully into the top drawer, leaving its contents inside.

"None of our sisters know that you're a virgin."

"Yeah, but that's totally different. That's private."

"You didn't bring any of the sisters out with you when you were hitting those clubs to find Mel," she said. And then, her voice a bit softer: "Not even me."

"Those clubs are not exactly the sorts of places that Deltas would appreciate," Joanie said with a warm smile. Their eyes met. "Not even you."

"Then bring Mel and her friends around here."

"They don't exactly seem like the Greek system types, if you know what I mean."

"People can surprise you."

"I'm meeting them at Jesse's show on Wednesday. You wanna come with?"

"Sure thing," Debbie said. "And then maybe you'll invite them to one of our events? We have the Theta mixer on Friday night. They were your sister's friends. Maybe they've been to fraternity parties before."

"Maybe." Joanie tried to imagine Mel, with her massive mohawk, at a fraternity mixer. Or Jem, with the bleached white hair and red tips. Or Mikki, with the tattoos running up her arms. Michele's friends would probably cause the Delta sisters to clutch their pearls and hide under their pastel cardigan sweaters.

And Jesse. What would they say about Jesse, with his violet eyes and painted-on leather jeans? With his punk music and his too-loud band? She shook her head as if to get Jesse out of her thoughts. She should not be thinking of another man when she had Matthew. He was down at the hardware store, getting wood for a shelf, since Joanie mentioned that she needed a place to store her jewelry. That's who should be filling her mind. Not some other guy she barely knew.

"Secrets or not, I just wish your sister had asked for help. I wish the sisters had known. That's what the Deltas are all about."

"No one knew."

"Let's make a pact. We tell each other everything, no matter what. Especially if we need help."

"Deal," Joanie said, putting out her hand. Debbie sat down next to her, leaned over, and gave her friend a hug.

"Now that you're living in the dorms, you can come and go as you please. You can do anything you want."

"I can't wait."

"But not tonight. Tonight we have a mixer with the Kappas. And not tomorrow night. We have a mandatory meeting in the Chapter Room about the Delta fund-raiser. But after that, you can totally do whatever you want."

"You make it sound so glamorous."

"And speaking of whatever you want, I bet Matthew's pretty excited to have you just a few floors away."

"He may have mentioned something about that."

"What did Matthew say?"

"He said that I might as well not bother making my bed, because I'll be sleeping in his every night."

"Oh, well, excuse me," Debbie said, in a faux-angry voice. Then, her face turning serious: "But I don't mean about moving into the dorms. I mean about Michele."

But Joanie hadn't told him yet.

FORTY-TWO

The seamstress
Paris, 1958

"Diana insisted I drop in to see how the dress is coming along," Robert said.

Rose was startled. She didn't think she would see him again while Diana was away.

He held out a telegram for Rose to inspect:

Dear Brother. STOP. Please visit Madame's atelier to check on progress of dress. STOP. Very important that the creation of the dress not be delayed in my absence. STOP. If dress not ready in time, my wedding will be ruined. STOP.

"You can tell your sister she needn't worry," Rose said. She spun the dress form around for Robert to see. She wanted him to send a good report to his sister—she wanted there to be no mistake that the dress construction was going well, that Diana would be happy with what she was creating. "I'm very pleased with the progress so far."

"It's extraordinary," Robert said, a flush coming over his face as he grinned in Rose's direction. "But I do, of course, have to make sure you haven't had any troubles crossing the street as of late."

"I stop and look both ways each and every time."

"One must always be careful." He smiled warmly and she smiled back in return. "Forgive the intrusion on your work. I'm sure by now you've realized how difficult it is to say no to my sister."

He was correct; Diana was the sort of girl who was impossible to say no to. "Yes," she said. "I have noticed that."

"And I know how hard it is to be doing something so important—planning this wedding—without our mother around, so I want to support her in any way that I can."

"How sweet you are," Rose said, getting lost in his eyes. Seeing his eyes soften, she then quickly qualified: "You're a very good brother."

"Thank you," Robert said. "I certainly am. In fact, I'm stuck with two tickets to the opera tonight because of her. I was supposed to go with my fiancée, but since she is with my sister, searching the far ends of the earth for a specific swath of lace, I'm afraid they'll go to waste."

"That's terrible," Rose said, and tried to parse his meaning. Was this Robert's way of inviting her to the opera? Or was he simply making conversation? Either way, it shouldn't matter. It didn't matter. As Julien was fond of reminding her, the Laurents were important clients. She was not to befriend them. She surely was not to fall in love with them.

"Would you care to go with me?" Robert asked, his face open and unguarded.

"Yes," Rose said, already forgetting herself. As the word left her mouth, she knew that she should take it back. She knew she should tell him no, she had made a mistake, and she could not attend the opera with him. It would be so simple to say no, so simple to deny her feelings. She could say that she had to work. She could say that she had plans with her "beau" Charles that evening. She could say a million different things, all of which meant that she could not attend. All of which meant that she did not want to see him. But then, even though she knew she shouldn't, she said: "I would love to go with you."

The rest of the afternoon ticked by slowly, minute by minute. At five o'clock, Rose told Julien she was heading home. As he said goodbye, she felt a tug at her heart. Lying had been coming more easily for her. She hated lying to Julien, but wasn't he the one who'd essentially taught her to lie? She found the more she lied to Diana about where Madame was, the easier it was to lie in every other part of her life. Even to Julien.

Rose met Robert at a small café a few blocks away from the opera house. She couldn't help herself from looking around, making sure that she wouldn't get caught. But what was wrong with what she was doing? After all, if Diana had offered her tickets to the opera, surely Julien would have understood. Even though the Laurents were clients, not friends, Rose had never been to the opera before and that counted for something, didn't it? And as for meeting for a light supper before the show, she certainly had to eat, didn't she?

Rose caught Robert's eye from across the restaurant. As he stood up and made his way to her, Rose held her breath. She felt giddy, buoyant. She knew that this man belonged to another, but what was wrong with enjoying one night in his company? Feeling as if she belonged to someone, for just one evening. What harm could that do? And this was about the opera. Just the opera. She simply couldn't let an expensive ticket like that go to waste. It wouldn't be right.

"May I take your coat?" Robert asked, and his hand brushed against hers as she spun around. She tried to suppress her tremendous smile as she turned back to face him, but it was no use. No use at all. She was positively beaming.

They sat down at a tiny round table, and Rose's knees knocked into Robert's as they sat.

"Oh, I beg your pardon," Rose said, giggling nervously. Already she had embarrassed herself.

"Not at all," Robert assured her. "I'm too tall for this table, it seems."

Without thinking: "You're perfect." The moment the words escaped her lips, Rose gasped and put her hand over her mouth.

"What was that?" Robert asked. "I'm afraid it's so noisy in here that I couldn't hear you."

"It was nothing important," Rose said, and let out a deep exhale, put her hands back down into her lap.

"Then let's order a drink." He summoned the waiter.

Rose sat back in her chair. As Robert asked her if she preferred white or red wine, she thought about what life would be like with this man. A harmless fantasy. It would be a life so different from the one she was living. Instead of going home to a lonely boarding house room, she would go back to a proper home. Instead of eating dinner by herself, gazing out the window at the people passing by in the street, she would have a dining room, and eat a home-cooked meal with Robert. Instead of going to the cinema on her own, she would have a constant companion—even though she resisted at first, she had to admit that it had been fun sitting with Julien and Charles the previous week. Having someone to walk you to your seat. Having someone to discuss the film with once it was over.

As she sipped her wine throughout dinner, she allowed herself to imagine that she was on a date. Surely, she knew that he had only asked her because he probably felt sorry for her—after all, wasn't that what Diana meant when she told Robert to look in on her?—but Rose didn't mind.

When Robert helped her on with her coat after supper, Rose

allowed herself to imagine that she was his fiancée, that they had a light supper like this all the time, and that it wasn't just this one time. They walked to the opera house side by side, Robert standing on the outer side of the sidewalk, like a gentleman, and putting his arm around her protectively when they crossed the street.

Rose was overjoyed to find that they had box seats—an entire little section all to themselves—for the performance. By then, she'd completely forgotten to look around to make sure they weren't spotted. She felt emboldened by the wine, warm and happy, and quickly forgot all of her cares.

Rose felt she was so close to the opera singers, she could see their every emotion played out on their faces. She was utterly captivated. So much so that she almost didn't notice it when Robert's knee knocked into hers again during the first act. Almost.

Rose sat through the opera, transfixed by the sights and sounds, overwhelmed by the emotion of it, and the feel of Robert's knee occasionally bumping into her own. She was hypnotized, under a spell that she hoped never would break.

And then, when it came time to walk home from the opera house, when Robert's hand brushed against Rose's, she didn't pull away. She let their hands touch, ever so slightly, the entire way home.

FORTY-THREE

The bride
Brooklyn, 2020

"Maybe we should just run away."

"From this bar? I kind of like it here."

"For our wedding," Rocky said, swatting Drew on his arm, leaning into him. "Maybe we run away and get married, just the two of us. No one else."

"Is this because you don't like the hashtag?" The bartender set their drinks down on the bar and Drew took a slow sip of his beer.

"First of all, we don't need a hashtag."

"I could never do that to my mom," Drew said.

"Have a wedding without a hashtag?"

"Elope."

Rocky sipped her beer and set it back down on the bar. She looked at Drew. She grabbed his hand, and he squeezed back.

"I thought it might be easier given what happened to your birth mother."

Drew looked down for a moment. Then, looking back up: "I appreciate that, but no. I want to have a wedding where we stand up in front of our parents and everyone we've ever met and tell them all how much we love each other."

"The wedding you've been dreaming of since you were a boy?"

"Something like that."

"Is this just to please your mom? Because she wants to see her only child get married?"

"So what if it is? Tradition is important in my family," Drew said, shrugging his shoulders. "It's important to me."

"I have a different relationship with my mother than you do with yours." Rocky stuck her fingernail under the label of her beer bottle. She pushed it until it gave way, finally coming off in one whole piece, and set it down on the bar.

"I know that," Drew said. "But don't you want more?"

Rocky did want more. Finding out about Drew's birth mother gave her a clarity she hadn't had before. It made her feel closer to Drew, more understanding, and it made her realize how important her relationship with her mother was. How lucky she was to have her, even if she didn't always see it. She may have always felt closer to her father, but the fact was: he wasn't around anymore.

"I want more. I don't know how," Rocky said.

"You could tell her how you feel."

"Every time I try, it always goes wrong."

"Because you're not telling her the truth. You're not letting her in."

"I try." Rocky picked up the beer bottle label again, rolling it in her fingers. It was sticky to the touch and after she put it down, the glue remained on her fingers.

"Be honest with your mom. Tell her the truth," Drew said, his eyes set firmly on Rocky. "Tell her you don't want to wear the dress."

FORTY-FOUR

The mother of the bride, as a bride herself
Long Island, 1982

"Do you ever feel like you don't know who you are?"

A voice shushed Joanie from a few carrels away. She wasn't sure who it was—the Thetas and Deltas had taken over the third floor of the library for mandatory "Study Hours" before midterms, which was really just another excuse to socialize—and she hadn't been speaking very loudly. Still, Joanie made a mental note to keep her voice down to a whisper. But she couldn't help it. Libraries always brought it out in her. The quiet made her feel safe, like she could spill all of her secrets.

"No."

"I just mean that I think I'm finding myself," Joanie said quietly, tentatively. "Or that I want to."

"Because of your sister?" Matthew asked, and Joanie didn't respond. He continued on in his regular speaking voice: "Joanie, just because you learned the real truth about how your sister died doesn't mean that you don't know who you are." The disembodied voice shushed them once again. Matthew stood up to see who was listening to them.

"Maybe I never did know who I was. Who I am." Her words came out in a jumble. It felt like the more she tried to explain herself to Matthew, the more her words got lost. Confused.

"You know who you are," Matthew said, softer. "I mean, you're you."

"But what if I don't know who I am?" she asked, her voice almost a whisper.

Matthew put his hands around her face and looked at Joanie. His thumb glided along the side of her cheek as he leaned in for a gentle kiss. "I know who you are," he said, firmer this time.

"Who's that?"

"The girl I'm going to marry, that's who!" he said, smiling broadly at her. He leaned over and kissed her again.

"Shhh!" the voice called out, and Joanie leaned back in her chair. Matthew stood up again and looked around before sinking back into his own chair.

"Right." Joanie smiled back broadly at her fiancé, but smiling felt like work. Unnatural. "Have you ever done it? Tried drugs?"

"Pot, sure," Matthew admitted. "But real drugs? Like cocaine? No."

"Me neither."

"Do you want to now?" He furrowed his brow and examined her face. He looked at her closely, as if he were trying to solve a puzzle.

"No, of course not."

"See that," he said, grabbing her hand in his. "You already know yourself a little more than you're giving yourself credit for."

Joanie considered his words. Maybe she did know herself more than she thought. But then her mother's words flooded her mind: Was she still a child? "Maybe."

"Have you given any thought to this summer?"

"Are we planning to get any studying done?" Joanie made a big show of opening her Psych 204 textbook and grabbing a highlighter from her knapsack.

"We'll study later," Matthew said, closing Joanie's textbook. "So, have you thought about the summer?"

The truth was, Joanie had not. She hadn't given much thought to anything lately besides her sister. "Of course."

"And, what do you think? I'll have a single room, all to myself." Matthew's face lit up whenever he spoke about their future. Joanie wished she could be as excited about it as he was. But whenever she thought about it for too long, it gave her a bellyache.

"My mother would flip if I went down to Florida to stay with you. She'd say we were living in sin, right before the wedding." Joanie bit the cap of her highlighter.

"It's only an eight-week internship."

"See? You'll be back before you know it. Then, we'll get married and start our lives together."

Matthew took the highlighter from Joanie's grip. "You can go two months without seeing me?"

"It's too hot down there, anyway. You know how much the humidity kills my hair." She shook her head from side to side, for effect. Her curls fell in front of her face, and she drew them back behind her ears with a finger.

"Don't you want to start the next phase of our lives together?"

"Of course I do!" Joanie didn't want to talk about this anymore. She felt the undeniable ache in the pit of her belly. She realized she hadn't given much thought to living together. Not just yet. Of course, after they got married, they'd live together. Wouldn't they? Joanie hadn't really thought much beyond that. That was "after" and Joanie was still stuck in "before."

Matthew challenged her with his eyes. He did not seem convinced of her words. Joanie leaned over and gave him a kiss.

Not a peck, a real kiss. A lean-back-and-enjoy-it sort of kiss. He murmured: "This conversation's not over, you know."

"Oh, I know," Joanie said, as she planted kisses all over his face, down his neck. Matthew kissed her back and Joanie remembered what a good kisser he was. How much she loved being in his arms.

"Keep it PG in here!" a Theta brother called out from a few carrels away. Joanie and Matthew laughed.

Why was she being so skittish about moving down to Florida with him for the summer? This was the man she wanted to marry. This was the life she wanted to have. And if her mother wasn't happy about it? So what. Her mother still thought of her as a child, but she was a twenty-year-old woman, and she would do as she pleased.

Matthew kissed her again and she hopped into his lap. She pressed her body to him, and his arms wrapped tightly around her back.

"Yes," Joanie said, her voice a murmur. "Let's do it. Yes."

Matthew's eyes brightened. "Should we go to my dorm room or the stacks? My room would be more special, but the stacks might be more fun." Matthew quickly threw his books back into his knapsack.

In an instant, Joanie realized it: Matthew thought that when she said *let's do it*, she meant sex. Did he really think she was going to lose her virginity randomly one night in the library stacks? How ridiculous! But then, an unwelcome thought passed through her mind. At the thought of sex, she couldn't help but think of Jesse. In fact, thoughts of Jesse had been coming to her more and more frequently as of late. When she got dressed in the morning, when she was in the shower, and sometimes when she woke up. Joanie shook her head, as if to dislodge him from her mind. She was with Matthew. She was engaged to Matthew. She would lose her virginity to Matthew.

"No, not yes to that," Joanie said with a nervous laugh. "Yes to Florida. I'll come down with you for the summer."

Matthew threw his bag back down onto the ground and let out a deep breath. "Right. I knew that."

FORTY-FIVE

The seamstress
Paris, 1958

"I revealed a secret to you, but you are keeping one from me."

Rose froze. Diana was newly back from her adventure—they had not been able to recover the exact swath of rose point lace that was used on Grace Kelly's wedding shoes, but not for lack of trying. They'd been out of the country for three weeks. Three glorious weeks where Robert visited the atelier nine times. They'd gone to the opera together, an informal supper, and a visit to the Petit Palais to see a new exhibit. He had walked her home from the atelier six times, and twice they walked through the Tuileries Garden on their way. Their hands had touched countless times, and on the last night that he walked her home, Rose had been sure that Robert was about to kiss her. Really kiss her. Not just an informal kiss on the cheek. They stood on her doorstep, face-to-face, and he took her hands in his.

"I've very much enjoyed getting to know you, Rose," he'd said.

"And I, you." She felt the weight of his hands in her own. They felt strong and assured.

"I am glad we had this time together." Robert squeezed Rose's hands. He brought them to his chest and kissed them gently.

"I, too, am glad." Her heart felt so full, did his feel full as well? When Robert looked back up at her, she felt as though her heart might burst. This was the moment. She knew it in her skin. He was about to kiss her.

But how could she kiss a man who was promised to another? She simply could not. How could she start a relationship like this? Rose didn't have much experience when it came to relationships, but she felt one thing was sure: it was not a good idea to start one when the man you loved was engaged to another woman.

"Thank you for walking me home." Rose gently pulled her hands away from Robert's. She knew that if she didn't do it quickly, she would lose her nerve. She spun on her heel and put her key in the door. Rose turned back to look at Robert one more time. He smiled warmly at her, and she returned his smile with one of her own. "I do hope I will see you again soon."

"You will," he said, still smiling. "Good night, Rose."

And now Diana was back in Paris. Rose knew that Robert would not be by the atelier to check in on her again. And she knew that he would be walking his fiancée through the Tuileries now, not her.

So, why did Diana say that Rose was hiding a secret? Had Diana's friends seen her with Robert? Did Diana know about Rose's inappropriate feelings towards her brother? She hoped not. The fate of the atelier depended on it.

"A secret?" Rose asked Diana. "Whatever do you mean?"

"Madame," she said, her voice measured and low. "I know about Madame."

"I don't understand," Rose whispered back. She took deep, even breaths, and tried to keep her nerves under control. Her hands betrayed her—they showed the slightest tremble, and Rose brought them under the table and into her lap to hide her guilt.

"I know that Madame is gone," Diana said. "And not just for another one of her work trips. On my travels, I met with many vendors who work with Madame. Not one has seen her in months. Not one has even spoken to her. They all seem to think she went back to America. Back to the moving pictures."

"America?" Rose said, stalling for time.

"You don't have to lie to me," Diana said. "I know that Madame went back to America. And what's more? I don't care. I love the work you are doing on my wedding dress. Your sketches are better than Madame's. Your eye is younger, fresher. Your work is impeccable, and you catered to what I wanted. Madame would not have done that for me."

Rose kept her face still, but she couldn't help a tear from forming at the corner of her eye. She didn't want to lie anymore. Not about the dress, not about Robert, not about any of it. But what to say?

"You don't have to say anything," Diana said. "I know that I am right."

Rose looked up at Diana and their eyes met. Slow tears fell from Rose's eyes and she quickly brushed them away.

"Your secret is safe with me. I have grown quite fond of you, and I would never do anything to bring you harm."

"Thank you," Rose said, and the moment the words escaped her mouth, she knew that they were as good as a confession.

"Now," Diana said. "I have a proposition for you."

FORTY-SIX

The bride
Brooklyn, 2020

"You want me to use a wedding tuxedo on a wedding dress?"
Greta asked.

Rocky looked down at her hands. "It was a stupid idea," she
said under her breath.

"It's a wonderful idea," Joan said, bursting with pride. And
then, to Greta: "Rocky would really like to honor her father on
her special day. And since his wedding tuxedo was so perfectly
preserved, we thought this could be a great way to make him
part of things. Perhaps we use part of the lapel on the cummerbund? Or the silk ribbon running down the pants leg could be a
bow? But I don't want to tell you how to do your job, of course."

Greta eyed Rocky carefully. "You don't like the dress?" the
older woman asked, and Rocky froze. She stared back at Greta
wide-eyed, unsure of how to respond. Could Greta see it on
her face?

"Of course she likes the dress," Joan answered for her daughter, as if she'd never heard something so crazy before in her life. "Who wouldn't like this dress? We're just trying to add another layer of meaning to it. And since we're updating it anyway…"

"I've never done something like this before," Greta said, partially to Joan, but mostly to herself. She picked up the tuxedo jacket, and turned it carefully in her hands.

"You can't do it?" Joan said, her patience suddenly gone.

"Don't rush me. I didn't say can't." Greta quietly, thoughtfully, fingered the lines of the jacket, putting her fingernail into the seams to see how it was made. "Give me a minute to think."

"We'll make it work," Joan said to Rocky, grasping her hands in her own. "It's going to be great."

Rocky smiled at her mother, but it wasn't genuine. Rocky did not, in fact, think it was going to be great.

"Maybe I should just wear the tuxedo." This wasn't Rocky's usual style, using a joke to get at the real truth of things—she liked to think of herself as a straight shooter. Someone who didn't play games. But dealing with her mother was different. This wasn't just anyone. And she couldn't just speak her mind when it came to Joan.

Drew's words rang out in Rocky's ears: *Tell your mother the truth.*

She could hear her father, too: *You can tell your mother anything, Kitten. She'll understand.*

"What on earth are you talking about?" A look of mild distaste crossed Joan's face. She quickly caught herself, and tried to hide it, but Rocky had seen.

"I just miss him, you know?"

"I do, too, honey," Joan said, her voice softening. Her expression becoming more gentle. She placed her hand over her daughter's and stroked it gently. "But you have me. You have Amanda."

"It's not the same," Rocky said, and as soon as the words left her mouth, she regretted them.

"No, honey," Joan said, patting her daughter's hand. "Of course it's not. Would you please excuse me for a moment?" She stood up and strode out of the room.

Rocky immediately jumped up and followed. She could feel Greta staring at her as she hastily left the room. She caught up with her mother on the sidewalk outside the bridal shop.

"I'm sorry, Mom," Rocky said.

"It's fine," Joan said quickly, smiling, but Rocky could see the tears gathering in her eyes.

"I'm sorry," Rocky repeated. Her mother looked around— she was never one to make a scene—but they were alone on the sidewalk. "I didn't mean it like that."

"I know what you meant," Joan said, pulling a tissue out of her purse. "Just go inside and I'll be back as soon as I collect myself."

"Mom, I just meant—" Rocky said, gentler this time, reaching out to touch her mother's arm.

"I know what you meant," Joan said, recoiling from Rocky's grip, her voice booming. "Just give me a minute here."

"I'm not leaving you like this," Rocky said, her arms back to her sides. "You're clearly still upset."

"I'm perfectly fine," Joan said, a strained smile on her face. "Now, please go inside. I don't want to be rude to Greta."

"Hey, I'm trying to talk to you." Rocky raised her voice just the tiniest bit to get her mother's attention.

"*You're* trying to talk to *me*?" Joan said, a nasty laugh leaving her mouth. High-pitched and unnatural. "I've been trying to talk to you your whole life."

"I'm right here." Rocky opened her arms out wide, to show her mother that she was there. To show her that she wasn't going anywhere.

"I get it. You want your father to be here," Joan said, speaking quickly. "Well, I do, too, Rachel. I do, too. But he's gone. He's gone, okay? You know who isn't gone? Me. I'm still here. I know you have this perfect memory of your father, and I love that, I really do, but I'm still here, you know. And I really can't compete with a dead person. A dead person stays perfect. But I'm still here."

"I know that, Mom," Rocky said. "I love you. I'm sorry for what I said."

"Do you think it was easy for me when your father died?" Joan said, her voice now a roar. She dabbed furiously at her eyes, at her nose. "It wasn't. I had two small kids, and you had all of your—all of your stuff—and I did the best I could. I know it wasn't good enough for you and you're filled with resentment towards me, but I did the best that I could. I do the best that I can."

"I'm sorry," Rocky said. It was all she could say, and she just couldn't say it enough.

"I am, too," Joan said. "I'm sorry you lost your father. I'm sorry you just have me. I'm sorry that I'm not good enough for you."

"You are good enough," Rocky said, tears now welling up in her own eyes. "Don't say that."

"It doesn't feel like it," Joan said. "You think I don't know that all you ever do is talk about your father? How you want to honor him at the wedding? How you can't walk down the aisle because he's not here. What about me?"

"What about me?" Rocky asked, pointing to herself. She could feel it—the sadness had given way and was being replaced by anger. She felt it building in her chest, bubbling as she spoke. Threatening to pop. "I could ask the same thing to you. Everything is always about Amanda."

"I have no idea what you are talking about," her mother said, finally finding another tissue and then blowing her nose loudly. "What is that supposed to mean?"

"Every time I see you, every time I talk to you, all you ever do is talk about Amanda."

Joan looked up at Rocky. "I think she would say the same thing about you."

"That's ridiculous," Rocky said, and felt her chest deflate as a laugh escaped. The anger was passing, she could breathe again.

"You can ask her," Joan said, shrugging her shoulders.

"I will ask her," Rocky said, "but the fact is, you are closer to Amanda than you are to me. You have two daughters. I'm your daughter, too. But sometimes I feel like it's just you and Amanda. I feel like I'm not a part of this family. I'm the one who gets left out. I'm on the outside."

"How could you say such a thing? You are a part of this family. I love you more than you could ever know, in a way that you won't fully be able to comprehend until you have children yourself. I have two children. And I love them equally."

"Do you?"

"Of course I do," Joan said, incredulous. She opened her purse for another tissue and came up empty. She sniffled the tears back and continued: "Do you have any idea how lucky you are to have a sister? I wish my sister were still alive. You have no idea what a gift you have. And you don't even appreciate it."

"I'm sorry about your sister," Rocky said. Breathe in, two, three, four. Out, two, three, four. *Control the anger. Don't let the anger control you.* "I really am. I wish I could have met her."

"I wish that, too," Joan said, grabbing Rocky's hands in her own. "And I wish we were closer, I wish we could be more honest with each other. I try. I've been trying for years. But you have this wall up, Rocky. You never let me in. Let me in. What is going on with you?"

"I don't have a wall up."

Joan took a finger and lifted Rocky's chin so that their eyes met. "What's going on with you?"

Rocky looked into her mother's eyes. She wanted to be honest with her. She wanted to have a better relationship with her.

And all of that started right here. Right now. Rocky took a deep breath and told her mother her truth. "I don't want to wear the dress."

FORTY-SEVEN

The mother of the bride, as a bride herself
Long Island, 1982

Senior Tea. It was the Delta house's biggest bash of the year, and the last hurrah of the school year. Every year, students clamored for an invitation. Each sister got three invites to distribute, three lucky friends who would get to attend the party everyone would be talking about all summer long.

The sorority house's common room was transformed into a magical place. A different theme each year, with decorations growing more elaborate as the years went on. Each year outdoing the year before. This year's theme? Alice in Wonderland, all grown up. You might be drinking out of a dainty tea cup, but that's not English Breakfast inside. It's vodka.

Costumes weren't mandatory, *per se*, but everyone knew to wear them. After all, when you've secured the hottest invite on campus, you may as well dress the part. That evening, Matthew was dressed as the Mad Hatter, Joanie, with her blond hair, was perfect as Alice, and Debbie made a fabulous Queen of Hearts.

Jenny and Missy rounded out their group quite nicely as a sexy Cheshire Cat and a sexy White Rabbit.

Joanie had used her three invites for Mel, Jem, and Mikki. She didn't need an invite for Matthew, as the president of the Theta house, and Debbie was right—she needed to bring Michele's friends, her new friends, into her world. The year was wrapping up perfectly—she was living in the city with Debbie, she'd be spending the summer with Matthew in Florida, and then, as they readied themselves to go back for their junior and senior years of college, they'd get married. She couldn't have planned things out better if she'd tried.

Joanie grabbed the giant clock that hung around Missy's neck. "It's almost midnight."

"What happens at midnight?"

"Nothing. I'm just surprised my sister's friends aren't coming. I was sure that they would."

"They might be on their way. Some people in the city don't even go out until midnight."

The DJ put on "We Are Family" for the second time that night, and Joanie was swept away by her sisters, all hitting the center of the dance floor for their song.

"I guess you were right after all," Debbie said to Joanie over the music. "Michele's friends never showed."

"I really hoped they'd come," Joanie said.

"Me too," Jenny said, dancing her way over to Joanie and Debbie. "Because otherwise it was a waste of three invites. You could've given them to Debbie to invite more boys."

"This place is packed past capacity. We really needed to invite more guys?"

"Think of it as a public service," Debbie explained. "I help fill the party with hot guys. Not just for me. For our sisters."

"You're very giving."

"That's what people say," Debbie said, winking at Joanie as she made her way towards the bar.

"Looks like things are about to get interesting," Missy said, pointing to the door, where Theta brothers were giving Jesse a hard time as he tried to push his way into the party.

Joanie strode across the dance floor. Jesse looked more out of place than Alice herself in Wonderland.

"He's with me," Joanie said to the brother who was at the door. And then, to Jesse: "Hey, stranger. Come on in."

"I'm not here for the party," Jesse said. He looked out of breath, as if he'd run across Manhattan to get there. His face was pale, and he ran his hands nervously through his hair, like a tic. "Joanie, it's Mel."

"Is she coming?"

Jesse shook his head from side to side. Tears welled up in his eyes. "Joanie, she overdosed."

FORTY-EIGHT

The seamstress
Paris, 1958

"Let's run away to America," Diana said, fire in her eyes.

"America?" Rose replied, utterly confused. Was Diana's big proposition simply a wild goose chase? Go off to America to find Madame? But Madame was not able to be found. What would Diana say when she discovered that Madame was not, in fact, off in America, but, in actuality, deceased?

"Why should Madame be the only one to chase her dreams in America? We could do the same. I think that you should have your own atelier," Diana explained. "You have the talent, you have the work ethic, and I see no reason why you should not have your own name on the door."

"My own atelier?" Rose said, puzzled. "Why, I could never."

"And why not?" Diana said. "You are single-handedly running this atelier—"

"Julien is running the atelier," Rose cut in. "I only make the dresses. I am just a seamstress."

"There is no atelier without the dresses," Diana responded, tilting her head to the side, as if to see Rose better. "Your work is the only work that matters. And you are far more than a seamstress. My wedding gown is based on your ideas, your sketch."

"I couldn't."

"This is what I've come to love about you, Rose," Diana said. "You are a good person. A good friend. Loyal. Trusting. Kind."

"Thank you."

Diana put her hand on Rose's shoulder. "So, what do you think?"

"I need this job," Rose said. "I cannot survive without this job."

"I'm offering you another job."

"I could never do that to Julien."

"We can bring Julien, too. I'm told that people in New York are far more accepting."

"I'm sure I don't know what you mean," Rose said, unable to meet Diana's eyes.

"I'm sure you don't," Diana said, a small smile on her lips. "I truly think the world of you. But you must know that already."

"Thank you," Rose said. "I think very highly of you, as well."

"Then let's open an atelier in America. You will be the talent, Julien will be the business know-how, and I'll be the one to keep us afloat. What do you say?"

Rose didn't know. What to think. What to do. *I will pay for it. I believe in you.* Had anyone ever spoken those words to Rose before? Her aunt must have, hadn't she? Surely she believed in her when she bought her that first sewing machine. She'd never said *I love you*, that just wasn't her way. But she had other ways of showing that she cared.

"I don't know," Rose said, her eyes fixed on the floor.

"It's been so wonderful having you here to help me with the dress," Diana said, a tremor in her voice. "It's been so very difficult to plan this wedding without my mother here. A wedding I don't even want."

"I know what it's like to feel alone," Rose said. And then she qualified: "To be alone."

"My dear friend," Diana said, placing her hand over Rose's. "I hope you'll excuse me for going on and on about not having a mother around for a few months when you lost your mother so long ago."

"You needn't explain. I understand," Rose said. It felt good to be honest with Diana. To speak words that were true.

"And you're not alone," Diana said. "You have me. You have Julien. You have my brother."

Rose cleared her throat. "We should get the dress on you. I don't want to keep you here all day for the first fitting. After all, there will be others after this one."

"I understand," Diana said, and Rose was unsure of what she was referring to. Was it about opening her own atelier? About being an orphan? Or about the fact that she would not speak of Diana's brother? As Rose stepped out of the fitting room for Diana to undress, she truly didn't know.

This would be the last appointment that Robert would accompany Diana on. The Laurents were due back in Paris in a week, and after that, Madame Laurent would be helping Diana to finalize the dress, along with the rest of the wedding plans. Rose worried about how they would keep up the ruse with Madame Laurent. Julien had thought Diana would be the easy one to fool, and it turned out they hadn't even managed that.

Rose walked down the entirety of the hallway before she knew where her feet were leading her. Once she stood at the base of the atelier, she realized. She had wanted to see Robert, one more time. He wouldn't be at the next dress fitting, and that meant that there were no more reasons for him to see her at all. He would go on planning the wedding to his fiancée, and Rose would have to forget about him. She would never see him again. Would she even see Diana again after her wedding?

She looked over to the chaise longue where he sat, thumbing through a newspaper. The sun hit his hair so that it appeared blonder than usual. His eyelashes glowed, like they were specked with bursts of light, and his skin looked healthy and bright. Even when his face was at rest, it seemed like he had just been smiling, as if he was thinking a happy thought. In her mind, she traced the curve of his lips, the sharp outline of his jaw. Rose longed to touch him one more time, take one more walk with him.

Robert turned to Rose and caught her staring at him. She wanted to look away, she knew she should look away, but she did not. Instead, she offered a shy little wave, and he waved back. Without meaning to, she giggled at the exchange, and quickly drew her right hand over her mouth. It only made Robert grin even more. The edges of his eyes crinkled, and his lips parted. Rose thought about how endearing his smile was, with the one tooth that was slightly crooked. The matching tooth on the other side was perfectly straight, and Rose wondered what Robert saw when she revealed her smile to him.

She felt silly standing so far from Robert; after all, he was the brother of a client, so it was only natural that she should go over and greet him properly. As she gathered the courage to make her way across the atelier floor, she felt a presence behind her. Had she left Diana in the fitting room too long? But it was not Diana. Over her shoulder, she heard Julien whisper to her angrily: "Rose, your client is waiting for you."

PART FOUR:
PUT THE PIECES TOGETHER

"Now is the moment you've been waiting for. Some have been waiting their entire lives. It is time to put your dress together. It is time to prepare for the future."

—Excerpted from *Creating the Illusion* by Madame Michel, Paris, 1954

FORTY-NINE

The bride
Brooklyn, 2020

Things Rocky would never forget: her father's funeral, quitting her job at Google to go out on her own, Drew's proposal. But now she had another thing to add to the list: the look on her mother's face when she told her she didn't want to wear her wedding dress.

Joan had assured Rocky that it was fine, she didn't mind, but her face told another story. It crumpled. She took a step back, as if Rocky had struck her, as if the pain of what Rocky said had hurt her physically. Joan tried to pretend that everything was fine, but tears sprang from her eyes and fell down her cheeks. Rocky did that to her. Rocky made her mother cry.

She would never forget that moment. And she had no idea how to make it better.

"She's not coming?" Drew's mother asked, and Rocky froze. She didn't know what to say to the Goodmans. It was so generous of them to offer to pay for the flowers for the wedding.

How could she tell them that her mother wouldn't be there to help pick them out?

Rocky hadn't spoken to her mother since the fight on the sidewalk. What was there to say? She had finally told her mother the truth, and it was just as awful as she thought it would be. Her mother had been crushed. Would she ever forgive Rocky?

"I'm so sorry," Rocky said, and she wasn't sure if she was speaking to Drew's mother or to her own.

"There's nothing to be sorry about," Drew's mother said, smiling widely. The smile did not reach her eyes. Rocky couldn't tell if she was upset that Joan wasn't there (Joan did have impeccable taste, after all), or if she was still conflicted over what had happened with Drew's search for his birth mother. Karen Goodman was nothing if not impossible to read.

"Shall we begin?" the florist asked, breaking Rocky from her train of thought. "I have a few things set up for you to look at."

Rocky and Drew's parents followed the florist to the back of the showroom. Her name was Iris and Rocky couldn't help but wonder if that was a fake name, if all of the women who worked there pretended they were named after flowers. She didn't look like an Iris. Rocky knew an Iris in college, and she was a homely girl from Kansas who had been homeschooled. This Iris did not look homely. She wore a tight black dress with impossibly high stilettos. How did she work on her feet all day with such impractical shoes? Rocky looked down at her own shoes, her beloved motorcycle boots, and thought of how her mother would chastise her for wearing something so decidedly unbridal to yet another wedding appointment.

"So, how did you meet the groom?" Iris asked, practically singing the words.

"It was hate at first sight," Rocky replied, on autopilot.

"Well, that's one I haven't heard before," Iris said, laughing. She motioned for them to keep following her.

Rocky couldn't bring herself to tell more of the story. This was where Joan would usually interrupt Rocky to sing Drew's praises, and Rocky would then take over, telling the part where she fell in love with him.

Rocky ached for her mother. She wished she hadn't let her mother out of the florist appointment so easily. She wished that when Joan had told her she had a migraine, and to go ahead without her, that she had driven to her mother's house in Connecticut and called her bluff. (Joan didn't get migraines.) But instead, Rocky had let it fester. And now Rocky had no idea where they stood.

Rocky almost bumped right into the florist as she stopped walking and pointed to the first floral arrangement. "We just did these lovely calla lilies at a wedding last weekend. Everyone loved them."

"Calla lilies represent death," Drew's mother said, putting her glasses on to inspect the floral arrangement more closely. She leaned in and squinted her eyes. "I don't think they're appropriate for a wedding."

Rocky felt a sneeze coming on. She could feel the pollen entering her nostrils, her throat. She rubbed her nose.

"No, they represent purity!" Iris argued playfully. "That's why so many brides carry them down the aisle!"

"We were just at a funeral," Karen said, leaning in a little bit more, fingering the petals of the flowers, "and every bouquet was filled with calla lilies."

"Ah, yes," the florist said, trying to keep the smile glued to her face, "we do use lilies in some funeral arrangements. You see, they are symbols of rebirth, tied to the resurrection of Christ. So we do use them for weddings *and* funerals."

Drew's mother turned to look at her husband and raised one eyebrow. He looked back at her and shrugged.

"What else do you have?" Rocky asked. As Iris spun on her heel to walk to the next arrangement, Rocky finally sneezed.

"Are you okay, sweetheart?" Karen asked, turning to face Rocky.

"I'm fine, thank you," Rocky said, brushing off her concern. "Let's see the other options."

"You don't seem fine," Drew's mother said quietly, as they passed over a footbridge to reach the next table setting.

"I'm fine," Rocky said, and smiled brightly to prove her point. But Karen wasn't convinced. She drew her in for a hug—one of her famous, full-body, *I've got you* kind of hugs—and Rocky immediately knew. Drew had told his mother about Rocky's fight with Joan.

But she wasn't going to discuss what had happened with her mother with Karen. If two FaceTime calls to her grandmother and one string of emails with her great-uncle couldn't help her figure out what to do, Karen certainly did not have the answers.

"The hydrangea really lend fullness to this one, don't you think?" Iris said, pointing to another arrangement, but Rocky could barely hear a word. She felt it happening—the anger threatening to bubble over. How could Drew tell his mother about the fight when Rocky was still processing it herself? Of course he had. *I tell my mother everything*, he'd said more times than she could count. She hadn't even had her appointment with her therapist yet. She wasn't ready to talk. He should have known that.

Rocky tried to take a deep, cleansing inhale—in, two, three, four, but the pollen in the showroom quickly took residence in her nose and she began to sneeze uncontrollably.

A chorus of "Bless you!" and "Are you all right?" rang out as Rocky doubled over, unable to stop sneezing. Three times, four times, five. Rocky could not stop. With each sneeze, she felt her head throb.

Drew's mother materialized with a handful of tissues and a

small bottle of water. "I think we should get some fresh air for a moment," she said to Iris, and directed Rocky to the front door.

"Are you sure you're all right?" she asked, once they were out on the sidewalk. Rocky finished the bottle of water in one gulp and looked at Karen. What was she asking her? About the sneezing or her mother? Rocky truly didn't know. Was she analyzing her, making her the subject of a therapy session? Rocky was always secretly scared that Karen was analyzing her.

"I'm fine," Rocky said plainly. "Thank you for the water. Are you all right?"

"Why, yes, of course," Karen replied quickly. "I don't have allergies."

Rocky wasn't sure if Karen had gotten her meaning. Did she really think Rocky was asking her about allergies? Or did she know what Rocky was really asking about, how Karen felt about Drew's birth mother?

Rocky held the silence for a beat. It was her own therapist's favorite trick—decline to speak so that the other party fills the air—and Rocky wondered if it would work on another therapist.

Each woman looked at the other, smiling, waiting for the other to fill the silence. It was like a very friendly game of chicken, one where you only used the crease of your forehead to win.

"I'm a little sad," Karen finally said, taking Rocky's hand and giving it a squeeze. "But I'll be fine. How about you?"

"Same."

"Weddings bring up a lot of things in a lot of different ways," she said. "But they are also beautiful, and ought to be celebrated."

"I agree," Rocky said.

"Why don't we reschedule this appointment for a time when your mother can make it?"

That would be great, Rocky tried to say. It's what she wanted to say, but she found her throat closing up and her eyes beginning to water. Whether it was the pollen or the sentiment, she couldn't be sure.

FIFTY

The mother of the bride, as a bride herself
Long Island, 1982

Joanie looked in at Mel in her hospital bed. She seemed so tiny, lying there. Her skin looked gray and her hair was matted, out of place. The mohawk that always stood proudly at attention, gone.

She was stable this morning, that's what Jem had told her, but the machines whizzed and blared out, making Joanie question whether or not Mel would really be okay.

Joanie caught a glimpse of her reflection in the hospital window. Her hair still curled into bouncy waves from last night's Alice costume, she looked ridiculous. When she had gone home in the middle of the night to shower and change into fresh clothing, Matthew was waiting for her in her dorm room. She'd had to explain why she'd run out of the party with a man he'd never met before, why she had been missing from midnight until four in the morning, and who, exactly, Mel was. By the time they'd been done talking, visiting hours at the hospital had begun, so she dressed and headed back to see if Mel had awoken yet. Matthew did not come with her.

Her mother's words rang out in her head: *In many ways, I'm afraid, you're just a girl.* And she was right, wasn't she? Joanie had been dancing at a sorority party when a friend was out there who needed her. Joanie knew that Mel's sobriety was a delicate balance. If she'd used half as much time on her outfit for the Senior Tea, maybe she could have helped Mel instead. Could have been checking on her, supporting her. Taking her to meetings, holding her accountable.

She wasn't there for her friend. Just like she hadn't been there for her sister. She hadn't even known that her sister needed help. Her sister hadn't told her about her addiction, but Mel had shared everything. And Joanie wouldn't take her friendship for granted again.

"Hey," Mikki said, walking down the hospital corridor with three cups of coffee. It had been a long night, and an even longer day, waiting for Mel to wake up.

"Thanks," Jem said.

"We should get her some things from home," Mikki said. "So that she's comfortable when she wakes up."

"That's a great idea," Jem said. "I can go. Let me just finish my coffee. I'm exhausted from being here all night. I'll hit her place, and then I can grab a pizza on the way back."

"Pizza would be great," Mikki said, rubbing her temples.

"I'll go," Joanie said, surprising herself with the sound of her own voice. But she wanted to go. She needed to move. To do something. She couldn't just stand there, keeping vigil over Mel's sleeping body.

"Get two pies," Jem said. "Jesse is on his way back."

Jem grabbed the keys out of Mel's knapsack and Joanie made her way down to Alphabet City.

Joanie gasped when she saw movement inside Mel's apartment. She knew the area was dangerous, but she hadn't counted on someone breaking into her friend's apartment as she lay in a hospital bed.

"I've got mace!" Joanie yelled, holding out her pocketbook as proof. She didn't have mace, but she hoped that her voice had enough conviction to fool whoever was in the apartment.

"I'm unarmed," the person said, turning around slowly to face Joanie. It was Jesse. She sighed in relief, and put her hands on her knees as she took a deep breath.

"You scared me."

"Hi," he said.

"Jem said you were on your way back to the hospital." They'd been together the previous night, keeping vigil over Mel's hospital room, and now, she somehow felt closer to him. Bonded to him. Like they shared a language that only a few other people knew.

"I was," he said, turning the television off. When he stood up, Joanie saw that he wasn't wearing his usual uniform of leather jeans. He was in sweatpants and an old T-shirt. No gel in his hair. It made him look younger, more vulnerable. "I just needed a break, you know?"

"I know," Joanie said. At one point the night before, Jesse had broken down into tears and Joanie sat down with him while he cried on her shoulder. When a nurse stopped by to ask Joanie if her boyfriend needed some water, she hadn't corrected her.

"It's strange being here without her."

Joanie looked around the apartment. She'd never been there before with Mel, much less without her, and being in Mel's personal space made her feel closer to her, another layer of her revealed. "I won't bother you, I'm sure you need space. I'm just here to pick up a few things to make your sister more comfortable at the hospital."

"That's nice of you. You're really nice, you know that?"

"Don't sound so surprised."

"You're nicer than your sister."

Joanie froze. "You knew my sister?"

"Yeah, she was into that whole art scene with Mel," he said, running a hand through his hair. "I used to see her all the time."

"And she wasn't nice?"

"She was nice," Jesse said, his eyes trained on Joanie. "You're nicer."

"Did you know that my sister died of an overdose?"

"Yes."

"I was the last to know." The things she didn't say hung in the air: *Both of our sisters overdosed, but mine died. You were close with your sister, and I thought that I was, too, but I didn't even know that mine was doing drugs. You are the only person in the world who understands how I feel.*

Jesse regarded her. "I think we need alcohol to continue this conversation."

He walked into the kitchen and came back with two beers.

"I don't drink."

"Well, now seems like as good of a time as any to start."

Joanie couldn't help but agree. She'd been trying so hard to be the good girl—no drinking, no smoking, no sex—but those things didn't make you good, any more than doing them made you bad. She could see that now. When she thought about all of the experiences she'd missed out on, simply because she was trying to be some version of herself that wouldn't hurt her parents, she couldn't help but laugh. Being a good person was about being there for your friends. Showing up for people, being accountable. She wasn't any of those things. And now she didn't want to think about it. She just wanted to be numb.

She took a tentative sip from the bottle. It was cold, ice cold, and the bubbles tickled the top of her lip. She quickly wiped her mouth on her shirt sleeve. She took another sip, this time bigger, and really tasted the beer. It reminded her of bread, somehow, mixed with something bitter. She took another quick sip, and then before she knew it, she'd finished the bottle. The aftertaste of citrus lingered on her tongue. Jesse handed her another as he disappeared into Mel's bedroom to get the clothes she came for.

As Joanie sipped her beer, she noticed Mel's Walkman sitting on the coffee table. She grabbed it—it seemed like the perfect thing for someone who was stuck in a hospital bed—and then browsed her cassette tape collection. She selected a few that she liked, Duran Duran, David Bowie, Culture Club, and then a few that she'd seen in her sister's room—The Runaways, The Clash, and Blondie.

Jesse came out of the bedroom with a duffel bag.

"Oh, great," he said, reaching for the Walkman and the tapes. "Great thinking."

Joanie looked up and saw tears forming at the sides of his eyes. "She's going to be okay. She's being well taken care of."

"I know that," he said, wiping his eyes with the backs of his hands. "I know."

"You're lucky that you have another chance with your sister. She's going to be all right."

All of the things they weren't saying lingered in the air. "I'm so sorry about your sister," Jesse said.

"Oh, it's okay."

"It's not."

"I know, but let's not think about it right now. Let's just focus on Mel. Getting Mel better."

"I forgot her sketch pad. *That* will make her feel better," Jesse said, snapping his fingers as he remembered. "Can you grab it? I'll get her pencils."

Joanie picked up Mel's sketch pad from the side table, as Jesse grabbed a set of pencils off the desk. She flipped through and couldn't believe how amazing Mel's work was. Mel was always talking about Michele, about how talented she was, but Mel had a ton of potential, too. They were mostly portraits, done in pencil. There was one of Michele, and Joanie ran her hands across it. Tears welled up in her eyes, so she turned to the next page. Each portrait was more beautiful, more detailed, than the next.

Joanie stopped at a drawing of Jesse. "It's you," she said, turning the sketch pad over so that he could see. "This is really beautiful."

Jesse sipped his beer as he walked back towards her. "You are."

Joanie could feel her face turn red. "Thank you," she said, and then immediately wondered if she should have said something different in response. But it didn't matter. An instant later, Jesse's hands were on her face, turning her towards him.

"I've wanted to do this from the first moment we met," he said. He kissed her gently and took the beer bottle out of her hand, setting it down on the table next to the couch.

"We shouldn't," Joanie murmured.

"I'm sorry. I thought..."

"You don't have to be sorry." She thought but didn't say: *I wanted to kiss you from the first moment we met, too. When I'm with my fiancé, I think of you. When I put on perfume, I think of you. I can't stop thinking of you.*

She kissed him back.

His kisses were frenzied, electric. He kissed her like he wasn't sure he'd ever have the chance to again. He kissed like he thought the world might end tomorrow. And Joanie wanted more.

Jesse put his arm around Joanie's back, lowering her onto the nearby couch. The weight of his body felt nice, nowhere near as heavy or muscular as Matthew, but Joanie tried not to think of him. There was no reason to think of him at all.

One by one, he unfastened the buttons of her Oxford shirt. Then, he pushed down the delicate spaghetti straps of her camisole and kissed her all over her collarbone. His kisses went lower. And lower still.

"We should get back to the hospital," Joanie said, as he reached around to undo the catch on her bra.

"Don't you want this?" Jesse whispered in her ear. His breath went down her spine, right to her toes. "I've wanted this for so long."

And she did. She wanted him to kiss her all over her body, kiss all of the places she'd applied her perfume. She didn't want to think about Mel. She didn't want to think about her sister. She didn't want to think about Matthew. She wanted to feel. And she wanted to feel with him.

She let him take her bra off. Then, without thinking, she helped him take his own shirt off as they kissed. But to call it kissing was an understatement. She'd never been kissed like this. She never felt like this. The urgency, the want. She pulled him closer to her, and closer still. She couldn't get close enough.

His hands went all over her body. "You're so wet," he murmured in her ear, and Joanie could feel her face flame red again. Matthew had never spoken to her like that before. No guy had. "I want you."

"I want you, too," Joanie said, and she didn't recognize her own voice. It was raw, animalistic.

He trailed kisses down her body, and then peeled off her underwear. Joanie gasped as he did to her what Matthew had never done.

"Does that feel good?" Jesse murmured.

"Yes," Joanie said, breathless. "Don't stop."

"I want to be inside you," Jesse said. "Do you want me inside you?"

"Yes," Joanie whispered. "Yes."

She had never wanted someone like this. Jesse took off the remainder of his clothes and Joanie examined every square inch of his body. He was thin and wiry, and his skin was even paler than she'd imagined. He had a small tattoo of a treble clef on his right hip. Jesse leaned down over her again and asked: "Are you sure?"

Without thinking: "Yes."

And then: pure bliss.

FIFTY-ONE

The seamstress
Paris, 1958

The only thing worse than knowing that she'd never see Robert again was this: having to meet with his fiancée to design her wedding dress. The gown Elisabeth would wear as she walked down the aisle with the man Rose loved.

"I really wish Madame were here," Elisabeth told Rose.

"She was so very much looking forward to this appointment today," Julien said. "But when she learned that the seed pearl merchant she's been trying to get an audience with for years would finally see her, she simply had no choice."

"I don't even want seed pearls on my dress," Elisabeth pouted.

"It's all part of the creative process," Rose explained, following Julien's lead. "Madame seeks inspiration everywhere in the world. While you might not want the seed pearls she brings back from Japan, surely her adventure there will help inform your wedding gown. And make it the dress of your dreams."

"I should hope so," Elisabeth said. "Because none of the

sketches she's created for me will do. Not one is right. I suppose that's why she left you here to do her dirty work and present them to me."

"I assure you," Rose began carefully, keeping her real feelings hidden, "Madame created these sketches entirely for you. She thought you would love them." Rose had spent the entire week creating these sketches for Elisabeth. Rose had pored over Madame's old dress designs for inspiration, used her signature design elements to make the dresses look like a Madame Michel original. She was proud of what she'd created, though it seemed Elisabeth could not appreciate the enormous amount of work that had gone into the sketches, each and every one.

"I hate them," Elisabeth said, sotto voce. "My dear Diana was right. Madame's ideas are old and stodgy. Perhaps you could draw something for me? The way you did for Diana?"

"Of course," Rose said. But when she put her pencil to the paper, her mind went blank. She could feel Elisabeth's eyes on her. Watching. Waiting.

"I have an idea," Elisabeth said.

"If you'll just give me a moment—"

"You'll meet me at the ballet this evening," Elisabeth announced.

"I don't—"

"Do you have plans?"

"No, but—"

"Then it's settled," Elisabeth said, already up from her chair, putting her coat on. "I'll send a car for you at seven."

"I want to look like that." Elisabeth pointed to a photograph of a ballet dancer, hanging on the wall next to the box office. Rose tried to pay attention, but she was overwhelmed by being at the Paris Opera Ballet for the first time. For a girl like Elisabeth, a night at the ballet was nothing special. But for Rose, it was extraordinary. Something she'd never had the privilege of doing before. And she wanted to take it all in. She wanted to appreciate every moment of her night, every sight, every sound, every smell.

"Of course," Rose said, finally turning her attention to the photograph. Certainly Elisabeth didn't mean that she wanted to wear a tutu as her wedding gown. (At least Rose hoped that she didn't.) Rose considered the design inspiration: how she could evoke the feel of the ballerina, and put that into Elisabeth's wedding gown, without making it a literal interpretation. "Graceful," she thought out loud. "An emphasis on the waistline, fitted throughout the hips." She put her hand on her own waist, hips, as she spoke. In her mind's eye, she could see the bodice come to life—a thick silk satin in ivory, heavy boning for it to keep its shape. She could hear Madame's voice ring out with Christian Dior's famous advice: *Without proper foundation, there can be no fashion.* That was it! She would create an attached girdle inside, to create the dramatic shape of the waist. It would suit Elisabeth's curves beautifully.

"Yes," Elisabeth said, dreamily, as if she could read Rose's thoughts.

"The tulle, billowing out. Even more beautiful when we make the skirt ballroom length." She thought back to one of Madame's early wedding dress designs that had a tulle ballroom skirt. Tons of volume, light as air. Rose would find the sketch when she was back at the atelier.

"Yes," Elisabeth repeated. "And wait until you see it move on stage. I want to look just like that when I dance at my wedding." She spun around like a dancer, on one foot, and it made Rose dizzy.

"I hope that doesn't mean I'll be expected to wear tights," Robert said, coming behind Elisabeth and giving her a delicate kiss on the cheek.

"Of course not, you silly man." Elisabeth fell into Robert's

arms and swatted him playfully. "Rose, you remember my fiancé, Robert, of course."

Rose had been so caught up in Elisabeth's spinning that she
hadn't noticed him approaching. She'd had no idea that Robert would be attending the ballet with them. If she had, she
surely would have told Elisabeth she was unable to make it. It
was one thing knowing Robert was promised to another, but
it was quite another to see their love on display right in front of
her. She couldn't bear it.

"Yes," Rose said quietly. "Of course."

"Lovely to see you again, Rose."

"Lovely to be seen," Rose said, so quietly it was practically
under her breath. Had she said it at all? Rose couldn't be sure.

"We should find our seats." Robert fanned the tickets out in
his hand.

Rose followed behind as Robert walked with Elisabeth, his
hand resting on the small of her back, the way he'd walked
home with Rose. She watched as he held the curtain open for
Elisabeth to pass into their box seats, remembering how he'd
done the same for her when they attended the opera together.

How foolish she had been. She allowed herself to get swept
up in her infatuation with Robert. He didn't have feelings for
her any more than he might have feelings for the other hired
help. The butler, the driver, the cook. There were people like
Robert and Elisabeth and then there were people like Rose.
How naive she'd been to think otherwise.

Elisabeth settled herself into her seat in the box. It was set up
with four chairs, two to a row.

"Why don't you sit up front with Elisabeth?" Robert said,
motioning for Rose to take his seat.

"I couldn't possibly."

"Don't be ridiculous, Robert," Elisabeth said, patting the seat
next to her. "Come sit next to me."

"I just want her to be able to see the show," Robert explained. "After all, isn't she here to see what it is you want in your dress?"

"I can see everything very clearly from here," Rose said, settling into the seat behind Elisabeth.

The curtain came up, and the ballet began. Rose tried to keep herself focused on the performance, the costumes that she was there to see. But it was difficult. She couldn't stop thinking about her night at the opera with Robert. But Elisabeth now sat next to Robert—the seat belonged to Elisabeth. Rose had only been keeping it warm for a short spell.

Elisabeth reached over and grabbed her fiancé's hand.

"I should go," Rose said, as the house lights came on at intermission. "Thank you so much for a lovely evening."

"You mustn't leave," Robert said. "The ballet isn't over yet."

"I've seen all I need to see." Her eyes teared up, and she hoped that Elisabeth and Robert would think that it was from the stunning performance they'd just witnessed, and not from her breaking heart.

"Is it clear what you need to do?" Elisabeth asked Rose.

"Yes," Rose said, nodding her head in assent. "It is perfectly clear."

FIFTY-TWO

The bride
Brooklyn, 2020

"I knew you weren't paying attention."

"I was paying attention," Rocky said, like a reflex. She put her phone down and looked up at Drew. She was happy to see him smiling. It had been such a rough couple of months, with the aftermath of his discovery about his birth mother, and he was slowly getting back to himself, bit by bit.

"My parents are already in a cab," Drew said. "I'll explain on the way."

Rocky racked her brain. Drew's parents, not paying attention…nothing. She was coming up dry.

Drew grabbed her hand as they walked out of their building and then swung their arms, the way you do when you're a kid. "That day we were at my parents' house. You were on your phone, but you said you were paying attention. Busted."

"I'm not busted," Rocky covered. "I was totally paying attention. Just remind me?"

"My mom and dad made us an offer. I said, 'Would you like that?' And you said, 'I think that's a great idea.'"

Drew was correct: Rocky was totally busted. She had not been paying attention that day. Not even a little bit.

"Well, what is it?" Rocky said, finally conceding defeat.

"I'm going to let you squirm a bit," Drew said, laughter in his voice. "It's something for our wedding, and it's something you agreed to wear."

Rocky stopped in her tracks, but it was too late. They were at the restaurant. How had they walked there that quickly?

Something for their wedding. Rocky felt sweat gathering on her brow—not this again. Something else that she was expected to wear at her wedding. First, the dress, and now Drew's parents had something that was special to them. And she had already agreed to wear it.

Drew held the door open, and she walked through with a smile. Could it be a veil? A tiara? Karen didn't really seem like the tiara type. Whatever it was, she would just smile and say thank you. It would be fine.

Drew's parents sat on the back patio, a bottle of wine, glasses poured.

"We are just so excited," Karen said to Rocky as they hugged hello. It was good to see Drew's mother happy again. It had been a difficult time for her, too, getting through the news about Drew's birth mother, getting through the fact that he wanted to find her in the first place.

Rocky pulled out her chair and noticed a gift bag at her seat.

"Open it," Drew's father said. He was smiling from ear to ear.

"Yeah, Rock," Drew said, challenging her with a devilish smile. "Open it."

Rocky smiled tentatively. She picked up the gift bag and sat down. She took a big swig of wine and then examined the bag. It wasn't very large, so that was a relief. But what could possibly be inside?

She pulled the first of five ribbons. The wrapping was ornate, and Rocky felt her hands get hot as she negotiated the ties on the top of the gift bag.

Inside, there were two ring boxes. She carefully took them out of the bag and set them on the table.

The rings. Drew's parents must have bought them wedding bands. Rocky smiled and looked up at Drew and his parents. Such a strange gift, she thought. So personal. Of course, Rocky hadn't thought about picking out wedding bands yet, so it was thoughtful. But still. How could they know what she wanted?

Rocky opened the first ring box. Inside was a delicate band of gold. Plain with no adornments.

"The rings that we were married in," Drew's father gushed, unable to keep it in. "We're so thrilled that you want to be married in these rings, too."

So, that's what she'd agreed to. Using the rings in her wedding ceremony that Drew's parents had used in their own ceremony.

"I know it's not as special as a wedding dress," Drew's mother said carefully. "But these rings mean so much to me—they belonged to my grandparents—so the fact that you've agreed to use them means a lot to our family."

Rocky opened the other box. Another plain gold band, this one a bit thicker. Drew's ring. She handed it to her fiancé and he tried it on.

"Perfect fit," he said, standing up to give each of his parents a big hug and a kiss. "Thank you."

"In the Jewish religion," Drew's father explained, "the wedding band must be unadorned and a simple unbroken circle. It symbolizes a marriage unmarred by conflict."

"It's beautiful," Rocky said, turning it in her fingers, examining every square inch of it, shiny and bright.

"And technically," Drew's mother said, taking the ring box from Rocky and handing it to Drew, "we gift it to our son first, and then he gives it to you as a gift."

Drew took the ring out of the box and held it out for Rocky. She moved her engagement ring over to her right hand and tried the wedding band on. She held her left hand out for a moment to admire the ring. It was so gorgeous in its simplicity. And it fit Rocky's finger as if it had been made for her.

"So, you think you'd like to use them for your wedding ceremony?" Drew's mother asked, tentatively.

"Of course we will," Rocky said. "This is so meaningful. Thank you." She loved the way the ring made her fingers look long and elegant. She snapped a quick photo and texted it to her grandmother and great-uncle. Her grandmother immediately texted back that she loved it. Rocky knew that her great-uncle wasn't as good with his phone or iPad as her grandmother, so she made a mental note to make sure her grandmother showed it to him.

Rocky glanced over at Drew. He looked so sexy rocking a marriage band. *That's the man I'm going to marry*, Rocky thought, and in that moment, it was as if she could see their future laid out: marriage, children, a house, grandchildren, and the day she would hand these rings down to the next generation.

They had the rings. Now all Rocky needed was something to wear down the aisle.

FIFTY-THREE

The mother of the bride, as a bride herself
Long Island, 1982

"C'mon!" Matthew called out as he ducked his head into Joanie's room. "We're going to be late."

"I'm not sure I can go today."

"It's the End of the Year party," Matthew said. "You have to go. Everyone goes. Even people who don't go to NYCU go."

And he was right. Even nonstudents descended on Hamilton Square Park for an NYCU tradition: the all-day End of the Year party. An excuse to drink beer all day long, make out with that person you've had a crush on all semester, and just blow off adult life in general, the End of the Year party was the day that all NYCU students looked forward to.

But Joanie didn't want to go.

"We need to talk," Joanie said. She tried to steady her tone, but there was no use. Her voice was shaking. Her whole body was.

"No time to talk. Time to party!" Matthew grabbed Joanie's

left hand and rubbed his fingers along hers. He looked up at her in surprise. "Where is your ring?"

"That's what I need to talk to you about," Joanie said tentatively.

"Did you lose it?" He dropped her hands and looked around the room. "Did it happen just now? I knew I should have called first. I didn't mean to startle you."

"That's not it." Joanie sat down on her bed, tried to keep herself steady. She wasn't the type to lose things, and he knew this.

"You lost it sooner? You could have told me. I have insurance." He looked into her eyes and his face was so open, so honest. Joanie doubted what she was about to say, what she was about to do. After all, wasn't Matthew exactly the type of person you should marry? Stable. Smart. Dependable. Someone who reacts perfectly reasonably when he thinks you've lost your two-carat diamond ring.

Then it hit her: this was the problem. She didn't want that. Not now, at least. She didn't want stable. She didn't want dependable. She wanted excitement. She wanted to live and be young for a little while longer. Wasn't that why she'd slept with Jesse? Sure, she could say they were caught up in the moment and worried about Mel, that their emotions got the best of them, but that wasn't the truth, was it? The truth was more simple than that: she wanted to do it. And she wasn't ready to get married.

"I didn't lose the ring," Joanie said, shaking her head. Tears sprang from her eyes as she looked at Matthew. He sat down next to her on the bed.

"I don't understand."

Joanie took a deep breath. "Matthew," she said, gathering her strength. "I can't marry you."

"Don't be silly," he said, grabbing her hand and rubbing his thumb across her palm. "Of course you can. I can't wait to marry you."

"I don't want to get married."

"Are you having cold feet about the whole big wedding thing? We can postpone the wedding, you know. We can push it later, if you'd like," Matthew said, holding her hands. He laughed nervously. "Or we can just run away together. Ditch the whole big country club thing. All I really want is you."

"It's not about the wedding," Joanie said, getting up from her bed. She couldn't face Matthew. Not when he was being so kind and she was breaking his heart. "I don't want to marry you."

She walked over to her jewelry box, sitting on the shelf that he'd lovingly made for her, and retrieved her engagement ring. It sparkled brightly in her hands, two perfect carats that any woman would be proud to wear. As she walked over to Matthew, she saw how it caught the light so beautifully, what a spectacular piece it was. And she was giving it back to him.

"You can't possibly mean this," Matthew said. "I thought we were happy."

"We were."

Matthew looked at the ring as Joanie placed it in his hand.

"This is just cold feet," he said, smiling at her. He pressed the ring back into her hand and kissed her forehead. "You hold on to this, and we'll postpone the wedding. Indefinitely, if you want. I'll marry you tomorrow. I'll marry you a year from now. Five years from now."

"I'm so sorry," Joanie said, tears welling up in her eyes. "It's not cold feet. I'm so sorry, Matthew, but I've done something horrible. The worst thing I could do."

"Hey, it's okay," Matthew said, wiping the tears off her cheeks. "Whatever happened, it's okay. We can fix it. You can tell me anything."

"I slept with someone else."

"What?"

"Another guy. I slept with another guy."

He sat perfectly calm, next to her, brow furrowed. He didn't yell. He didn't scream. He didn't react at all. He looked pro-foundly confused, as if disappointments weren't the sort of thing that happened to people like him. And they didn't. Peo-ple like Matthew were the presidents of their fraternity. People like him became astronauts. People like him got married and had 2.4 children, a beautiful house in the suburbs.

"Is this a joke? Or a prank or something? I don't get it."

"It's not a joke," Joanie said, tears streaming from her eyes. "I'm so sorry."

"Are you telling me that you lost your virginity to someone else while you were engaged to me?"

Joanie nodded her head yes. She was crying so violently now that she couldn't speak.

Matthew shook his head, as if he couldn't process what she was telling him. He looked at her, and she could see it wash over his face. "How could you do this to me? To us?"

"I don't know. I'm so sorry."

"I was the perfect fiancé to you."

"I know. You are perfect. But that's the thing. I'm not. I don't even know who I am. What I'm going to be. I didn't realize it, but I have so much growing up to do. I can't possibly marry you like this."

"I suppose I can understand that you feel that you're not ready to get married. We're young. I get it. But why did you have to betray me in the worst possible way? How could you do this to me?"

"I'm sorry. I'm so sorry."

"I will never forgive you."

"I'm sorry. I don't know how else to say it. I'm just so, so sorry."

He stood up from her bed. Without looking at her: "You're making the biggest mistake of your life." He walked across the room and paused at the door frame for an instant, and then turned to face Joanie. "You can't come back, you know. When you change your mind, and you *will* change your mind, I will not be waiting for you."

"Please forgive me."

"I will never forgive you," he said, and walked out the door.

"I'm so sorry," Joanie said again, but he was already well down the hallway and could no longer hear her.

FIFTY-FOUR

The seamstress
Paris, 1958

"My daughter speaks very highly of you," Madame Laurent said.

Rose was on edge. Madame Laurent had returned to Paris and had requested a private viewing of Diana's wedding dress. Rose felt good about the dress—she knew Diana loved the youthfulness that Rose had brought to it—but what would her mother think? Rose feared she might wonder where Madame's touch was. Would Madame Laurent immediately know that the dress was designed solely by Rose? That she was not Madame Michel's protégé, but rather, her replacement? A replacement that had not been chosen by the master herself. Rose hoped not. That was certainly not what the Laurents were paying for.

This was the moment they'd been waiting for—the final step in the ruse. Would Madame Laurent like what she saw? Everything had led up to this.

Julien sat at his desk, pretending to be busy, but Rose could feel his nerves all the way across the room. She only hoped that

Madame Laurent couldn't sense them, too; Rose hoped that she would be fooled.

"Thank you," Rose said. "I think very highly of your daughter. She is lovely."

"She is brash," Madame Laurent said, with laughter in her voice, a sly smile playing on her lips. "Unbridled."

"She is ahead of her time," Rose said.

"That, my dear," Madame Laurent said, "is a very nice way of putting things." She turned to Rose with a smile on her face, and Rose felt her shoulders begin to loosen, her breath return to normal. There was nothing to be afraid of. The dress was impeccably made, and Madame Laurent had no reason in the world to be upset. But Rose couldn't help but think of the worst thing that could happen: Madame Laurent canceling the dress.

Madame Laurent turned back to the dress form. "Your workmanship is outstanding. I can see why Madame Michel trusts you."

She fingered the delicate rose point lace that covered the bodice, careful not to disturb it. She put her hands on either side of the dress form's waist to embrace the cummerbund. It lay beautifully between the blouse and the skirt; all of Julien's direction had been correct. Crafting the dress in four parts made the whole come together perfectly.

Madame Laurent's eyes traveled down to the bottom of the smooth skirt, where Rose had hand-sewn flowers that she'd painstakingly cut from the lace onto the silk faille. They created a delicate border traveling around the bottom of the dress. Rose loved the way it danced—the way the roses would move with the bride as she walked down the aisle.

"The way you've cut these roses out from the rose point lace is exquisite," Madame Laurent said.

"Each rose was done by hand," Julien said. "One at a time, by Rose herself."

"Roses made by Rose." Madame Laurent looked at the embroidery. "It was meant to be. What a beautiful touch."

"Thank you," Rose said, her hands folded carefully at her waist.

"You've truly made this dress your own."

Rose loved the dress—she'd tried it on herself more times than she'd cared to admit, more times than she'd even confessed to Julien—but she knew it belonged to Diana. She knew that she would soon give it over to her bride, just like she'd done every other wedding dress she'd worked on. This one felt different, though, because she'd designed Diana's dress herself. Had worked on each individual piece of it herself.

"Every great designer has a signature, and I think you've found yours. Madame Michel has certainly chosen her protégé wisely."

"Thank you," Rose said, looking down at her feet.

"Clients are just mad about our Rose," Julien said, slowly rising from his desk. He walked over to Rose and put his arm around her shoulders. "She is a genius. And she has created something very special for your daughter."

"I agree," Madame Laurent said. "I only wish Madame Michel were here to see it."

"She has been checking in with us in between her travels," Julien said. "In fact, she was just here the day before you arrived. She gave her seal of approval on this final design. But then she left for Tangiers just before you came, unfortunately."

"That is unfortunate," Madame Laurent said, looking directly into Julien's eyes. "I'm sure you're aware that there are whispers."

"Whispers?"

"About where Madame really is," Madame Laurent said, as if it were the most natural thing in the world. "People are saying that she's abandoned her atelier and moved back to America."

"Why, that's just ridiculous. I can assure you, she did not go to America."

Rose felt her back getting hot. Yes, what Julien said was the truth: Madame Michel was not in America. But the actual truth was far worse. And Rose felt like she wanted to crawl out of her skin, out of the office, and out of the atelier.

"Well, then," Madame Laurent said, "I suppose it was just a silly rumor, then."

She and Julien both laughed. Silly rumors. Yes. There were quite a lot of them going around town.

As Rose looked at Madame Laurent, she tried to find Robert's face in hers. He'd inherited his deep smile from her—when she laughed, Rose was buoyed, as if she felt the happiness she projected inside of her own chest. And the hair. They had the same shade of dark blond hair, the same thickness and unruliness. Madame Laurent had hers up in a chignon.

"Thank you for being so kind to my Diana in my absence," Madame Laurent said, and clasped Rose's hands in her own. She felt the weight of Madame Laurent's ring—an enormous ruby surrounded by small diamonds. Rose hoped that her hands weren't too hot. She did not want to embarrass herself in front of a lady like Madame Laurent.

"It is my pleasure," Rose said back. "I adore your daughter."

"It has been difficult for her these past few months, with my husband and me traveling. I have been comforted in the knowledge that she was taken care of by you."

"She is not just a client," Rose said to Madame Laurent. "She has come to be a friend."

Rose could feel Julien's eyes on her, but she refused to turn his way. What she was saying was the truth. She knew that she wasn't supposed to fall for her, wasn't supposed to become her friend, but Rose simply could not help herself. Diana had become a friend. She had shared confidences, and Rose felt that Diana truly cared for her, reciprocated her feelings.

Madame Laurent eyed Rose slowly, with an expression that Rose could not quite decipher. Eyes narrowed, head slightly tilted. And then, quickly finding herself: "The dress is perfect. I have never seen a more beautiful wedding gown in my life."

"I created a dress that I, myself, would be proud to wear."

"That's sweet of you to say," Madame Laurent said. She smiled at Rose, and for a fleeting moment, Rose imagined what it would be like to have her as a mother-in-law. Afternoon tea, just the two of them, sprawling family dinners, a confidante to talk to. So many of her brides confessed that they hated their fiancés' mothers, but she knew that Robert's fiancée was lucky. Madame Laurent was a special woman. Kindhearted and generous. Rose imagined herself wearing the dress, getting ready to walk down the aisle with Robert. Happiness flooded her heart.

But then she thought of what would really happen: Madame Laurent would never accept a poor, orphaned seamstress as her daughter-in-law. She would expect her son to marry someone of the same social standing as the Laurents, not the help. Rose's dream of marrying Robert was just that: a mere dream. It could never become a reality. Rose hung her head and chastised herself for dreaming so big.

Julien made an appointment for Diana's final fitting, and then walked Madame Laurent out of the atelier. They didn't speak much that afternoon, and Rose knew that she should not have told Madame Laurent that Diana was her friend. But it was the truth. Diana wouldn't break her heart, because Rose knew she felt the same way about her.

It was only later, when Rose was in bed, unable to sleep that night, that she realized how she misspoke: all that talk about roses for Rose. How she had made the dress her own. How she'd created the dress that she would be proud to wear herself. Nonsense, all of it. Madame Laurent may have been polite in response, but Rose had forgotten herself. Had forgotten her place. She was merely the hired help. The dress was Diana's. It did not belong to her.

FIFTY-FIVE

The bride
Brooklyn, 2020

"I think I have to say goodbye to you."

Rocky couldn't be sure if she'd said the words aloud, or just in her head. She felt unsettled, unmoored, since the fight with her mother. Grand-mère repeatedly insisted that Rocky call her mother, that the only way out was through, but Rocky hadn't yet gotten the courage to do it. She couldn't have another tough conversation that left her mother in tears. She just couldn't.

Rocky closed her eyes as she sat still on the stone bench across from her father's gravestone. She took a deep breath in, two, three, four, and out, two, three, four.

When she opened her eyes, she visualized her father sitting next to her: handsome in the tailored suit he wore to work each day, his eyes bright and not yet crinkled with age; he would never get old enough for them to crinkle with age. He wore the infectious smile that was his trademark. Whenever people spoke of her father, they always spoke of his ever-present smile.

It was the smile that had been there for her when she broke her leg at four years old, jumping off the couch. It was the smile that had been there for her when she was afraid to walk into the elementary school building on the first day of kindergarten. Amanda had rushed ahead, eager to see her school friends after the long summer break, but her father stayed by her side, waiting until Rocky was ready to walk in by herself. It was the smile that had been there for her when she learned how to swim, how to ride a bike, how to fly a kite. And now she had to let go.

I don't think that's true, Kitten, she imagined her father saying to her.

"I've made a mess of things with Mom. I've been awful to her, and all she wants to do is help. I have no idea how to be close to her, and it's because I'm holding on to you."

Is that really the problem?

Rocky looked down at her feet. She kicked the dirt with her motorcycle boot, and watched as it formed a tiny cloud before settling back down onto the ground again.

"Isn't it?"

I'm a part of you, Kitten, he said. *And you're a part of me. I'm always going to be there. Always going to be in your heart. You don't have to let go of me just to get closer to her. Love makes us stronger, bigger. The heart expands with love. There isn't a finite amount.*

Rocky wiped a tear from her eye. Her father was right. She knew what she had to do.

FIFTY-SIX

The mother of the bride, as a bride herself
Long Island, 1982

"Why don't you come with me to the beach club today?" her mother suggested. "It's too hot to go into the city."

"I think I'll just stay home today," Joanie told Birdie. "Rest up a bit. I have a migraine."

"You don't get migraines," Birdie said knowingly.

"My head…"

"I'm glad you decided to move back home for the summer."

"Me too."

"There were so many parties at the end of the semester. And then final exams. And…the engagement. Rest is a good idea. What could be more relaxing than a day at the beach?"

"I'm just too tired," Joanie said. "I'm sorry." She could barely look up to meet her mother's eyes. She felt such profound shame over what she had done; she was unsure if she'd ever be able to look her mother in the eyes again.

"You know, you look like you could use a little sunshine and salt water," Birdie said. "Whenever I feel worn out, just the feel of the sand between my toes can bring me back to life."

Joanie burst into tears. She couldn't lie to her mother any longer.

"Oh, honey," her mother said. "If you really don't want to go, you don't have to. I just thought you could use some fresh air after all the time you've been spending in the city."

"It's not that," Joanie said, the truth spilling out of her like a fountain. "I've made a huge mess out of everything."

Her mother walked over and enveloped her daughter in a warm hug. She held on tightly, rubbing her daughter's back. "Whatever has been done can be undone."

"It can't. I don't know what to do," Joanie said through her tears. "I don't even know who I am."

"I know who you are," her mother said. "You are my daughter. You are the love of my life, and your father's life, too. You are smart and beautiful and kind. Being your mother has been the greatest source of pride in my life."

"I've made so many mistakes." Joanie couldn't stop the tears from falling. It felt as if they might never stop. Her chest heaved as her mother held her close.

"Nothing is irrevocable," her mother said, kissing the top of her head.

"Isn't it?" Joanie asked. *If only you knew what I did*, Joanie thought. *You might not feel the same.*

"I will love you no matter what," her mother said. "No matter what."

"If you knew what I did..."

"No matter what," her mother said, loosening her grip. She held Joanie by her arms and wiped the tears from her eyes.

"I broke off our engagement."

"I know, honey."

The tears came full force, once again. "But you don't know why. I slept with someone, Mom. Another guy. It's horrible, I know. But I was so upset about Michele, about Mel, and it's like I wasn't even myself."

"Oh, honey," her mother said, grabbing her in for another hug. "My goodness. It's okay. I've got you."

"It didn't even mean anything."

"Sex can be complicated," her mother said. "But it's just sex."

"That's so French of you," Joanie said, her tears giving way to laughter. "What sort of mother would say that to her daughter?"

"Oh, I just mean that you don't have to beat yourself up about it. I'm sure you wanted it to be different, but it wasn't, and the next time will be different. Hopefully."

"How could I do that to Matthew?"

"We all make mistakes. Some are bigger than others."

"I didn't mean to do this to you."

"You didn't do anything to me," her mother said. "People call off weddings all the time. There's no shame in admitting that you're not ready to get married."

"I'm more lost than ever," Joanie said, looking into her mother's eyes.

"I think you know more than you're letting on." Her mother reached over for a tissue. She passed it to Joanie.

"I didn't want to marry him," Joanie said, pressing the tissue to her mouth, as if to hold the thoughts inside. "That's the truth. And I don't know why."

"I'll support you no matter what," Birdie said. She leaned over and hugged her daughter. Joanie grabbed hold of her mother and squeezed tightly.

"Will this be the biggest mistake of my life?" Joanie asked into her mother's shoulder. "The thing that defines me?"

"There's no such thing as the biggest mistake," her mother said. "There's only what you do and what you don't do. But you certainly should not get married only because you want to be married. You should only get married if you truly love the man. And only if you're ready."

"But if I don't marry Matthew," Joanie said, "how do I come back from that? What if I'm never ready? What if I never find someone again?"

"Not everything is right the first time," her mother said carefully. "Take Grace Kelly's wedding dress. Do you think that was the first design Helen Rose came up with?"

Joanie reached over for a tissue and dabbed at the corners of her eyes. She smiled. "The dress is utter perfection."

"It took two tries to get it that perfect," her mother said. "In 1952, Helen Rose created a dress for the actress Dorothy Mc-Guire to wear for a wedding scene in the film *Invitation*."

"We never saw that one," Joanie said, thinking of all of the Sunday afternoons spent watching old movies with her mother.

"It looks very similar to the dress she made for Grace Kelly's 1956 wedding. Wait here." Birdie disappeared upstairs for a moment, and when she came back downstairs, she had a shoebox filled with old magazine clippings.

Joanie could hardly believe her eyes. It was just as her mother described—a first incarnation of the dress Grace Kelly would eventually wear down the aisle. The bodice of the dress was similar: the delicate neckline, the rose point lace overlay. The cummerbund. The skirt was slightly different: it had a bubble bustle on the sides and the back, as opposed to the clean lines that would become the trademark of the Grace Kelly dress.

Her mother was right—the same woman designed both dresses. And the second one was a more refined and elegant version of the first.

"I'd say Helen Rose got it right the second time, wouldn't you?" Birdie asked.

FIFTY-SEVEN

The seamstress
Paris, 1958

"Rose?"

Rose looked up from the book she was reading. It had become a habit—on Sunday afternoons, she would come to the
Tuileries to sit on a park bench and read. She had grown to love
the Tuileries Garden, and not just because it reminded her of
Robert. Or rather, solely because it reminded her of Robert, of
the time they had when his fiancée was away.

And now, he stood before her.

"Robert," she said, by way of greeting. She was unsure of
what was appropriate in this circumstance.

"It's so lovely to see you," he said, sitting down on the bench
next to her.

"It's lovely to be seen," Rose said, shocked, her voice a
whisper. When she looked back up to Robert, she held her
tongue—she couldn't possibly say all of the things she was feeling, inappropriate, all of it.

"I was so sorry that you left the ballet in such a hurry."

"It was time for me to go. You understand."

Robert nodded. He understood. "It's a beautiful day," he said, looking out at the grounds.

"It is," Rose agreed, staring down at her hands.

Robert edged closer to her on the bench. He regarded Rose for a moment. "I've been thinking about you."

"Oh," Rose said, in place of all the other things she wanted to say, but wouldn't dare utter. She would not tell Robert she had been thinking of him, too. She would not tell Robert she missed seeing him. And she certainly would not tell Robert she was in love with him.

"My mother told me that the dress is beautiful," he said. "Even more beautiful than she could have imagined."

"Thank you," Rose said, her voice quiet and careful. "I appreciate that."

Rose's eyes teared up. Robert took a handkerchief from his jacket pocket and handed it to her. She dabbed carefully, so as not to disturb her mascara, and as she handed the handkerchief back to Robert, she noticed that it was not a handkerchief at all—it was a linen napkin, embroidered with the crest from the opera house.

She looked up at him, confused. "Is this from the opera house?"

"I wanted to remember the night, so I took a napkin home with me," he said. "I hope you won't tell."

"I won't tell."

"I want to see you again." With one finger, he brushed away a lock of hair that had blown into Rose's face. His hand cupped her cheek, and he held it there for a moment. Rose closed her eyes at his touch, as if to memorize it. She brought her hand to his and held it.

"Robert?" a familiar voice called out, bringing Rose back to the present. She opened her eyes and saw that Robert had dropped his hand back into his lap. The spell had been broken. Rose turned her head to the source of the voice.

Elisabeth, Robert's fiancée. His sister, Diana, stood next to her, mouth agape.

"What are you doing with my fiancé?"

Rose held her breath.

"I was heading over to the restaurant to meet you and I saw Rose sitting here alone," Robert said, standing to greet them. "I sat down to say hello."

"It looked to me like you were holding hands with the help," Elisabeth said, her voice angry.

Shame flamed in Rose's chest. She had forgotten her place. Her head dipped down, like when she was a child in the confession booth.

"Lovely to see you, Rose," Diana said quietly.

"Lovely to see you, too," Rose said, her voice small and uncertain. Rose silently cursed herself. She was supposed to be drumming up more business for the atelier, trying to keep it afloat. Trying to keep her job. Instead, her careless actions were threatening her very livelihood. If Elisabeth canceled her dress and alerted others to Rose's behavior... Rose couldn't even think of the repercussions.

"Robert," Diana said, making a show of checking her delicate wristwatch. "We're late for our lunch plans. I don't want to keep Bertram waiting."

"Let's go," Elisabeth said. And then, turning to face Rose: "Do be a dear and tell your boss that I won't be buying a dress from your atelier, after all. Would you?"

"But I'm almost done with the final sketch," Rose said, her voice choking on the words. "I know that you'll love it."

"I don't think that I will," Elisabeth said, walking off with her arm woven territorially through Robert's.

Rose's face fell. She tried to think of something to say, something that would reverse what had just happened, but she couldn't think of a thing that would salvage the situation. She watched Elisabeth walk off. With the man she loved. With the dress commission the atelier desperately needed. How could she have done this? How could she have ruined everything?

Diana offered Rose a warm embrace before she joined Robert and Elisabeth. Her hug said, *It will be all right*, even though Rose knew that it would not. Julien would be furious with her. He'd warned her about Robert, and now Elisabeth was canceling her dress contract. Could Diana be far behind?

Rose hurried home. She could no longer sit in the park, could no longer do things that reminded her of Robert. Could no longer think of him. It wasn't right. He didn't belong to her, just as the dress didn't belong to her. Thinking about either one would only cause her pain.

As she arrived back at the boarding house, Rose was surprised to find Julien standing in the door frame. He looked distraught. His hair was mussed and his vest was unbuttoned.

Was it her? Was he cross with her? There was no way he could know that Rose had just bumped into the Laurents. No way to know that they'd lost the commission for Elisabeth's dress. There had to be another reason for his visit.

"Is everything all right?" Rose asked carefully, after she had greeted her friend.

"It most certainly is not," he said. Julien held out the newspaper for Rose to see, and pointed to the headline:

Acclaimed Dress Designer Madame Michel, Author of *Creating the Illusion*, Dead at Age 63

FIFTY-EIGHT

The bride
Brooklyn, 2020

"I wasn't expecting you."

"May I come in?" Rocky asked.

"Yes, of course," Joan said. "Come in."

Rocky walked in and took a deep breath. She loved the scent of her childhood home. Even when her mother wasn't cooking, it smelled like holiday. Like roasted garlic and rosemary and cinnamon. Joan led her to the family room and motioned for her to sit down.

"Tea? I was just making myself some chamomile, so—"

Joan turned toward the kitchen, but Rocky grabbed her mother and held her close. Joan had not been expecting the hug. But what could Rocky do? The second she saw her mother, it overcame her. This feeling of love, of appreciation.

"I'm so sorry. I'm sorry we fought. I'm sorry I didn't tell you the truth sooner. I'm sorry I made you cry."

"Oh, honey." Joan brushed Rocky's hair off her face—lavender this week—and pressed her lips to her forehead, the way she used to do when Rocky was a little girl and she was testing to see if Rocky had a fever. "You don't have to be sorry."

"I do."

"Then, I accept your apology."

The kettle screamed out, and Joan rushed into the kitchen. She met Rocky back at the couch with two cups of tea.

"I'm so sorry for everything."

"I've already told you that it's okay. I'm sorry for the way I reacted. I was just so taken off guard. But everything is fine."

But Rocky couldn't stop. Her thoughts came out in a jumble: "It's not fine. I'm sorry for everything I said, the way I made you cry. I'm sorry I took you for granted. I'll wear the dress."

"It was never about the dress," Joan said, her hand on Rocky's face. "I wanted you to have it. It was something that was very important to me, and I gave it to you to mark the occasion. But you don't have to wear it if you don't want to."

"So, you don't want me to wear it?"

"Wear it. Don't wear it. Use it for a tablecloth. It's yours now. It belongs to you."

Rocky furrowed her brow and tried to come up with a re-sponse. But she couldn't think of a thing to say. Her mother took her hand and spoke: "This is not about me. It's about you. It's your wedding. Your day. But as you get older, I think you'll come to see why these heirlooms are so important."

"I don't hold on to things. My life is about things that are new. Throwing out the old and replacing it with what's current."

"New is great. But sometimes the old stuff is meaningful, too. These things are a tie to our past, they remind us what is important."

"And what's that?" She honestly didn't know. Rocky didn't give much thought to things that were old. She never formed emotional connections to things. Never found it hard to leave behind something old once it was replaced with something newer, better. After all, why would you want outdated technology once there was an alternative?

"Love. Family," Rocky's mother said. "The care it took to make that dress means something. It is a reflection of how your grandmother felt about your grandfather, about how I felt about your father, about how you feel about Drew. It binds us together."

"I get that, but what if the dress is just not me?"

"These things we hold on to, they are more than just things. They prove our history, who we are, where we came from."

"So, you *do* want me to wear the dress."

"The dress only means something if you want it to. What is important are the people behind it. When it comes to these things that are handed down from generation to generation, each woman leaves her own mark on it, so that it tells our story, stitch by stitch. Whether you decide to wear the dress is entirely up to you. But your grandmother and I want you to have the dress. The dress belongs to you. If you choose to keep it preserved in the back of your closet like you do the pearl necklace I gave you on your sixteenth birthday, that's up to you."

"I wear that necklace."

Her mother laughed a deep, throaty laugh. "Oh, honey, it doesn't matter if you wear it or not. That's not what's important. What is important is that you know how much I love you. How much your father loved you. Your whole family, in fact. And on your wedding day, we will stand proudly by your side as you marry the man you love. No matter what you're wearing."

Rocky looked at her mother. Her face, warm and open. Maybe she'd been right, maybe Rocky *did* have a wall up. But now, as she looked into the eyes of the second woman to wear the wedding gown, Rocky understood. This dress was a part of their family history. Part of where she came from. Part of who she was. "I'm going to wear the dress."

"There is another option, of course."

"What's that?"

"You want something new." Joan moved her fingers to look like a pair of scissors cutting. She sliced through the air with her hands, snip, snip. "So, make it into something new."

"I could never do that to your dress. To Grand-mère's dress."

Joan laughed. "I don't know how many different ways you want me to say it to you: the dress is yours. Do what you want to it."

"But—"

"Do you think Grand-mère liked it when I took the sleeves off and put on the Princess Diana sleeves?"

Rocky regarded her mother. She hadn't considered that. To her, her mother was the way she'd always been as long as she was born, a rule follower. A good girl. The sort of girl who would never disappoint her mother. It hadn't occurred to her that Joan would ever do something that Grand-mère disapproved of.

Joan looked back at her daughter and smiled. "It's yours now. Make it yours."

FIFTY-NINE

The mother of the bride, as a bride herself
Long Island, 1982

"Here, drown your sorrows in this," Debbie said, passing a wine
cooler over to Joanie. Joanie took the bottle from her friend and
waited for the cabana boys to set up their beach chairs and um-
brellas in the sand.

"I don't deserve a wine cooler," Joanie said, looking out at the
ocean. Two weeks later, she had finally taken her mother up on
her offer to spend a day at the beach club, and Debbie had taken
the Long Island Rail Road out for the day to join her. "I don't
deserve anything. I can't believe I did that to him."

"I can't believe you did that to yourself," Debbie said, clear-
eyed. "You had the guy, you had the ring, you had what every
girl wants. Why would you throw that away? Tell him you
made a mistake."

The cabana boys finished setting up the chairs and smiled
at Joanie. "Thank you," she said, and gave the older one a tip.

"Now, this is heaven," Debbie said, plopping herself down

in a beach chair. She angled the umbrella so that her chair was completely in the sun.

"That's the thing," Joanie said, sitting down on her own chair. The umbrella covered her beach chair in shade. "I don't think that I did make a mistake."

"I'm telling you," Debbie said, leaning back in her beach chair. "You made a mistake. Pass the baby oil."

Joanie passed the bottle of baby oil and gazed out at the ocean. It was so vast, and so wide. It was beautiful, but it made Joanie feel small to look at it. There was this giant world out there, and there was so much of it that she hadn't seen. So many things she had yet to experience.

"Earth to Joanie," Debbie said, breaking her friend out of her spell. "Are you even listening to me? I said it's not too late. Call him today. Tell him you were out of your right mind and will do anything to get him back. Anything."

"I couldn't go back even if I wanted to," Joanie said, placing her wine cooler on the side table set up between their chairs. "He made that clear."

"I'm sure that's not true," Debbie said, flipping her hair off her shoulders. The ends were drenched in the baby oil she'd slathered all over her body. "He still loves you, I know he does. And you still love him. You still want to marry him, right?"

Joanie thought about Debbie's words. But she couldn't think of an answer.

Debbie regarded her. "Oh."

"Should we go into the ocean?" Joanie asked.

"You know I only want what's best for you, right?"

Joanie took a deep breath of the salty ocean air. "I'm still trying to figure out what that is."

"You know I'll be there for you, no matter what, right?"

Joanie looked to her friend. "I do know that."

Debbie hummed a few bars of the song "That's What Friends

Are For," from the movie they'd just seen the previous week-end, *Night Shift*.

"I'm getting in the water. You coming?"

"I need to get a little more sun first," Debbie said. "Then, when I feel like I'm about to burn, I'll go into the water to cool down."

"I'm going now," Joanie said, and she didn't wait for a response. She threw her cover-up onto the beach chair and walked down to the water. It was starting to warm up—the water was always so cold in June and got warmer the closer they got to August—and she stood at the edge for a moment, feeling the ocean water lap at her feet. She watched as the water ebbed in and out, melting her feet farther into the wet sand. Off in the distance, she saw people diving off speedboats, swimming towards the shore.

She took a step deeper into the water, felt the small shells under her feet. Another step, feeling the water hit her knees, splash her arms. And then, taking a deep breath, she dove right in.

SIXTY

The seamstress
Paris, 1958

Julien hung up the telephone soberly.

"Another one?" Rose asked. Julien nodded his head slowly. Yes, another one. It wasn't just Elisabeth who had canceled her wedding gown. It was yet another bride. Like dominoes falling. Another dress order canceled in light of the news that Madame Michel had died.

"I'm almost finished with Diana's dress," Rose said, hoping that news would cheer Julien up. He had been utterly inconsolable. Word had spread like wildfire through high society— Madame was gone, and an orphan seamstress was creating all of the dresses in her stead. Overnight, the shine of a dress custom-made by Madame Michel had faded into nothing.

Julien studied the ledger after every cancellation, rubbing his temples as the numbers went into the red.

"I'm glad to hear it," Julien said. "We'll need the final payment on Diana's dress if we're going to keep the lights on for another month."

Rose didn't dare say what they both were thinking: *If the Laurents choose to give the final payment.* What if they, too, refused to pay because of the subterfuge? They wouldn't be wrong— Julien and Rose had deceived them. The Laurents had agreed to the price of the dress based on the fact that Madame Michel was designing it. Rose knew that Julien wouldn't argue with the Laurents, just as he hadn't put up a fight with Elisabeth's family, or any of their other clients.

Rose tried to thread her needle. Her hands weren't as steady as they usually were; it was as if she had forgotten all of the basics of how to sew.

"We'll need to write up a list of instructions on how to get the dress on," Julien said.

Rose hadn't thought of that—they had practiced getting all four pieces of the dress onto Diana's lithe frame, but Rose had always been there to help. When it came to the day of Diana's wedding, she would need assistance. "Should I offer to—"

"No," Julien said, cutting her off. He knew exactly what she was going to say before she could utter the words, that she should offer to help Diana get dressed on the morning of her wedding. Julien was adamantly against it. Just as he had warned her, the Laurents had broken Rose's heart. Diana, whose friendship was conditional on the making of her wedding gown. Robert, whose heart was never really open to Rose, even though she had opened hers to him.

Rose busied herself with the blue ribbons she was planning to sew onto the inside of the dress. Grace Kelly's dress had little blue satin bows attached to the stiff lace-edged net ruffles on the inside of the skirt, and Rose wanted to give Diana a little surprise to find on her wedding day. She, too, sewed tiny handmade bows onto the underside of the dress support, and left them for Diana to discover on her own.

Julien saw what she was doing and questioned her: Why spend so much time on a part of the dress that no one will see? That isn't needed to support the garment? But Rose couldn't help herself. Just because no one would see what she was doing didn't make it any less important. It was as if she was sewing her very heart and soul into the underside of the garment, giving the dress a part of herself. With each ribbon that she painstakingly tied into a delicate bow, she was leaving her mark on the dress. She was making the dress her own, telling the world that this was not a dress custom-designed by Madame Michel; this was a couture piece from Mademoiselle Rose. And just as wearing a wedding dress designed by Madame Michel was said to guarantee a happy marriage, so too would a dress from Mademoiselle Rose.

Oh, the look of delight that would form on Diana's face the day of her wedding. Rose hoped the ribbons would convey everything she felt for Diana—that she wished only happiness for her, that she valued their time together.

But of course, Rose would not be there on Diana's wedding day. She would have to rely on her work to communicate all of this to the bride.

Rose wondered what Madame would think of everything that had happened since she was gone—of Rose becoming her protégé, posthumously, of the plan she and Julien carried out, of the dress she created for Diana Laurent. Would Madame be proud of her? Would she approve of her work? Rose knew it didn't matter now. The only opinion that mattered now was that of the Laurents, but that still didn't stop the thoughts from coming. She'd worked for Madame for so long, had studied at her elbow for so many years, that it was impossible to stop thinking about how Madame would see things.

"What would Madame think of all this?" she asked.

Julien rose from his desk and stood at Rose's side. He surveyed her work, the dress, and clasped his hands together, in front of his face. "She would say," Julien said, quietly, reverently, as if calling to the spirits beyond, "'Dear child, you have created a true masterpiece.'"

SIXTY-ONE

The bride
Brooklyn, 2020

"What girl wouldn't want to look like a princess on her wedding day?" Amanda asked, a dreamy look in her eyes. "You're not going to change the dress *too much*, are you?"

"The dress is mine now. I'll do what I want with it." Rocky motioned to the bartender to bring over two glasses of wine.

"Just remember, it is a dress that is fit for a princess."

"Do I look like the sort of girl who cares about princesses?"

"Mom cared about princesses."

"Princess Diana did humanitarian work that is still important today," Rocky said, looking at their reflection in the mirror over the bar. Her hair was still lavender, and she liked the way it looked next to her sister's honey waves. She'd let her own shag dry naturally that morning, and as Rocky looked at their reflection across the bar, she felt that they matched. That a passerby could tell they were sisters.

"That's not why Mom put those sleeves on her wedding

dress," Amanda said, looking down at her sister with a smirk. "Those sleeves were not about humanitarian work."

Rocky laughed as the bartender set down two glasses of wine and nodded at Rocky. Out of the corner of her eye, Rocky could see him wink at her sister. What's more, Amanda winked back.

"Why did she tell you that?" Rocky asked.

"Tell me what?" Amanda took a sip of her wine, the first sip, and purred like a cat. "Mmm, this is good."

The bartender heard Amanda's murmur and made his way back over. He started to say something about the top notes of the wine, but Rocky cut him off. She wasn't letting someone interrupt their night alone. She cleared her throat. "About me changing the dress."

"All she ever talks about is you," Amanda said, rolling her eyes dramatically. "It's annoying."

"No," Rocky said slowly, "all she ever talks about is *you*." She pointed to her for emphasis. She would not allow Amanda to make this thing hers.

"I think she would say that it's called keeping us all in touch, keeping us in the loop," Amanda said, all of it in air quotes, as if this very idea annoyed her. "Letting us be a family, letting us know what's going on in each other's lives."

"Did she say that to you?" Rocky asked, leaning in. She eyed her sister suspiciously.

"No," Amanda said, laughing. "My therapist did. But she thinks that's why Mom always talks to me about you. Mom lost her sister when she was young. It's important to her that we're close."

Rocky turned to look at her sister.

"My therapist says—" Amanda began, only to be cut off by Rocky's laughter. "What's so funny?"

"Quoting your therapist like that," Rocky said, taking a slow sip of wine. Despite herself, she let out the same murmur that Amanda did on her first sip. Everything her CFO had told her about this wine bar was right—you couldn't pick a bad glass. "It's funny."

"Well, I don't really care what you think," Amanda said in a way that made clear that the opposite was true—she very much cared what Rocky thought.

"Yes, you do," Rocky said with a smile. She edged her seat a little closer to her sister's. "You absolutely do."

"Okay, I do," Amanda said, throwing her hands up in defeat. "I care what everyone thinks."

"Your therapist say that?" Rocky asked, taking another sip of her wine.

"Yes," Amanda said, bowing her head in defeat. Then, looking up to face her sister: "But you know, you care what I think, too."

"I don't care what anyone thinks," Rocky said, flipping her hair off her shoulders. Evidence. Would a person who cared what people thought dye her hair a different color each week? No. Absolutely not.

Amanda let out a roaring belly laugh. "Of course you do."

"No, I don't," Rocky said. Once the words left her mouth, she felt embarrassed that she sounded like a petulant child. But she didn't care what people thought. She really did not.

"Everyone cares about what other people think, to some extent. Society couldn't function otherwise. But please don't fool yourself into thinking that the crazy hair colors, the tattoos, and the combat boots mean that you don't care. You do. Just in an entirely different way. You may not want to look like a princess on your wedding day, but you care about how you project yourself to the world."

"I definitely do not care about looking like a princess on my wedding day," Rocky said. And then, with her lip firmly pouted: "They're motorcycle boots, not combat boots."

"Grand-mère cared about looking like a princess on her wedding day," Amanda said dreamily, as if she were summoning up memories of their beloved Grand-mère.

Rocky took a beat to consider this. "Grace Kelly was an accomplished actress before she was a princess," she pointed out. "I'm not entirely sure that one counts."

"Anyway, princesses are more a metaphor than anything else," Amanda said. "No one really wants to be a princess, not if they really think about it—the way they made Kate Middleton walk out of the hospital mere hours after giving birth, the way they've got Meghan Markle wearing pantyhose. Pantyhose!— but it's more the idea of what a princess represents. This idea that you've found 'your prince,' meaning your one true love. It's more romantic to think that the universe has just one true love in store for you. It's not romantic to think that lots of different people could have been that mythical one, if only for better timing. And when you're getting married, don't you want it to be romantic?"

"I guess," Rocky said, considering her sister's words.

"And the whole princess thing is really a metaphor for having a happy, charmed life. Who doesn't want that?"

"You're a very good lawyer," Rocky told her sister, swirling the wine in her glass. "You could basically convince anyone of anything. It's like an evil superpower."

"It really is," Amanda said, smiling broadly back at her sister. She tilted her head conspiratorially and asked her sister: "Would you like to know the latest victim of my evil superpowers?"

"Sloan."

"Sloan."

"Sloan."

"How did you know?" Amanda asked.

"After you fainted, when you came to? You told her you loved her."

"Did I?"

"You did," Rocky said, and took a sip of wine. "Do you?"

"I might," Amanda said. "Think my wedding invite will include a plus one?"

"I think that can be arranged."

"So, what are you going to wear?"

SIXTY-TWO

The mother of the bride, as a bride herself
Long Island, 1982

Joanie had to check the address Mel had written down—this couldn't possibly be the place, could it? There were no floor-to-ceiling windows, no high ceilings, like at the bigger galleries she'd been to before. In fact, this one wasn't even announced with a sign on the street. They had to take a service elevator to the eleventh floor, and there were handwritten signs directing toward the Red Gallery.

"You made it!" Mel called out, just as Joanie and Debbie walked in. Joanie gave her sister's friend, now *her* friend, a warm hug.

As Mel walked them through the gallery to see her work, the wood floors creaked. It wasn't as grand as the gallery that had hosted the group show for Mel and Michele, but it was a solo show, a huge achievement.

Joanie moved slowly through the space. Mel's work: traditional paintings, with a twist. She used fluorescent colors, like the clothing sold at Trash and Vaudeville, to create something that felt almost alive. Joanie had never seen anything like it. Each painting was a different portrait. The paintings themselves were a mix of classic styles, but the vibrant colors—neon pink, fluorescent yellow—made them look new and fresh in a way that got Joanie excited.

When they passed the portrait of Jesse, done in oranges and yellows, Mel said, "He just left. But he'll be back later, if you want to see him?"

Joanie shook her head no.

"You two could be good together, you know. I see the way he looks at you."

"I don't think I could be good with anyone right now," Joanie said. "I need a little time on my own."

Jesse had been a mistake. A mistake that she'd come to terms with—it might not have been the way she'd always envisioned losing her virginity, but it took her a step closer to figuring out who she was and what she wanted. But still, it was in the past. She was only looking to the future now.

Mel led the way to her next piece. With the more intimate space, Joanie felt more in sync with the art, more comfortable. She stopped at a portrait of two girls standing next to each other, one with blond hair, the other with black.

"Oh, my god," Debbie said, joining her. "That's us."

Joanie had to admit—the painting did bear a resemblance. She turned to Mel, who pursed her lips, as if to say something.

"I love it," Debbie said before Mel could speak. "We're buying it."

"I couldn't take your money. And anyway—"

"You're a starving artist," Debbie said. "For sure you can take our money. Quick, before someone else buys it first." She rushed off to find the manager, leaving Joanie alone with Mel.

"Your stuff is really amazing," she said.

"Not as good as your sister's," Mel said, eyes fixed on the

painting, as if she were critiquing it, still. "But I think I have something, all the same."

"You have a real signature style." Joanie pointed at the lines of the figures, the colors. "It feels alive, you know?"

"Thank you," Mel said. "You know, I'm really glad you came."

"I wouldn't miss it for the world." Joanie reached over and gave Mel's hand a little squeeze.

"Another sale!" a voice sang out. The manager of the art gallery came over and put a sticker onto the side of the painting. "You're on fire, Mel."

"Go easy on them," Mel said. "They're college students."

"Sure," the manager said, laughing slyly.

Debbie handed over her father's credit card and Joanie looked more closely at the plaque. She leaned in and saw the name of the painting: "Michele."

SIXTY-THREE

The seamstress
Paris, 1958

Rose sat at the worktable, waiting. The dress for Diana hung in the fitting room, ready to be boxed up and sent off.

Rose wiped her hands on a linen napkin, nervous. Would the Laurents agree to pay the final installment on the dress? Would they even take the dress with them? Would Diana hate her for lying all this time? Rose truly didn't know.

The door to the atelier opened, and a tiny chime rang out.

"How lovely to see you," Julien said, rushing over to Diana and her mother. A flurry of greetings followed.

"Rose!" Diana called out to her friend. "I can't wait to see the dress."

Rose felt her shoulders soften, her breath come back to her body, as she brought Diana into the fitting room. She opened the dressing room door with a flourish, and her client slowly walked through. Diana was silent as she gazed upon her wedding gown, finally complete, set up on a dress form. Although

Diana's back was to her, Rose could see her reflection in the mirror. Diana was crying softly.

"It is the most beautiful dress I have ever seen," she said through tears, slowly taking in every detail. Her head moved this way and that as she gazed upon Rose's creation.

"I'm so honored to hear you say that."

Diana fingered each of the delicate silk-covered buttons that ran down the back of the bodice. Her eyes traveled across the cummerbund, and then down to the silk faille skirt. When her eyes caught the delicate lace detail at the bottom of the gown, she smiled. "Roses made for me by my Rose," Diana said, gently holding the bottom border of the gown. "These are exquisite."

"Your mother liked that part, too," Rose said, a smile overtaking her face.

"Did you cut each one of these by hand?" Diana looked closer at the hem of the gown.

"I did."

"Why, that must have taken hours upon hours," Diana said, turning the material over in her delicate hands.

"My aunt taught me the value of hard work," Rose said. "She always told me that hard work paid off. And I think it did here."

"Oh, it did," Diana said. "It truly did. I can see you in every stitch on this gown. Every last detail."

"I'm so delighted that you're pleased with it," Rose said, and Diana rushed toward her and enveloped her in a hug.

"I love it," she replied, hugging Rose even tighter. "I love what *you* created. It was *your* design I wanted. *Your* vision."

"I'm sorry about what happened in the park," Rose whispered in Diana's ear. She found she only had the courage to say this to Diana as they embraced, and only in a whisper; if she had been facing Diana directly, she wouldn't have been able to say the words out loud.

"Sorry?" Diana said, breaking away and looking at Rose with tearstained eyes. "Why on earth would you be sorry?"

"I'm so filled with shame over how I behaved," Rose said, tears now stinging her own eyes. "Please forgive how I acted with your brother. I should apologize to Elisabeth as well."

"But, Rose," she said, laughter in her voice. "There's nothing to forgive."

"He is an engaged man." Rose's spine straightened as she prepared to own up to what she had done. Her aunt had always told her to look someone in the eye when you wanted to be heard. When you had something important to say. When you admitted that you were wrong. "I should not have been spending time with him the way I had. I should not have let him touch me."

"He doesn't love her the way he does you," Diana simply stated. "I see it in his eyes, the way he looks at you. Elisabeth and Robert have always been pushed together, since we were kids. It's not really love. It's just something familiar. Something expected. Something for our families."

"The way he tells it, they're soul mates. And always have been."

"Then you weren't listening to the story very carefully," Diana said, focusing her attention on Rose.

"Wasn't I?"

"Why do you think I forced the two of you to spend time together?"

"I'm afraid I don't understand," Rose said, shaking her head.

"The futile search for the rose point lace that would match the lace used on Princess Grace's dress?" Diana said, laughter rising in her voice. "You didn't think I actually thought I would find it, did you?"

"Well, of course I did," Rose replied, furrowing her brow. What was Diana saying to her? "Why else would you have gone off to try?"

"Silly girl," Diana said, her smile filled with warmth. "I only did that to distract my dear brother's fiancée. To give you and my brother time to spend together. Alone."

"I don't know what to say."

"Say that you love him, too." Diana's face lit up from within. "Tell me that I'm right."

"Even if you were," Rose said. "I could not start a relationship like this. It wouldn't be right. And what about Elisabeth?"

"She feels the same way," Diana said, her voice softening. "They were simply always expected to be together, to get married—and now neither one knows how to extricate themselves. You'd be doing her a favor."

"By stealing her fiancé?" Rose's hands shook and she felt unsure on her feet. She held on to a nearby chair for support. "That hardly seems like a favor. And that is not the sort of woman I am. I could never do a thing like that."

"But you love him and he loves you," Diana said. "Surely that is all that matters."

"No. You're wrong," Rose said, shaking her head. "I never loved him."

SIXTY-FOUR

The bride
Brooklyn, 2020

"My style is a bit different from my mother's," Rocky explained, and Greta nodded. Rocky was back at the dress shop, but this time she was by herself. Free to do whatever she wanted to the dress that belonged to her.

"I understand," Greta said.

"Well, the first problem is that I don't wear dresses," Rocky said quietly, as if it were a secret she was afraid to reveal. "Or skirts."

Greta regarded her for a beat. And then, catching on: "You want to wear pants?"

"I think so," Rocky said. Slowly, tentatively, like she wasn't even sure herself. "Have you ever done that before?"

"I have not." Greta let her pencil lazily hit her sketch pad and began to draw as she spoke. "But that doesn't mean that I couldn't try."

The first rough sketch she drew was a pair of cigarette pants. Slim-cut and cropped to just above the ankle.

"Those are impossibly chic," Rocky said. "I'm not sure I could pull those off."

Greta didn't respond; she merely let her eyes travel up and down Rocky's body. Rocky looked down and remembered that she was wearing cropped skinny jeans, clearly the inspiration for Greta's design. "That's not my only idea," Greta said, and let her pencil do the work once again. The next sketch was just as elegant as the first: a pair of wide-legged palazzo pants that were so long they kissed the ground.

"Those are beautiful," Rocky said, pointing at the drawing.

"Or perhaps we do them cropped," Greta said, pulling out an eraser and making the pants shorter. "It depends on the shoe. What sort of shoe do you plan to wear?"

"I have no idea."

"I should have guessed." Greta laughed. She looked at Rocky and smiled warmly. "We could also make the pants wider, more dramatic, and mimic the look of a skirt."

Again, her trusty eraser altered one design and let her create something entirely different.

Rocky's eyes widened as she looked at what Greta had drawn. "That's stunning."

"We could have it fall to the floor so that you could wear a heel or a flat."

"I don't really wear heels," Rocky said, fingering the sketch, letting the ball of her finger rest on the lines of the pant leg.

"If you like the idea of it, I can refine it for the final sketch."

"I'd love that."

"Then let's move on to the bodice," Greta said, picking up her pencil once again. "We have that beautiful cummerbund." She drew the bodice of the dress and the cummerbund on top of the palazzo pants. "We can make changes to the bodice, of course, too, if you want to show off your tattoos. I saw that mother and daughter did not really agree on the sleeve length."

Rocky laughed. "Right. I'm sure you don't understand, but my tattoos are important to me. They mean something to me."

"Why do you think I don't understand the meaning of having your skin marked?"

"I don't exactly think it's the sort of thing your generation did," Rocky said, nervously laughing.

Greta removed her cardigan and rolled up her shirt sleeves. "I understand what it means to have your body marked."

Rocky sat breathless. She did not know what to say. She had never seen the tattoo of a Holocaust survivor before, but now here was Greta, laying herself bare, showing Rocky the tattoo she had been given in Auschwitz.

"Why are you crying?" Greta said. "I didn't mean to upset you. I meant to share something with you."

Rocky hadn't realized she was crying. "I'm sorry," she said. "I'm so overwhelmed. I'm so sorry for what you went through. You must think I'm awful, getting all of these tattoos when you yourself—"

"I don't think you're awful at all," Greta said. "I am not judging you."

Greta reached over and grabbed a tissue. She passed it to Rocky. "You have nothing to be sorry about. I'm glad that you came back to me. And I'm honored to be helping you create the wedding dress that will truly belong to you."

"But what you've been through," Rocky said, and then she blew her nose into the tissue. "That tattoo is a terrible reminder."

"It is important to remember our past," Greta said. "Don't you think? After all, that's why this dress is important to your mother. We must never forget where we came from. Isn't that why you get the tattoos? To remember?"

"Yes," Rocky said, throwing her tissue in the trash and grabbing for another. "Each one marks something important in my life, something that defines me. I think it's important to re-member."

"We need to remember the past so that we can more clearly see where we are going," Greta said quietly. The room had be-come silent, as if they were the only ones in the shop. "I see nothing wrong with honoring the past however you see fit. For your mother, it's this heirloom dress. For you, it's the tattoos you wear proudly on your body. But they are the same thing, are they not?"

"You know you don't have to convince me to wear the dress, right?" Rocky said. "I've already decided."

Greta smiled widely. She erased the drawing of the bodice and cummerbund and got ready to sketch something new, just as she'd done with the skirt. "So, then, let's tear this thing up, shall we?"

SIXTY-FIVE

The mother of the bride, as a bride herself
Long Island 1982

"Are you ready for school to begin?" Birdie asked. She looked down into her food, trying to pretend she wasn't prying, and even though Joanie knew this trick of her mother's, she still opened up.

"I'm excited. And nervous. And a whole host of other things," Joanie said.

"A new year," her mother said, smiling warmly at her daughter. "Another chance to have a fresh start."

"Here's to a fresh start," Joanie's father said, raising his wineglass.

Joanie sighed. If only he knew all of the things that had happened this summer. They clinked their wineglasses for a toast, and then ate their Sunday night dinner.

Joanie and Birdie had spent the day packing up boxes, returning engagement presents. It was hard work, but sending the gifts back was the easy part, it turned out. There was still another thing they had yet to do.

Putting the dress away would be the hard part, and they'd saved it for after dinner. It wasn't that they'd planned it that way, nothing had been said about the dress explicitly, but it had been the task that hung over them the whole day. The thing they both knew they needed to do.

As they packed up the last of the engagement gifts, Birdie had casually said: "There's one last thing to box up. Shall I take care of the dress on my own?"

Joanie hadn't known what to say. Should she simply ask her mother to bring it to the cleaner's herself, and then she wouldn't have to deal with it anymore? Or should she look at it one more time, say goodbye?

But just then, the kitchen timer for Birdie's chicken went off, and they rushed downstairs to get dinner on the table.

When the dishes were cleared, Joanie made a beeline to her childhood bedroom, knowing she needed to say goodbye alone. The dress sat in its box, on top of her old toy chest. The juxtaposition was not lost on Joanie. In some ways, she was still a child. Was that why she wasn't ready for marriage yet? In other ways, she was very much a woman. But she wasn't ready for her mother's life just yet, wasn't ready to give up this part of her life, this part that straddled both worlds. There was still so much to do, so much to see.

Joanie opened the box and took one last look at the dress. She couldn't bring herself to touch it—was it because she wasn't wearing the cotton gloves her mother insisted on or was it because she knew she would not be wearing it?—and she simply let her eyes trail down the intricate rose point lace. Noticed detailing in the fabric that she'd never noticed before.

"Do you want to try it on again," her mother asked, standing at the door frame, "before we take it back to the cleaner's for preservation?"

"I don't think that I do," Joanie said, carefully putting the lid back on the box.

"I'll take care of it for you," Birdie said, and walked across the room to give her daughter a hug. "I'll make sure it's perfect for when you're ready to wear it for real."

"What if I never get the chance to wear it?" Joanie said, tears welling in her eyes.

"One day, you will find the right man at the right time, and you will wear the dress. The only mistake you could have made was going through with a wedding when you weren't ready."

"I'm sorry for all of the pain I've caused you."

"Pain you've caused me?" Birdie said, wiping a tear from her daughter's eye. "You haven't caused me any pain."

"I try to be good for you," Joanie said. "I always try. I know that I'm all that you have left."

"Oh, Joanie," Birdie said. "You shouldn't feel the weight of the world like that. What happened to your sister isn't your fault. And it's not your burden to bear. You know that, don't you?"

"I do," Joanie said carefully. "But I just don't want you to ever go through that sort of pain again. I have to be good."

"The only thing you have to be is yourself," Birdie said, grabbing her daughter by the shoulders, as if to make sure Joanie heard what she had to say. "You can be whoever you want to be. You belong to me and I belong to you, no matter what. And I will love you no matter what."

"I love you, too," Joanie said.

"Your sister loved you, too," Birdie said. "She just didn't know how to show it. But you meant something to her. That's why I got you this."

Birdie jumped up from the bed and walked over to the closet. She brought back a box. Joanie turned it over in her hands before opening it. Inside was a small canvas. It was painted in shades of pink and red, and Joanie could make out the faint outlines of the map of their street on Long Island. Then, laid over that, was a series of photographs, the type you get out of a photo booth, and Joanie could see that all four pictures were of her parents, her sister, and her. It took Joanie an instant to recall where those pictures came from, but she remembered a family vacation spent in Atlantic City. Lazy days on the boardwalk, eating saltwater taffy and walking from hotel to hotel at night. They stayed at the Golden Nugget, which had a big pool that Joanie would spend hours in. Michele was more drawn to the arcade, where she'd play video games for hours on end. That was where the photo booth was—in the arcade. Joanie could remember taking the picture, Michele in her father's lap, Joanie in her mother's, how they all squeezed their faces together to fit in the frame.

"Your sister made this her freshman year at NYCU. I've been saving it for you. Now seems like the perfect time to give it to you," Birdie said. "I want you to remember that all you have to be is you."

Joanie shook her head and closed her eyes, as if to preserve the thought. She took a deep breath in, and considered who that might be.

SIXTY-SIX

The seamstress
Paris, 1958

"This is the way to heal a broken heart," Julien said. "I know it."

He took her hand and they rushed off into the dark night. They were meeting Charles for a late supper in town. Julien had promised that keeping busy would take Rose's mind off Robert, but Rose was unconvinced. Nothing could take her mind off Robert. She saw his face in the clouds, heard his voice in the music they listened to in the atelier all day. Everything reminded her of him.

He had been sending bouquets of roses to her at the boarding house. Each time, the card asked if he could see her, but Rose never responded. The notes all went directly into the trash. As for the roses, she would give them to the children in the boarding house, and they would bring them back to their rooms, a touch of beauty in an otherwise barren place. Rose couldn't bear to have them in her own room, in her own space, near her bed. Still, as she drifted off to sleep each night, she could swear that she smelled them, the faint scent of fresh roses entering her dreams.

"How are we doing?" Charles asked by way of greeting, mostly to Rose, but also to Julien.

Rose held back tears as she smiled at Charles and he swept her up into a warm embrace. "You deserve someone wonderful," he whispered in her ear. "If it wasn't him, there will be another. I'm sure of it."

"Thank you, Charles," Rose said, and she struggled to smile at her friend.

"I tried to warn you, dear child," Julien said, and squeezed Rose's arm. "I only wanted to keep your heart safe."

"I know," Rose said, looking up at Julien.

"I know you feel heartbroken now," he said. "But you have me. And I love you. I will never stop loving you. So, when you feel disconsolate, I want you to remember that."

"And how are you doing?" Charles asked Julien. He rubbed his arm, but that was as far as their affection would go in public. Never a hug, never a kiss hello.

"More cancellations each day," Julien said, matter-of-factly. "We'll be closing within the month."

"My love," Charles said, his face crumpling, and Julien smiled meekly back in response. His smile said that it was okay, that everything would be all right, but Rose knew that his heart was breaking over the loss of his aunt's legacy.

"Perhaps we should skip dinner and go to a picture instead," Julien suggested. "A movie always cheers my Rose right up."

Julien and Charles had tried everything they could think of to brighten her mood—musical performances, dinners, and even the theater, but nothing worked. Rose was utterly inconsolable.

They walked arm in arm to the theater. Being surrounded by her two friends was the one thing to look forward to in her day. No matter how awful she felt, she at least knew that she was no longer alone in the world.

"It's better this way," Charles said to Rose as they crossed the street. "Men like Julien and me know a thing or two about unrequited love, and it's better that it's over now, before you gave that man more of your heart."

Rose didn't know how to respond. She'd given every ounce of her being to Robert. When she worked on the dress for Diana, she was really putting all of her love into it. Everything she felt for Robert was in that dress. And now they both were gone. The dress. And the man.

"Now, let's go forget our problems at the cinema," Julien said. He put his arm around Rose's shoulders, and Charles put his arm around the other side as they approached the box office.

After the movie, Julien and Charles saw Rose home. She walked into the boarding house and found her next-door neighbor Marion waiting for her in the entryway. She pointed to a vase filled with red roses. "Another one," she said, and handed Rose the card.

But Rose didn't need the card to know who the roses were from. Each card was the same: "Roses for my Rose. I need to see you."

Rose picked a flower out of the vase and brought it to her face. Her fingertips felt the soft skin of its petals. It never ceased to amaze her how smooth the rose's petals could be, how sharp its thorns. She took a deep breath, letting the beautiful fragrance fill her body. She closed her eyes and thought of Robert. What was he doing at that moment? Was he with his fiancée? Did his heart ache for her as her heart ached for him?

She opened her eyes and threw the flowers in the trash.

SIXTY-SEVEN

The bride
Brooklyn, 2020

The number eight is said to signify resurrection and regeneration. Some people say the number eight means that an angel is communicating with you, and others say it stands for achievement and success in life.

Some tattoos were easy. Rocky's second tattoo, angel wings to commemorate her father, had been an easy one. Top of her right foot. Her third tattoo, the zip code of Stanford, had been hard. (What if she moved off campus to another zip code?) Right ankle.

Some were ill-advised: the small Google logo that she got on her left shoulder after accepting the job right out of college. That one was covered up by tattoo number five: a drawing of the Brooklyn Bridge. Her home.

There were tattoos she treasured most: the infinity symbol, her first, right hip. The logo of her company—a small black cat for Kitten Games—etched on the inside of her right wrist. Drew's name on the inside of her right arm. Easy.

Her eighth tattoo was hard. How do you mark an occasion like your wedding? It seemed so important, so momentous. There were so many components to wedding planning, so much tension to work through.

Rocky had considered doing the date of her wedding. But after seeing Greta's tattoo, there was no way she'd ever mark her body with numbers again. She had considered doing her initials alongside Drew's, but that seemed too similar to the tattoo of Drew's name she'd gotten on the day they moved in together—he had a matching one on his own arm. She wanted something different, something that was meaningful.

"You want me to tattoo a duck?" Jimmy, Rocky's favorite tattoo artist, asked now.

"It's a wild goose, actually," Rocky said. "It's a Korean wedding tradition."

"I thought he was Jewish?" Jimmy went over the sketch with his fingers, getting a feel for the design.

"He was born in South Korea. He was adopted by a Jewish family."

"So, what's with the ducks?" Jimmy readied his instruments.

"They're wild geese," Rocky repeated. "Not ducks. It's traditional that before the wedding, the groom gifts the bride's mother a wild goose."

"To eat?"

"No," Rocky said. "To symbolize harmony and structure. Geese mate for life."

"Man, that's beautiful," Jimmy said, and stopped what he was doing for a brief moment. "So, this one's for Drew?"

"It's for Drew. It's for the birth mother he never got the chance to meet. It's for my mother, too."

"So, I guess that means we won't be doing another cover-up job in a few years, huh?"

"Nope." Rocky took off her jacket. The tattoo would sit at the nape of her neck.

"Then, let's get started." He laid the paper over Rocky's skin and paused. "Isn't this going to show when you wear your wedding dress?"

"Yes," Rocky said, relaxing herself into a comfortable position. Seven tattoos in, she knew that you needed to keep yourself still and quiet while the artist did his work.

"That's the idea."

SIXTY-EIGHT

The mother of the bride, as a bride herself
Long Island, 1982

A pall had been cast over the entire week.

The start of the semester had been difficult—stops and starts, characterized by deep bouts of sadness, but this week was worse than anything that had come before. And there had been a lot.

First, it had been the Theta house Back to School Party, when she bumped into Matthew, still the president of his fraternity. Joanie tried to say hello, as she imagined a mature adult might, but Matthew simply looked at her and acted as if he'd never seen her before. This was a man she'd been engaged to, a man she'd promised her life to, and there he was, pretending they'd never once before met. Joanie felt like she'd been knocked off her feet.

Then, in Psych 305: she walked into the lecture hall, excited to see old friends gathered together, but Matthew's friends acted like they didn't know her. No one to sit with, she was banished to the back of the lecture hall where she had trouble hearing the professor over the din of the students who were only there to socialize, and not to actually learn from the class.

And finally, at the Student Union: when she'd walked in to see Matthew cozied up in a booth with one of her sorority sisters. Apparently, they were already an item.

But this weekend she would go home. It felt only right, to be home in her mother's house, after something so tragic had happened. On Monday, Grace Kelly had been in a car accident, and died the following day. Joanie would be home on Long Island in time to watch the televised memorial service, laying to rest the legend, along with the rest of the world.

Her mother had been distraught all week. Grace Kelly had been such a large part of her life—wearing a wedding dress based on Princess Grace's iconic gown had changed her life irrevocably.

The dress hadn't yet changed Joanie's life, but it would one day. Five years after her broken engagement, Joanie would find herself engaged once again. Six years after her broken engagement, she would wear the dress.

It would not be love at first sight. It would not be hate at first sight. It would be tentative and slow. She would fall in love gradually. She would fall in love not based on what he looked like, or who he was, or what family he came from, but the sum of all of those things, or perhaps none of them at all. It would be because he was handsome and kind and smart. It would be because he came from a lovely family and he wanted the sort of family life that Joanie wanted, too. It would be a love based on mutual respect and understanding. It would be because he was a good man, the sort of man you could count on, and he would see the same things in her. It would be because she was ready for it. They would agree on where to get the best bagels in the city, they would disagree on whether milk chocolate or white chocolate was better, and they would compromise on all the rest.

It would not be love at first sight like what her mother had experienced. It would not be hate at first sight, like what her own daughter would eventually experience. It would simply be love. And it would be all her own.

Joanie would have the big wedding she'd always dreamed of. (And she would get the fairy-tale Princess Diana sleeves she'd always wanted, too.) And on her wedding day, her mother would remind her: "To wear a custom-designed Madame Michel wedding dress is to guarantee a happy marriage." And it would.

It was a beautiful day in Monaco for the funeral. How could the weather be so lovely when the day was so awful? Joanie wondered. It didn't seem fair. Didn't seem right.

Joanie and her mother were perched on the couch, watching the funeral procession. When Prince Rainier appeared, flanked by his children, Birdie burst out crying. Joanie wasn't far behind. They held hands as they watched, supporting each other through their sadness, entwined.

"Those poor children," Birdie said, her eyes not leaving the television screen.

"I can't imagine losing you," Joanie said, glued to what was unfolding. "I can't imagine what Stephanie must be feeling right now."

"All fairy tales come to an end," Birdie said through tearful eyes.

"Why do they have to?" Joanie wondered out loud.

"Because fairy tales aren't real."

"You're right," Joanie said. "Oh, but they're beautiful to think about, aren't they?"

"Princess Grace herself said, 'The idea of my life as a fairy tale is itself a fairy tale,'" Birdie said. She looked over at her daughter, still transfixed by the images on the screen. "In time you will find something real, something true."

And Joanie would. She just didn't know it yet.

SIXTY-NINE

The seamstress
Paris, 1958

"But, Mademoiselle," the man said, "that would be impossible."

"Then you don't have to cancel the order," Rose reasoned. "Just stop sending the flowers."

"I cannot," the florist said, his hands up, as if in surrender. "Monsieur Laurent has placed a standing order. I must comply with his wishes."

"I don't want the roses," Rose said, slowly, articulating each word, and the florist looked confused. After all, what woman would not want dozens of lush red roses? Rose didn't know how to get through to him. How could she explain to this man that her heart was broken, that she needed to forget about Robert, that the roses only served to remind her of him, over and over again?

"I cannot stop sending the roses until Monsieur Laurent tells me to stop. The Laurents are good customers of mine. I could not possibly risk making them angry."

This was something Rose could understand. After all, hadn't she been in a similar position? The atelier was dying, and Rose would do anything to keep it afloat. So, how could she fault the florist, a man who, like her, simply wanted to protect his business? She, too, had been careful to keep the Laurents happy for the sake of her business.

Rose offered an alternative: "You don't have to cancel the order. What if you simply sent the roses somewhere else? Perhaps to the hospital, to cheer up the sick and elderly?"

"I must comply with Monsieur Laurent's orders," he said. "If I do not fill the order properly, they will know."

"The flowers are being sent to me," Rose pled. "How could they possibly know?"

And then, as if to prove his point, the bell rang out to signal the arrival of a client, and when Rose looked over at the door, she saw Diana. The florist greeted Diana warmly and Rose looked around the store, searching for a back door so that she could leave discreetly without being seen. But it was no use. Diana saw her immediately, as if she'd known that Rose would be there all along.

"My dear Rose," she said warmly. "It's lovely to see you."

"It's lovely to see you, too," Rose said. "I was just leaving."

"Rose," Diana asked, as if she simply could not help herself. "Have you been enjoying the roses?"

"Yes. Or rather, no," Rose said, struggling to compose herself. She straightened her spine and kept her voice strong. "I cannot accept the roses. In fact, that is the reason that I am here today. I came here to cancel the standing order."

"Madame, I can assure you, I explained to this lovely mademoiselle that I would not cancel an order placed by your brother," the florist said, piping in.

"Didn't you find them lovely?" Diana looked hurt, her brow furrowed. She put her hand to Rose's shoulder, as if the act of her touch would make Rose tell the truth.

"Of course they are—"

"He thought roses would be so perfect," Diana said, seemingly lost in thought. "And I couldn't help but agree, especially after I saw the rose detail you had added to my wedding dress. I'm so sorry the roses weren't to your liking."

"It's not that I don't like them. I love them. Or rather, they're beautiful. I simply cannot accept them. Not when he is promised to another."

"You are a good person," Diana said, a sense of understanding washing over her face. Her expression softened, her eyes crinkled as she spoke. "You have a good heart. This is why we are friends. I can see why my brother is so fond of you."

"Thank you," Rose said, and looked down at her hands, folded in front of her.

"My brother would be so fortunate to end up with a girl like you."

"His fiancée is a very lucky girl," Rose said quietly, still unable to meet Diana's gaze.

"Why, he called off his engagement weeks ago," Diana said, looking puzzled. "Didn't he tell you?"

SEVENTY

The bride
Brooklyn, 2020

The first time Rocky walked into the wedding salon she'd felt out of place, like she didn't fit in. Like she didn't belong. But being back, creating the dress that truly belonged to her, had changed that. Now, when she heard the little chime that signaled her arrival for the dress appointment, she didn't feel fear. She felt only joy.

Rocky smiled as her mother said hello to everyone in the shop, introducing her own mother, Rocky's grandmother, around. Something had changed between Rocky and Joan, something had shifted. Rocky couldn't put her finger on it, couldn't describe it to Drew, really, when he asked, but she felt it. Something was different. Something good.

Rocky walked into the back office, embraced Greta warmly and introduced her to her beloved Grand-mère. The dress, the one that her grandmother and mother had both walked down the aisle in, was set up in pieces on three separate mannequins in the shop. It was strange to see it deconstructed like that—after all, any other time that Rocky had visited the dress shop, it had been put together as one dress.

Rocky saw that her grandmother had the same reaction. She stood silently before the dress in pieces, as if in prayer.

"Are you ready?" Greta asked.

"I can't wait," Rocky said.

And with that, Greta revealed the final sketch of the dress. It reflected what she and Rocky had discussed, but somehow seeing all of the ideas down on paper, drawn so beautifully that the picture itself looked like a work of art, made Rocky lose her breath. She examined it more closely. The bodice was completely transformed, as Greta had suggested. The big Princess Diana sleeves had been removed, but the original sleeves didn't make the cut, either. Now sleeveless with the edges rough and unfinished, it had a sexy, modern edge to it. It was fresher, and completely new. Completely Rocky.

The cummerbund remained, but in place of the skirt, there were those palazzo pants Greta dreamed up on the fly. Only these pants were now a more refined version of what Greta had first sketched. They almost looked like the original skirt, if you weren't looking closely enough.

But all three women were.

Down each side of the pants was a single stripe, done in white silk. A subtle nod to tuxedo pants. But it was more than just a simple design detail. Rocky looked over at the elegant white dinner jacket that Rocky's father wore to his own wedding, draped over a mannequin. She turned to Greta, who smiled. Then, she looked to Joan and shrugged. "You were right. His tuxedo belongs on the dress."

"The sketch is absolutely beautiful," Joan said. And then, to Greta: "You've done a masterful job."

"I really love it," Rocky said, tears now brimming in her eyes. "Thank you."

"How are you planning to handle detaching the bodice and underbodice from the slip?" Rocky's grandmother asked, putting her glasses on, leaning in.

Greta looked up, her face full of surprise and delight. "I see we have someone who knows a little something about Grace Kelly's wedding dress. Well, what you don't know is that the bodice and skirt waistband can be detached with these snaps." Greta pointed to the snaps, smiling.

"I do know that," Grand-mère said, walking over to the mannequin which held the bodice and the attached skirt support and slip. "But aren't you going to use the skirt support in order to give the pants volume? How else will you create the look of the skirt?"

"Yes, I was puzzling over that," Greta said thoughtfully. "I was thinking of using a thicker silk faille on the pants to give it the structure I need. Possibly with some boning, depending on how we do in the fittings."

"I'm afraid that won't work." Grand-mère ran her fingers along the ruffles with Valenciennes lace. "The only way to get the volume that you need on the pants is to use the skirt support. You will have to detach the slip that's attached underneath very carefully, stitch by stitch."

"That seems impossible," Greta said, kneeling down on the floor to examine the dress from underneath.

"It is possible. Just very difficult."

"Aha," Greta said, under her breath, as she seemed to find what Rocky's grandmother was describing. "But tell me, how on earth do you know so much about dress construction?"

"Simple, my dear," Grand-mère said. "I didn't just wear the dress. I made it."

SEVENTY-ONE

The seamstress
Paris, 1958

"Did you know that Grace Kelly wanted to elope?"

His voice punctured the silence that filled the atelier. Julien and Rose both looked up from their task for the day—they had been wordlessly packing up boxes all morning, the atelier having delivered its last dress. There were no new orders coming in, and the books had gone completely into the red. The atelier had closed its doors the day before, sent all of the seamstresses home. Julien had done everything in his power to keep his aunt's business afloat, but still, it was not enough. Nothing they had done had been enough. Her legacy, it seemed, would die along with her.

Julien would shutter the doors of Madame Michel's Bridal Atelier once they'd packed everything up and gotten it out of the building. It was difficult work: they'd had to separate the things they were able to sell to other shops—the sewing machines, reams of pristine fabrics, the office furniture—and decide on what to do with other things—the bulk of Madame's private possessions, unfinished muslins, and nearly completed dresses that had been canceled. Julien had been unsuccessful in his efforts to stage an auction of the items from Madame's atelier, like the completed dresses that would never be picked up or paid for, her sketches. Although she, at one time, had maintained a nine-month-long waiting list for her designs, that did not seem to matter anymore. Overnight, her dresses had gone out of fashion, her name had become utterly meaningless. The dresses would later sell for pennies on the dollar, Julien's heart breaking just a little bit with each sale. But it couldn't be helped; he needed the money to pay the seamstresses the last paychecks they were owed.

Julien had discovered that the building itself was worth more than the business, than his aunt's very name, so he'd sold it, the entire thing, including the atelier, the offices, the apartments. He couldn't afford to pay anyone to help clear out the atelier— oh, how the seamstresses had no loyalty! Not one offered to volunteer her time after everything that he and Madame Michel had done for them—so it was just he and Rose who were left with the massive job. Charles had offered to come and help out after work, but Julien and Rose were exhausted each night after toiling all day, and by the time Charles arrived, they could no longer lift another box, dust another surface, and ended up going home for a light supper instead.

This was not how Rose wanted to see Robert Laurent for the first time since learning of his broken engagement. After she had spoken to Diana, Rose had no idea how to approach Robert. Surely, that's why he'd been sending her the roses—he'd wanted to tell her the news in person. But she had thrown out each note he'd sent her, each note that asked to see her; she'd had no idea of the truth.

She should have known that he would come to her, but in her mind's eye, she imagined seeing him again much differently.

She would be beautifully dressed, with her hair set and makeup freshly applied. They would meet at the Tuileries, the gardens that Rose had come to think of as a space that belonged to them, and they would sit down on a bench. The sun would be shining, the birds would be singing, and she would finally be happy.

Instead, Rose saw Robert Laurent for the first time since learning of his broken engagement as they stood in the dusty atelier, Rose looking a fright. She wore work jeans and had her hair up in a ratty old scarf. Her face was free of makeup. But she would not send him away again. She would not take the chance that he wouldn't return to her a second time.

"Grace Kelly wanted to elope?" Rose asked Robert, walking over to the doorway where he stood. She removed the scarf from her head and smoothed her hair. "Why on earth wouldn't a girl want a wedding fit for a princess?"

"Ah, yes," Robert said. "A very good point. But in Grace Kelly's case, she said all she cared about was the man, not the big, splashy wedding. Wedding planning had taken a toll on her nerves, it had made her so overwhelmed that she wished they could just elope."

"That sounds utterly mad," Rose said, smiling despite herself. It seemed she could not stop smiling in Robert's presence.

"When you're in love," Robert said, looking deeply into her eyes, "you're in love." And then, as if remembering something, he reached into his jacket pocket and handed her a letter.

"Is this another one of your love notes?" Rose asked. "Roses for my Rose."

Robert smiled. "This one is from my sister. One last favor she asked of me."

Rose quickly opened the envelope.

My dear Rose,
You have been a very good friend to me, and over the course of these months, I have cherished our friendship.

You are a special person, and I have grown to think of you as not merely a friend, but as family.

I have decided to elope. I simply cannot live my life based on my parents' wishes anymore, and I must do what is in my heart. Although she didn't want to, my mother has given us her blessing. Bertram and I leave for America tonight.

I gift this dress to you. It is still the most beautiful thing I have ever laid eyes on, but what I've come to realize is that even though I love the dress, it truly belongs to you. It would be my honor if you would accept this gift, and wear it on your own wedding day.
All my love,
Diana

"I don't understand," Rose said. "I couldn't possibly accept this." She looked up at Robert, and he had dropped to one knee.

"Rose, I have a message of my own to deliver to you," he said. "From the moment I saw you, I felt an inescapable pull. I don't believe in love at first sight, or any of those silly things that you see in the movies, but still, there is no other way to explain the way that I feel. Getting to know you only confirmed what I felt the first day I met you. Rose, I am in love with you. Madly and truly in love with you. I can think of no other, and I hope that you feel the same way. Will you marry me?"

Rose couldn't speak. She looked at Robert and saw him reach into his jacket pocket. He pulled out a ruby ring—the one surrounded by diamonds that she had seen his mother wearing—and held it out. She took the ring and put it on her finger. It fit perfectly.

"So, is that a yes?" Robert asked, laughter rising in his voice.

"Yes," Rose said, breathless. "Yes."

Robert stood and took her in his arms. For the first time, his lips met hers and they kissed. She felt her knees grow weak, and she held on to Robert tightly as she kissed him back.

"I love you, Robert Laurent," Rose whispered. "I love you."

Rose heard the sound of a champagne cork popping and she spun around to find Julien walking toward them, carrying a bottle of champagne and three flutes. "I think congratulations are in order," he said, and pulled Rose in for a hug.

As Rose poured the champagne, Julien and Robert shook hands. She gave each of the men a glass, and they clinked them together in celebration.

Rose took a sip of champagne, and looked to the two men who meant the most to her in the world. She had never been so happy in her entire life.

Robert held up an enormous box, a box that Rose recognized. "Don't forget this. I think this belongs to you," Robert said.

Without even opening it, Rose knew what was inside: the dress she'd designed for Diana. The dress that she'd crafted by hand. The dress that truly belonged to her. The Grace Kelly Dress.

SEVENTY-TWO

The bride
Brooklyn, 2020

Her something old: the heirloom wedding dress that her grandmother had made for someone else, only to wear it herself.

Her something new: the perfect wedding shoes, a pair of white satin ballerinas with black leather straps and thick silver buckles, mismatched grosgrain ribbons that wrapped around her ankles.

Her something borrowed: her mother's white leather cuff bracelet, a bracelet Rocky had never seen her mother wear before. A bracelet Rocky didn't even know her mother owned. But she did own it, and made it very clear that it was to be returned after the wedding. The leather was soft to the touch, in contrast to the hard silver grommets and pyramid studs it was covered in.

Her something blue: her hair, freshly dyed baby blue for the wedding.

Guests gathered on the rooftop of Rocky and Drew's apartment building, where they danced all night under white paper lanterns to a band that Rocky and Drew heard on their fourth date. Amanda tried to get guests to post pictures on social media using the hashtag #FoundAGoodMan, but abandoned her efforts when she saw her new (old? former? did it even matter?) girlfriend Sloan come out of the kitchen in a tiny black dress that left very little to the imagination. After taking Sloan's hand, she quickly forgot all about social media.

Rocky danced with her new husband. She danced with her new father-in-law. She danced with her great-uncle Julien, newly back on his feet after his hip replacement surgery.

"*Oncle,*" Amanda said, cutting in on Rocky's dance. "There's someone I'd like for you to see. *Oncle,* you remember Sloan, don't you? Sloan, you remember my *Oncle* Julien."

"It is a pleasure to see you," Julien said, taking Sloan's hand in his and kissing it delicately.

"I almost forgot where Amanda got her charm from," Sloan said, smiling widely.

"He owned the atelier that created this dress," Amanda told Sloan, pointing at Rocky's wedding dress. "So, when it's our time, he'll put the skirt back together for us."

"I took care of the business end of things," Julien said. "It's your Grand-mère who made the dress."

"Also, it's my dress," Rocky said, but no one was listening to her. As she walked away, she heard her Uncle Julien ask Sloan to dance with Charles and him. And then she heard Sloan tell her Uncle Julien that they didn't need an intermediary to appear in public anymore, and they certainly didn't need one in order to dance—it was 2020, goddammit, and men danced with men now. He could, and should, share a dance with his long-time partner, Charles.

"Oh, we know that, dear child," Rocky heard Uncle Julien reply to Sloan. "But can you blame two old men for wanting a dance with the infamous Sloan?"

Rocky's grandmother grabbed her hand. "You are the most beautiful bride I've ever seen in my life."

"That's not true," Rocky said, feeling a flush across her face. "You were the most beautiful bride in the world."

"What about me?" Joan asked, materializing as if out of thin air.

"The sleeves, Mom," Rocky said, shaking her head from side to side. "No one can get over the sleeves."

"They were the height of fashion at the time," Joan said defensively. "I was very fashionable. You have no idea."

Rocky stood in the middle of the dance floor, surrounded by her mother and her grandmother. She reached out and took the hands of both women in her own. Wearing the dress, her hands entwined with the women who came before her, Rocky could feel it. That she was a part of something larger than herself, something larger than all of them, being the third generation to wear the dress. A dress that meant something different to each one of them; a dress that reminded them of where they came from, and where they had gone.

"Let's get a picture," Joan said, motioning for the photographer to come their way.

Rocky's grandmother put her arm around Rocky's waist and got ready to pose. She leaned her head into Rocky, and Rocky could smell the faint scent of ylang-ylang, the perfume her grandmother always wore, the scent that reminded her of Madame Michel, the woman she would name her first daughter after, the woman who changed the course of her life.

Rocky's mother glided into the frame effortlessly, as if she'd been next to Rocky the entire time, and the flash went off.

"Don't forget about me!" Amanda called from across the dance floor, and hopped into the picture before the next flash.

That picture—the four women, together—would be the one that Rocky displayed proudly in the apartment she shared with Drew, and then later, when their family expanded, their town house in Prospect Park. It would be the photograph that Rocky's daughter would display in her own home, after she, herself, got married, and the sterling silver picture frame, gifted to Rocky and Drew by Sloan, would become something of a family heirloom in and of itself. Rocky would give the picture, in that original sterling silver picture frame, to her own granddaughter at her own bridal shower.

"This is your family," Rocky would tell her granddaughter, as she looked at the picture. (Her granddaughter, of course, had always admired the picture and knew exactly who was in it, had heard her grandmother utter these exact words many times before.) "Those are the two women who wore the dress before me, and the one who would wear it next."

Rocky's granddaughter would smile, and two months later, wear the dress herself. On her wedding day, Rocky would tell her granddaughter, just as her own grandmother once said to her: "To wear a custom-designed Madame Michel wedding dress is to guarantee a happy marriage." And it would.

★ ★ ★ ★ ★

ACKNOWLEDGMENTS

Thank you to my superstar agent, Jess Regel, and her team at Foundry Literary + Media. I know I say this all the time, but let's get it in print: Jess, you're a genius and I feel so lucky to be working with you.

Thank you to my wonderful editor, Melanie Fried, and her fabulous team at Graydon House Books. Thank you for taking a chance on me and this book! Melanie, you are so incredibly smart and always help to steer me in the right direction—I'm so delighted to have you on my side.

Thank you to my phenomenal publicity and marketing team: Heather Connor, Roxanne Jones, Justine Sha, Pamela Osti and Ana Luxton, as well as my copy editor, Jennifer Stimson. Special thanks go to Loriana Sacilotto, Dianne Moggy, Margaret Marbury, Susan Swinwood and Heather Foy. And for that cover art that still makes me swoon, thank you to Quinn Banting.

Special thanks to Tara Block and the entire team at PopSugar.

Thank you to Kristina Haugland, the Le Vine associate curator of costume and textiles and supervising curator for the Study Room at the Philadelphia Museum of Art, and author of the wonderful book *Grace Kelly: Icon of Style to Royal Bride*. Your insights on the Grace Kelly wedding dress, and dress construction in general, were invaluable. All mistakes are mine and mine only.

Librarians are my superheroes. Thank you to my wonderful librarian and friend, Jackie Ranaldo from the Syosset Public Library. Thank you to Brenda Cherry from the Syosset Public Library. Thank you to Rebecca Federman, research coordinator at the New York Public Library. Thank you to Allison Piazza, health sciences librarian at Seton Hall University.

Special thanks go to my family, the Janowitzes and Luxenbergs.

Thank you to Shawn Morris for the boxes of books, Jessica Shevitz Rauch for the read, Danielle Schmelkin for the tote, Kim Kramer for the rings, Rachel McRady for the pitches and Andrea Peskind Katz for the hashtags. And for going the extra mile: Robin Kaplan, Bobbie Nottebohm and Melissa Vallone.

Writing can be such a solitary endeavor, and it's wonderful to have author friends who help you along the way with their brilliant advice and warm friendship: Cristina Alger, Mary Kay Andrews, Jenna Blum, Jamie Brenner, Julie Buxbaum, Jillian Cantor, Laura Dave, Fiona Davis, Liz Fenton, Elyssa Friedland, Emily Giffin, Jane Green, Kristin Hannah, Elin Hilderbrand, Pam Jenoff, Caroline Leavitt, Emily Liebert, Elinor Lipman, Lynda Cohen Loigman, Jo Piazza, Sarah Pinneo, Amy Poeppel, Alyson Richman, Kristin Rockaway, Eve Rodsky, M.J. Rose, Susan Shapiro, Lisa Steinke, Alix Strauss, Heather Webb, Jennifer Weiner and Lauren Willig.

Endless thanks to my readers.

Finally, the biggest thank-you goes out to my husband, Douglas Luxenberg. Thank you for everything.

And to my children, Ben and Davey, you'll never know how much I love you until you have kids of your own, so for now, I'll just say this: I may have written six novels, but you are, by far, the greatest things I ever created.

READING GROUP GUIDE

1. *The Grace Kelly Dress* is about an heirloom wedding gown that's been passed down through three generations of a family. Do you have any heirlooms in your family? How important are these items? How did they become heirlooms?

2. What does the dress mean to each woman in the novel? What impact does it have on their lives, and how does it shape their expectations for love, marriage, and family?

3. How does the dress reflect the times in which each woman is living? Discuss the role fashion can play in forming (or performing) identity and in pushing societal boundaries.

4. Which woman's version of the dress was your favorite? Why? How did you feel about the alterations each generation made? Do you think the women should have made changes or kept the original version?

5. Family roles define many of the women in this book: Rose is an orphan, Joanie is an only child following her sister's

death, and Rocky struggles with her relationships with her sister and mother. How can familial expectations define a person? Can you ever step outside of these roles?

6. Discuss how each woman in the story is touched by loss. How does the death of a loved one affect our daily lives? How do you keep those you've lost in your life and honor their memory?

7. In chapter twenty-four, Diana tells Rose that her friends are like family to her. Discuss what this phrase means and how it applies to your own life.

8. Do you think Birdie was right in keeping the truth about Michele's death from Joanie? Have you ever had a family secret you withheld from loved ones? How important is it to shield our children from life's more difficult moments?

9. Why do you think Grace Kelly—and her wedding dress—have inspired so many? How does her influence live on today, half a century after her wedding and decades after her untimely death?

10. Discuss the importance of tradition. How can family tradition both bond people together and cause tensions and misunderstandings?